Tyco...
by K...

Corrine Martin was dangerous.

Rand emerged from the bathroom to find her waiting. He didn't know *why* she made him react the way she did, only that she did. And he didn't like it. He wanted to blast through her icy exterior and make her the vulnerable one, not him—never again.

If she were a different kind of woman, he would take her. But there was no way he'd be able to remain uninvolved with her. Already the tension was intensifying, making him shake with a weakness he refused to acknowledge.

'Hi,' she said softly.

Her voice brushed over him, making him feel heavy and lethargic. His groin tightened, and he could only nod at her. He was used to playing and winning, even with women. Winning made him feel in control and sure of himself. But there was a vulnerability in Corrine's eyes that warned this wasn't a game. Or at least not one that would leave behind a victor…

Sleeping with the Playboy
by Julianne MacLean

ෆ ✿ ෧

She ignored him, and that intrigued him.

He caught a perfumed whiff of her dark, shoulder-length hair as she strode by him.

'You are definitely in need of help.' She handed him her business card and turned to the door.

He glanced down at the card, then followed her out to the lift. 'Wait a second. Does this mean you're taking the job?'

She pushed the button. 'Yes.'

'But…when will you start?'

The lift dinged and the doors opened. She stepped inside. 'Right away.'

'But how do we do this? If you're going to be my bodyguard, shouldn't you be staying here? Where are you going?'

As she pushed the down button inside the lift, a tiny infectious grin sneaked across her lips. 'I liked the look of those feathery pillows in your guest room, Dr Knight, so if you must know, I'm going to get my toothbrush and pyjamas.'

The doors closed in front of Donovan's face.

He stood in the vestibule holding her card, feeling transfixed and suddenly exuberant, and totally surprised by the fact that his cool, reserved bodyguard actually had a sense of humour.

Things were definitely going to get interesting around here.

Available in May 2004 from Silhouette Desire

Where There's Smoke...
by Barbara McCauley
(Dynasties: The Barones)
and
Beauty & the Blue Angel
by Maureen Child
(Dynasties: The Barones)

Marooned with a Millionaire
by Kristi Gold
and
The Gentrys: Abby
by Linda Conrad
(The Gentrys)

Tycoon for Auction
by Katherine Garbera
and
Sleeping with the Playboy
by Julianne MacLean

Tycoon for Auction
KATHERINE GARBERA

Sleeping with the Playboy
JULIANNE MACLEAN

SILHOUETTE®
DESIRE™

First published in Great Britain 2004
Silhouette Books, Eton House, 18-24 Paradise Road,
Richmond, Surrey TW9 1SR

The publisher acknowledges the copyright holders of the
individual works as follows:

Tycoon for Auction © Katherine Garbera 2003
Sleeping with the Playboy © Julianne MacLean 2003

ISBN 0 373 04985 4

51-0504

Printed and bound in Spain
by Litografía Rosés S.A., Barcelona

TYCOON FOR AUCTION
by
Katherine Garbera

KATHERINE GARBERA

lives near Chicago with the man she met in Fantasyland and their two kids. She started writing to prove to herself that she could do it and found herself addicted to it. Creating worlds where everyday people find love and balance it with already full lives appeals to her. She loves revisiting the places that have influenced her and has once again returned to Orlando, which is an especially fond place for the native Floridian. Readers can visit her home page on the web at www.katherinegarbera.com.

This book is dedicated to Mavis Allen,
for her insight and her laughter.
It's a real pleasure to be working with you!

Acknowledgements

This book is a different direction for me, and I have to
thank many people for the opportunity to try it.
Joan Marlow Golan and Mavis Allen, who pointed out
my first version of the hero was a little weak and then
encouraged me to try something new.

Teresa Brown, Pam Labud and Catherine Kean,
who helped with every Orlando question I had.
Any mistakes are my own. Eve Gaddy, who spent
endless hours on the phone with me talking about
this story and how to make it stronger, plus just
offering her support—the words *thank you* really
aren't enough!
And thanks to Nancy Thompson, who double-checked
some facts on Orlando for me.
I wish we could still meet for lunch at Dexters!

As always, thanks to my family for their love
and support, without which I'd probably
accomplish nothing.

One

Lust wasn't something Corrine Martin was comfortable admitting she experienced. It didn't fit with the image she'd carefully cultivated—cool sophistication from the top of her blond head to the toes exposed by her slinky gold sandals. She'd done a good job of ignoring the surging feelings and the man who inspired them—until tonight.

Maybe it was something in his wizard-green eyes. Or maybe it was just that she was tired of having him stare through her as if she wasn't there. Whatever the reason, tonight she'd thrown caution to the wind and had purchased Rand Pearson for three corporate dates.

Of course, she'd only bid on his services as a corporate spouse. She even had an airtight excuse for doing it. She needed an escort to the upcoming business meetings she'd be expected to attend.

The ballroom at the Walt Disney Dolphin Hotel had been transformed into an old-fashioned buy-a-bride auction. All the money raised tonight would go to the Collation for the Homeless, an Orlando-based charity that fed and sheltered the homeless. This was Corrine's first year attending. She'd bid on and won the services of Rand Pearson.

Though they'd been working together for the last five months on a training project, she really didn't know him. He'd been one of only three men on the auctioning block representing the company he was a partner in—Corporate Spouses. The company provided business-etiquette lessons as well as dates for executives for business functions.

Corrine's boss, Paul Sterling, the CEO of Tarron Enterprises, had won a similar package the year before. Corrine had been Paul's secretary until his promotion to CEO when Paul had promoted her to a midlevel manager. Corrine loved the challenge her new role provided.

But she needed to show her boss that she wasn't in danger of becoming one-dimensional and focused only on her job as a middle manager at Tarron Enterprises. And on a more personal level she needed to remind herself that she was still a woman.

Rand Pearson made her feel dangerous and alive. She didn't like it, but she knew she needed to deal with it and get her life back on track. She had her eye on the vacant vice president position and knew that she'd need to be focused one hundred percent at work.

"Dance with me, Corrine?" Rand asked, coming up to her. His tuxedo was obviously custom-made, making him look like royalty, which, if gossip was true, he'd descended from.

"Why?" she asked. She'd never had any finesse when it came to men. They made her nervous. Probably because of her experiences in foster care during her teen years.

"When a man asks you to dance, Cori, yes or no is the appropriate answer," he said, with that gleam in his eyes that made her want to do something shocking. Which was how she'd ended up bidding on him.

She sighed and reminded herself that she was known as the ice queen for a very good reason. Life was safer that way. "My name is Corrine. And I know that."

"Do you?" He slid closer to her in the crowded ballroom. His hand glided up her arm—*her bare arm. Why had she listened to Angelica Leone-Sterling, her friend and boss's wife, and purchased this strapless dress? It wasn't her, and it made her feel like someone she knew she couldn't be.*

His palm was rough and rasped her skin. Tingles spread up her arm and across her chest, making her nipples tighten against the lace of her strapless bra. She shivered and stepped away from his disturbing touch. He arched one eyebrow but made no comment.

"Yes," she said at last, knowing only that she needed to do something to take control of the situation before she forgot about her plans. Rand was a stepping-stone to the next level, she reminded herself.

"Shall we dance?" he asked again.

She nodded. His cologne—a spicy, masculine scent—surrounded her as they stepped onto the dance floor and he pulled her into his arms. *I'm in charge.*

But as his arms came around her and he settled her close against his chest, she didn't feel like she was in charge. She didn't want to be. Delicious sensations spread out from the hand he'd placed on the small of her back, radiating throughout her body and making her blood flow heavily through her veins.

She shuddered and tried to break the spell his touch was weaving by looking at him. But his eyes held a lambent gaze that pulled her further under his spell. The slow, sensual sounds of a jazz saxophone filled the room, and then the trio's lead singer, a tall black woman with a sultry voice, began to sing about wishing on a star.

Corrine had spent her entire childhood wishing for something that had never come. She thought she'd grown beyond that, but the temptation to rest her cheek on Rand's shoulder was strong and she knew she'd made a mistake. She had to get away.

She tugged free of Rand's grasp and hurried off the dance floor. What was with her tonight?

She headed for the bar and ordered a Stoli straight. She needed something to shock her back to her senses. Maybe she could blame this funky mood on the fact that her closest female friend, Angelica Leone-Sterling, had just announced she was pregnant.

Corrine knew she'd never have children. She wasn't ever going to do something as dicey as bring a child into this chaotic world. This world where nothing lasted forever and death came quickly and swiftly, taking no notice of those left behind.

Damn, she was getting maudlin. Maybe she shouldn't be drinking. But before she could rescind her drink order, she sensed Rand behind her.

"Make that two," he said to the bartender.

The bartender set the drinks in front of them. Rand paid for hers before she had a chance to get her money out.

"Here's some money for my drink," she said when the bartender moved away.

"I see that you are going to need some etiquette lessons as well as an escort for business functions."

"Why do you say that?" she asked. She knew she had manners. Mrs. Tanner, one of her foster mothers, had drilled manners into Corrine when she was eight years old. She didn't think she'd ever forget those lessons.

"Because you don't know how to say thank you. Put your money away."

She slipped the folded bill back into her beaded handbag. When you grew up on charity it was hard to accept a handout. And Rand wasn't her date for the night, he was a man she'd bid on. When she thought about it, maybe she should have paid for his drink. "I don't like to take advantage of people."

"I didn't think you were."

She took a sip of her drink, uncomfortable with the

silence that had fallen between them. The liquid burned going down, but she didn't flinch. Rand held his glass with a casual grace that made her feel awkward. She put her glass on a passing waiter's tray and noticed that he did the same.

"What happened on the dance floor?" he asked at last.

She shrugged. No way was she going to tell him that he'd taken her by surprise. That the rich boy who liked to win had needled his way past the barrier she thought would keep her safe from any man. "I just didn't feel like dancing."

He arched one eyebrow at her again.

"That's the most condescending thing I've ever seen anyone do," she said.

"What?"

"That lord-of-the-manor eyebrow thing you do."

He did it again. "It bothers you?"

"I just said so."

"Good," he said, caressing her cheek with his fingers.

"Why good?" she asked, trying to keep her mind off the shivers spreading over her body.

"Because you seem too removed from life."

"I'm in control. Something you should appreciate."

"I do. It's just fun to needle you out of your comfort zone."

"Rand, if we are going to have even a slim chance of getting along for our three 'dates' you are going to have to remember one thing."

"What's that?" he asked. Putting his hand on her elbow, he moved them out of the traffic path near the bar.

She waited until she was sure she had his attention. "I'm in charge."

"Where did you get that idea?"

"I don't know for sure, but I suspect it was when I wrote out the check to buy you."

"Did you say *buy me?*" he asked.

"Do you have a hearing problem? I might have to trade you in."

"You're playing with fire, Cori."

Why did he have to call her by that ridiculous nickname? No one had ever given her a nickname. In her first foster home they'd called her Corrine Jane. After that she'd made sure no one knew she had a middle name. When he called her Cori it was as if he was seeing inside her soul to the lonely little girl she'd been. And she didn't like that.

"I know how to keep from getting burned," she said carefully. Though with Rand she wasn't sure of anything. They'd known each other casually for almost a year, and she still felt uncomfortable when she was near him.

"How?"

She looked straight into those devastating eyes of his. Why had she started this? There was no way out of this, and she knew she had to retreat now before she did something really foolish and tell him she was afraid of the fire in his eyes.

"Stay away from the fire," she said, and turned to walk away.

"What if the fire doesn't stay away from you?" he asked.

She pretended not to hear him and continued across the ballroom to her table. She told herself she hadn't just issued a challenge to Rand but knew she had, and a part of her tingled in anticipation of what he'd do next.

Rand knew better than to follow her. A crazy kind of excitement buzzed through his veins. This was the first time a woman had inspired the feeling, and he wasn't sure how to handle it. The logic part of his brain said that Corrine was a woman and a client and he should leave it at that, but deeper instincts called for him to probe deeper into her psyche until she had no secrets left. Nowhere to hide from him.

He detoured by his partner's table. Angelica Leone-Sterling had the glow typical of a newlywed. More surprising to Rand, her husband, Paul, shared that same luminescence. Though they were both involved in separate conversations, Rand noticed their joined hands on the table.

For a moment he felt a pang at the loneliness of his life. Despite having four sisters and two loving parents. It was the same feeling that had dogged him since he was sixteen and a car accident had changed his life when his twin had died. But he'd learned to live with that missing part of himself. And until tonight he hadn't realized that he wasn't really living with it, rather just ignoring it.

He didn't want to examine it now. He had to settle for flirty banter instead of meaningful conversation with the opposite sex. But then he knew that everything in life was a trade-off.

He was a successful businessman. He had a trust fund most people only dreamed of. And on most days that was enough. But tonight wasn't one of them. Tonight his personal demon was rearing its ugly head and Rand fought to keep his jovial attitude. He really wanted to escape back to his dark corner of the world and go numb until he could escape.

He never should have followed Corrine to the bar and joined her for a Stoli. He knew better than to dance with a woman he wanted so badly that her perfume seemed etched in his memory, and her scent filled his every breath.

His reactions to Corrine weren't helping, either. He could still feel her in his arms, dammit. She'd fit perfectly, and he'd wanted to nudge her head onto his shoulder and keep her cradled there all night long.

That woman needed someone to cradle her, even though she'd never admit it. Unfortunately, he couldn't be that someone. The vow he'd made when he was twenty-one prevented him from being any woman's "forever" man, yet he wanted to remind Corrine Martin she was a woman. There was something in her cool gray eyes that made him want to shake her up.

She's a client, he reminded himself. "Never let the

client get personal'' was his mantra, but he wasn't behaving true to form tonight. He blamed it on the fact that he'd been conned into going on stage at this charity event when he'd sworn never to do so.

The problem was he'd never been able to resist a challenge. He wasn't sure when it had started, but he could remember having his first broken arm at age six when his older cousin Thomas had dared him to climb a tree. At thirty-five, he should be old enough to know better, but he liked the thrill he got from riding the edge of a dare.

It was a Super Bowl wager that had led to his participation in the themed ''Buy a Bride'' charity auction. Though he hadn't been the only man on the stage, it was still humiliating to participate in such an event.

Angelica looked up as he approached and smiled at him. She'd changed a lot since her second marriage last year. She was happier and more willing to take a chance. Their friendship had started with her first marriage to Rand's best friend, Roger. He and Roger had been roommates at military school and then in college. They had been closer than brothers.

Rand approached the table and made small talk until the right moment presented itself. He wanted a few minutes alone with Angelica.

''Want to dance?'' he asked her, needing to talk to her without her husband around. Also, he needed to erase the memory of Corrine Martin in his arms.

''I don't know. Your technique must be off. I saw Corrine leave you earlier.''

Great. He'd forgotten they were in a virtual fishbowl at these events. Usually he liked the attention and the feel of eyes on him. But when he'd held Corrine in his arms he'd forgotten all about being on display and had immersed himself in the sensations she elicited in him.

What was it with these women tonight? "The answer I'm looking for is yes or no."

She sighed. He knew she'd probe into what had happened, and he should probably leave her sitting at the table with her husband. But he needed to talk to his best friend and congratulate her on the pregnancy she'd just announced. He wanted to warn her about life and how one had to be cautious when you got close to having it all.

He'd have to be on his guard around Angelica. Watch over her at work and make sure that she stayed safe for Paul and the baby. He owed Roger that much—after all, Roger had saved his life. He felt a little more pressure tightening the back of his neck.

"Yes. I think they're playing our song," she said.

The band had begun to play "I've Got a Crush on You." It was the song they'd danced to at her first wedding so long ago. And over the years that song had helped them survive. Rand had held Angelica while she cried to that song on the anniversary of her first wedding.

There'd never been anything sexual between them; instead, she'd become like a sister to him. Though his own sisters would describe him as cold, he and Angelica had a warm relationship. Rand knew that was because of his debt to Roger.

Roger had guarded Rand's secret addiction and pulled him back from the edge. He owed Roger at first. Then he'd come to know and care for Angelica.

Rand knew a moment's fear for Paul and Angelica. It seemed as if they had too much. Rand had a healthy respect for the balance of the universe and the fact that you couldn't have it all. He prayed that Paul and Angelica would be the exception to that rule.

"Congratulations on your pregnancy," he said as they danced around the floor. They'd been partners in Corporate Spouses for more than ten years and friends even longer. Things were getting back to normal now. The tension at the back of his neck eased.

"Thank you. I'm a little nervous about it."

Her confession robbed him of the advice he'd been about to give. He couldn't tell her that fate never let anyone have it all. Because Angelica already knew that.

"I'll make sure you have everything you need, kiddo," he said.

"Oh, Rand. Thanks, but I think that's Paul's job now."

He swallowed, realizing it was true. The one woman he'd allowed himself to care about belonged to someone else now. That's good, he thought. Really, it is.

He tried to think of something else to say when he noticed one of the Tarron vice presidents, Mark something, escorting Corrine onto the dance floor. He didn't like how low the guy's hands were on Corrine's hips.

He maneuvered himself closer to the couple. Corrine's gaze met his and she seemed to want something from him. He looked closer at Mark and realized the man was drunk. Rand knew better than anyone how too many drinks could change the world around a man.

"Kiddo, you feel like using your power as the CEO's wife?" he asked Angelica.

"How?"

"I'm going to cut in and rescue Corrine from a man who's had one too many."

"I get to dance with a drunk. Boy, Rand, you sure know how to show a girl a good time."

"As you just pointed out, that's not my job anymore."

"You're right. Who is it?"

"Mark something, I think." He turned them so Angelica could see the man.

"Mark Jameson. His wife left him on New Year's Day—what with it being Valentine's Day—he hasn't been the same since then."

"Can you handle him?"

"No problem."

Rand spun them neatly into Mark and Corrine's path and tapped the other man on his shoulder. "May I?"

Mark's eyes were blurry and he looked a little confused. Angelica stepped into his arms as Rand tugged Corrine free. He heard Angelica use her most soothing voice as she took the lead in the dance and moved Mark to the edge of the dance floor.

"Thanks. I owe you one," Corrine said.

"I think I'll collect now," he said, even though he knew he should be escorting her off the dance floor and then collecting his keys from the valet and heading home.

"What do you want?"

That was a loaded question. "Don't walk away again."

She glanced up, obviously startled. "Ego problems?"

"Do you think I'm that shallow?"

"Yes," she said.

He laughed. There was a part of him that was shallow, and he did his best to make sure that was the only thing people saw.

"Maybe I just wanted to hold you for the three minutes or so that the song lasts."

"Don't say things like that."

"It's the truth." God, he wished it weren't, but his body had already decided that there was no way Corrine was going to be a hands-off client. She called to parts of him that he'd put away a long time ago. Nothing was going to be normal until he'd mussed up her cool exterior. Until he had her blond hair spread out on his pillow and was buried deep in her sweet body with her legs and arms wrapped around him.

"We have a working relationship, Rand. It can't be anything else."

"I'm aware of that," he said. He'd been working

with Corrine on the new training module he and Corrine were developing at Tarron.

"Why'd you bid on me tonight?" he asked. It was out of character for the woman he knew her to be. She'd given not only him but most of her co-workers the cold shoulder. She was cordial and polite, but she kept a distance between herself and others. The only person he knew who'd gotten past her barrier was Angelica. But then, Angelica had a way with people.

"You looked lonely up there."

He stopped dancing and glanced down at her. This was the second time she'd sassed him tonight. "Are you saying pity motivated you?"

"Well…yes."

"Darling, I seem to remember a brisk bidding before you finally won me."

"Cling to that memory," she said with a laugh.

He joined her, even though she was having fun at his expense. There was something warm and almost adorable in her eyes that made him want to protect her. Much the same as he'd wanted to earlier when he'd realized she was trapped on the dance floor. But he'd never been anyone's protector except Angelica's. And she'd been safe because Rand couldn't really fall in love with her. And he'd been doing it to pay back a debt. Business was the one thing he'd always been good at.

He was a loner by nature and he didn't want to get too involved with Corrine. He let his arms drop, and the music ended a second later. There was confusion in her eyes. He knew he had to get away before he gave in to the temptation to take everything she had to offer. Because the woman he'd just held had a softness that she didn't usually let the world see.

And that softness called to everything masculine in him. Made his chest swell and his muscles flex. It made him want to defend and protect her from everyone except himself. And Rand Pearson was no woman's hero.

He'd learned that the hard way.

He pivoted to leave.

"Is this payback?" she asked.

He stopped and took her elbow to escort her off the dance floor. He'd never forgotten his manners before. He prided himself on always being a gentleman. Something his parents had instilled in him since he'd first known the difference between boys and girls.

He stopped at the edge of the dance floor and turned to thank her for the dance. But those gray eyes of hers made the words die unsaid.

"I'm sorry," he said.

He walked away from her, knowing that he was going to need more than the words "never let the client get personal" help him this time. Because there was something about Corrine Martin that made him want to forget rules and lessons learned in life. And he was old enough to know better.

Two

Corrine neatly managed to avoid spending time with Rand until her first official date. She'd even corresponded with him through e-mail instead of calling him. His last e-mail had been brief to the point of seeming curt, but that didn't bother her. She regretted the impulse that had led her to bid on him and wished that she had some way to go back in time and change things. Although she knew that time travel didn't exist, she wished she could go further back than Rand Pearson's appearance in her life and make some huge alterations.

Today was a sunny Saturday in March, and Paul Sterling, Tarron's CEO, was having his annual staff party on his yacht moored in West Palm Beach. It

was a two-hour drive from Orlando and Rand was
picking her up.

She'd suggested meeting him there, but he'd sent
back a reply saying only that he'd pick her up at ten.
He pulled up at five till, and as he climbed out of his
car and came toward her front door she wished again
she'd never bid on him. Her pulse hammered, and
everything feminine in her came to life.

She didn't have time for this. She'd wanted to have
an escort to social functions because she always
seemed to be the only one alone. And it made her
stand out. She hated to have attention drawn to her.
She liked blending in with the background.

She knew there was no way she was going to survive the two-hour drive down the coast unless she had
a distraction. The doorbell rang and she glanced frantically around her neat house. Spotting her laptop in
the corner she grabbed it and her leather carryall and
headed for the door. Work had been her salvation
since she was fourteen. She realized early that at work
it didn't matter where you came from, only how well
you did the job.

She shoved her Ann Taylor sunglasses up her nose
and opened the door. The classic designer appealed
to Corrine. Rand was leaning negligently against the
porch railing, staring out at the street. She lived on
Kaley, in one of Orlando's older sections. Her home
had been built in the fifties and required lots of care,
but she loved it.

"Nice neighborhood," he said, glancing up and

down the street, which wasn't too busy this Saturday morning.

"Thanks. Ready to go?" she asked, not wanting to encourage him to be nice to her. The other night had shown her that he'd slipped between her defenses and that was something she refused to let happen again.

"What, no tour?"

"Not today. I don't want to be late."

"We won't be. We've got five minutes to spare."

"Traffic could be heavy. I don't share your confidence."

"Want to bet on it?" he asked.

She knew from Angelica that Rand would bet on anything. And he usually won. She'd never gambled in her entire life. Not even on the twice-weekly Florida lottery. She preferred the safety of investing her money over the risk of losing a dollar to a chance of becoming a millionaire. "No."

"Scared?" His eyebrow rose behind his sunglasses.

"Of a bet with you? I don't think so."

"Then, why not?"

There was only way to beat this man, she thought. And that was with wit, because he was too smart and confident for his own good. "You don't really have anything I want."

He pulled his glasses down to the tip of his nose and regarded her over the top of the lenses. "Really?"

"Really," she said.

"I'll take that as a challenge."

She pushed her glasses back on her head and gave him her haughtiest stare. The one that made people back off. "Will your swelled head fit in the car?"

"No problem. The car is a convertible. I'll put the top down if need be."

She laughed and closed her door, locking it behind her.

"Why are you bringing your computer?" he asked.

"I have some work I need to do. I hate to waste the time since you're driving."

"You can't take one day off?" he asked.

"Sure I can. I just don't want to."

"Don't you ever have any fun?" he asked, opening her door for her.

"I like working."

She knew it was an old-fashioned gesture, and yet she liked it. He probably did it without thinking, but it made her feel good. She dropped her bags on the floor and smoothed the skirt of her sundress under her as she slid into the car. She felt the heat of his gaze on her legs as the hem slid up on her thighs.

Was he interested in her as a woman? Since he'd kept his distance after their dance she figured his attraction to her had been posturing since she'd been the one in the position of power.

He slammed the door and walked around in front of the car. He wore khaki shorts and a golf shirt and looked like an advertisement for easy living. She pulled her sunglasses back into place, then smoothed her hair along her head, searching for any strand that might have escaped the ponytail she'd pulled it into this morning. Neat and tidy, she thought.

"I like my job, too, but that doesn't mean I don't take time to enjoy life."

"I'm not an unhappy person, Rand. And you're working today."

"I know."

"So why shouldn't I?"

"Never mind."

She pulled her laptop from its case and powered it up. Rand fastened his seat belt and neatly backed out of her driveway. The traffic was heavy, but he wove through it effortlessly. She pulled up the company memo template and pretended to be composing the memo in her head, but all she could concentrate on was Rand.

His muscles flexed each time he shifted the car. She could practically smell the testosterone as he drove. And she wondered if she'd really survive if he decided to take her words as a challenge.

Because without even trying to, he was engaging her senses and distracting her from her work. She knew then that she'd never claim the other two dates she'd purchased from his company because there was no way she was going to be this close to him again after today.

Rand knew it shouldn't matter that she was working as they drove down to West Palm Beach. Ivanna Marckey, the last client he'd provided a corporate escort for, had spent all the time to and from engagements on the phone or reading e-mail on her PDA. But for some reason it bothered him when Corrine did the same.

That wasn't true. Not only did her actions disturb him—she did. From the tips of her hot-pink toes to her sleek blond ponytail. She seemed aloof and he wanted to bring her down to his level. He wanted to see her hot and mussed. He lowered the windows so the air circulated around them, tugging the long blond strands from her neat coiffure.

She glanced over at him. He knew he should have asked before he lowered the windows. He'd been raised with more manners than most, and this was one of the reasons why he'd left Chicago many years ago. He sometimes reacted without thinking. Something that Pearsons simply didn't do. Especially ones who seemed to live a charmed life.

"Do you mind?" he asked at last.

She shrugged. "I guess not. I wish I'd brought a scarf."

She turned back to her computer and started typing again. Obviously not too concerned with the wind. Or too ruffled by it.

"We'll stop before we get to the yacht club so you can fix your hair," he said, trying to make up for his behavior.

"Okay," she said. Her pleasantness made him feel like a bully on the playground.

He wanted to push harder to see what it would take to get a reaction out of her. A few more miles passed, and when they got on I-95 heading south he couldn't stand the silence anymore. It just left his mind free to wander and he'd never been that comfortable with himself. Usually he blared the radio on a heavy-metal station, but today there was an interesting distraction right next to him.

Her sundress was demure on the outside, but it was encasing a body that was his version of heaven. Long, slim limbs and generous curves above and below the waist. In his mind's eye he could still see her white thigh from when she'd gotten into the car.

He imagined his hand sliding up that leg. He knew it would be as smooth as silk. He'd touched her arms and shoulders the night they'd danced together and his fingers still remembered her texture. The roughness of his callused hands on her soft skin. He wanted to touch her again. Now.

Sexual tension pumped through his body, making him heavy. Dammit, he needed a diversion. Too bad she was engrossed in her job.

Which he knew shouldn't bother him, but it did. Everything male in him wanted to rise to the indirect challenge she issued by ignoring him. And that was the one thing he'd never been able to resist. So he fiddled with the radio dial until he found a classic-rock station.

Instead of something hard and raunchy, the sensuous sounds of Dave Matthews and his band singing one of their ballads. The soft, emotional lyrics didn't help his situation as he felt the beast in him rising to the surface.

He tightened his hands on the wheel. She hadn't

even glanced at him when the music blared out of the speakers. Unable to help himself, he reached over and removed the elastic holding her hair back. She didn't move to stop him, only glanced toward him.

"Problem?"

"You're going to have to take it out later, anyway," he said. Which had to be the lamest excuse in history. But there was no way he was going to tell her more.

She held her hand out palm up, and though he wanted to toss the damn elastic out the window he gave it to her. "Thanks," she said quietly.

"For what?"

"I put vanity before comfort."

"I don't imagine you being vain."

"Well, not like ego. I just like to look...well kept."

"I'll keep you well," he said before he could stop himself. Damn, normally he wasn't such a hound, but he could think of nothing but her in his arms. Her in his bed. Her...just her, and that disturbed him.

"Rand?"

"Don't, okay?" Rand asked.

He concentrated on the road. Hardly noticed that the long, sunshine-colored strands of her hair brushed his arm every thirty seconds or so. Hardly noticed that her scent engulfed him. He wanted to bring her closer so he could breathe her in. Hardly noticed that for once a different kind of tension was pursuing him.

He felt like a big, mean bastard. He turned the radio down and concentrated on his driving, annoyed at her for ignoring him and mad at himself for reacting as if he were in junior high school.

He clicked off the radio and floored the accelerator.

"You okay?" Corrine asked.

He'd had enough of being a beast and wasn't about to say another thing to her until they arrived at the yacht. And then he'd find a way to make sure he didn't take her actions so personally. But she appealed to him on too many levels. "Yeah."

She closed her laptop and put it away. "I've always loved the smell of the beach."

"Me, too. One of the first times I beat my older twin brother was at beach volleyball. We played all afternoon and we kept switching off winning, and then finally I won two in a row," he said.

"You know, I grew up in Florida but never got to go to the beach until I was in college. That trip was my shot at freedom, and I stood on the shore looking out at the endless horizon and vowed to make the most of every opportunity given to me."

"You've kept that vow," he said.

"Yes, I have."

"Why is success so important to you?" he asked. He knew that he shouldn't get to know her better. That knowing the woman behind the executive would only make her more tempting, but there was no way he could resist learning more about her. And the few glimpses he'd had of the real Corrine told him they weren't well suited. There was a sadness in her eyes sometimes that made him believe she needed an average guy without the baggage he brought to any relationship.

"I'm an orphan."

Her words didn't make sense to him at first. He had so much family that he couldn't imagine a life without them. And even when his five siblings weren't around he had friends who were like family. "When did your parents die?"

"I'm pretty sure they are both still living somewhere."

"Have you ever tried to find them?" he asked. He liked knowing he was part of the past as well as the future through his ancestry. Though he and his father had never seen eye to eye on one thing, Rand wouldn't change his lineage. He liked knowing where he came from, and if the pressure of being a Pearson was too much to bear sometimes, that was a price Rand paid.

"No."

"You should think about it," he said.

"Rand, I'm never going to look for them."

"Why not?"

"I was abandoned when I was two days old."

Her words cut him. No one should have abandoned this woman. Why hadn't he let her alone? "I'm sorry."

"Why? It was a long time ago."

He reached across the gearshift and found her hand. It was clenched in a tight fist, nails digging into the flesh of her palm. Though her words sounded as if she'd gotten over it, the truth was her emotions ran deep and strong. He pried her fingers open and slid his hand around hers. And he knew how time could lessen the pain but not totally abate it.

He said nothing else as they drove along the highway, the wind in their hair and hands tightly clasped. She didn't speak, either, and when he pulled off the highway and had to let go to downshift, she reached for her handbag and pulled out a brush.

He knew he wouldn't be holding her hand again or seeing any more glimpses into her soul. Because as she put up her window, and he did the same, she morphed into someone he didn't want her to be. She smoothed her hair back into place, and she was no longer the woman he'd spoken to earlier but the corporate executive looking for her next promotion.

The party was fun in spite of being a work event. Corrine mingled through the crowd with Rand at her side. Tarron and Corporate Spouses had a strategic partnership for training—the project Rand and Corrine had been working on, so he knew many of her colleagues. As they circulated through the room, Corrine couldn't help being aware that this was how things might be if she ever had a husband. It was a little unnerving. Finally the party wound down and everyone started to leave.

"That went well," Corrine said as they helped tidy up after the party. Corporate Spouses had helped man the check-in table and had arranged for a caterer. Though Rand wasn't in charge of this event, he'd still made sure everything ran smoothly. And when Paul had asked her if she'd mind helping supervise the cleanup, Rand had said he didn't mind staying.

"Did it?" Rand asked.

He'd been distant since their conversation in the car and Corrine wasn't sure what to make of that. There was something about telling people that your own parents thought you weren't worth keeping that made them treat you differently. She'd revealed too much and had worked hard to keep him at arm's length during the luncheon. She shrugged. "I guess not."

He faced her suddenly, his green eyes intent. "It wasn't anything spectacular."

"Spectacular isn't necessary for success," she said.

"No, but it makes life more exciting."

She watched him working and realized that he craved excitement. It clung to him like a second skin. She knew then that if she hadn't bid on him they'd never have been intimate because they were in two totally different universes. Maybe they'd never been meant to meet. Every time she'd messed with fate it came back to haunt her. Just once she'd like to find a guy and have the kind of relationship that her peers at work seemed to take for granted.

"I like to blend in," she said.

He came over to her. The sun streaming through the windows behind him made it impossible for her to see his features. He touched her cheek, rubbing one finger down the length of her face, resting his hand against her neck.

"I noticed," he said.

She couldn't think while he touched her. She knew her pulse had increased. He probably felt her racing heartbeat. Could he see inside her? Did he realize that she wanted more from him than three cold impersonal dates? She stepped back. *I'm in control,* she reminded herself.

She felt like she should apologize but didn't. Quiet was who she was. "That's not your way, is it?"

"Not really. I like to shake things up."

"I noticed. I'm sorry I didn't want to play in that trivia game," Corrine stated, referring to the game many of the guests had played.

"No problem. I just thought we could win." She knew they would have. She'd always been good at those kinds of games but never played them in public. It seemed like the only people who participated at company events were the glory hounds and those who'd had too many drinks.

She had a strict rule about alcohol and work-related functions. She thought Rand must, too, because he'd drunk cola all day like herself. Actually, she'd drunk diet, but Rand didn't need calorie-free drinks. His body had been sculpted by years of being top dog. Of honing his body and skills until he was simply the best man in any room. Realizing an uncomfortable silence had fallen, she attempted to break the mood.

"Sometimes winning isn't the most important thing."

He grabbed his chest and staggered backward. "Say it isn't so."

Corrine chuckled. She liked his self-deprecating

humor. She liked that he'd let her set the tone for their presence at the party. She just plain liked him and that was…dangerous.

"What's wrong with him?" Paul asked from the other side of the room.

"I shocked him," Corrine said.

"How?" Paul asked.

"I told him winning wasn't everything," she said with a grin.

"Oh, no."

"Are you still weakened from the blow?" Paul asked Rand.

"Yes. That's my Kryptonite. Need a quick fix. Must win." Rand staggered around the room like a weakened man, clutching the table for support.

"Good. How about a quick match of beach volley-ball?" Paul asked.

Rand straightened slowly. "What did you have in mind?"

"Two on two. You and Corrine against me and Angelica."

Paul was looking at Rand, but Rand looked at her and Corrine wasn't sure what to do. She shrugged. "I don't have a change of clothes."

"Angelica keeps spare clothes on the yacht. I know she'd loan you some. I'll go check with her," Paul said, leaving the room.

She sensed Rand's eyes on her as she finished clearing the last table and put some things in the trash. She didn't want to look at him. Didn't want to see that challenging light in his eyes. But she glanced over her shoulder and was captivated.

"Wanna play?"

No, she thought. She wanted to retreat to her home ground—her safety area—and forget about her job and men and everything. At least until Monday when life would be normal again.

"I'm not good at sports," she said carefully. She prided herself on mastering whatever she attempted. When her prowess at sports never developed she'd given up on them.

"You said winning wasn't everything."

"But to you it is."

"How about we just have fun?"

"I can do fun."

"Really, without your laptop?"

"Make up your mind. Do you want me to play or not?"

"I want you to play, but it's up to you," he said.

She knew he'd be disappointed if she didn't play. Why did pleasing him matter? But for some reason it did. Before she could answer, Paul returned with Angelica.

"Come on, Corrine. It'll be fun," Angelica said.

Corrine nodded and found herself in a very short time standing barefoot in the sand wearing borrowed clothes. Rand wrapped his arm around her and pulled her close.

Her mind ceased functioning and all she could do was breathe in the masculine scent of his aftershave and feel the warmth of his body pressed to hers. His leg was hairy and tickled where it rubbed against hers.

"Here's the plan," he said, his words brushing across her skin.

"I can't hit the ball very hard," she said.

He smiled at her. It was the kind of smile that people always gave you when you were athletically challenged. "Don't worry. I can."

"Tell me what to do."

"I will."

"Don't let this go to your head," she said.

"How?"

"I'm still in charge."

"How can I forget it? You bought me, remember?" he asked.

She knew she didn't want to like him but realized it was too late. He served the ball and the game progressed. She realized that Rand Pearson was the kind of guy that made her wish she still believed in happy endings.

Three

Rand knew Paul had meant for the game to be friendly; the inclusion of the women pretty much said it without words. Angelica, though, was a fierce competitor and Corrine as well rose to the occasion, playing with more spirit than skill. But Rand had never been able to participate in any match and not give it his total concentration.

Even his demons demanded perfection from him. He did everything to the max without worry for the consequences. And sometimes the price he paid was high.

He forgot about winning the first time Corrine flinched, putting her hands up to block the ball instead of hitting it back over the net. But it soon became apparent that Corrine didn't like to be unsuccessful.

She watched Angelica and Paul and found weaknesses in their game that allowed her and Rand to stay even with them.

They'd probably be able to win if he could keep his eyes off her bare legs. It wasn't as if hers were the first he'd ever seen. But for some reason his eyes kept straying there. And his libido went into overdrive.

The sand was warm beneath his feet and he imagined only the two of them remained on the volleyball court. She was sweaty from the sun and from playing. Her T-shirt clung to her torso like a second skin, revealing all that her neat dress had hidden earlier. He wanted to toss the ball to the ground and pull her close to him. Not to huddle over game strategy but to taste those full lips of hers.

"Rand?" she asked. He imagined her calling his name in a much more intimate situation. Urging him closer to her body, bringing her mouth to his and whispering his name as her lips touched his.

"Rand?"

He glanced up to find Corrine staring at him. He became aware of the ball in his hands and the fact that he was supposed to be serving instead of ogling his teammate's legs. Damn, she got to him faster than any other woman he'd ever known. The tension that was always his companion settled in the pit of his stomach. It had been a long time since another person had affected him this deeply.

"Yes?" he asked, hoping his reaction to Corrine wasn't visible to the world. His beach shorts weren't made to disguise the hardening of his groin. He shifted a little and decided he had to concentrate on the game. The sexual thing he could handle if that were the only draw to Corrine. But the depths he kept glimpsing of this woman's soul made him wary.

"You okay?" she asked. She'd pushed her sunglasses to her head, and her eyes were serious as she watched him.

Did she suspect where his mind had been? "Fine. I was figuring out the score."

"Two-two," she said.

Okay, time to play and forget about the tempting woman whom he didn't want to like. The woman who'd shared some of her past with him and whom he realized he wanted to know more about. But he'd never ask. Because knowing more meant forming bonds and commitments. He wasn't a "forever" kind of guy. He couldn't ask anyone to share the life he lived because it was based on subterfuge.

He served the ball and the game ensued. It was fast and furious, and despite her claim not to be good at sports, Corrine played well. The next serve would determine who won the game.

Rand just couldn't wait for it to be over so he could hit the shower, preferably a cold one. And try to forget about how Corrine's shorts had ridden up on the curve of her buttocks as she'd lunged for the ball. She had a sweet, curvy rear that made his fingers tingle with the need to test the resilience of those curves.

"Time out," Corrine called, and walked to the center of the court. She stood there staring at him. Had she realized his mind wasn't on the game?

"You tired?" he asked. She was flushed and her eyes seemed exhausted.

She shook her head. "I want to talk to you."

He waited, but she gestured impatiently for him to join her. Angelica and Paul were huddled together, but it looked as if they were smooching rather than discussing strategy. Part of him hungered for what they had, but Rand quickly pushed it deep down and ignored it as he always did. Having it all came at a high cost and he wasn't willing to pay the price.

"What's up?" he asked.

"Umm…"

He waited. She didn't smell sweaty, he realized, but faintly floral and something else that he associated only with Corrine. He'd held her in his arms twice and some things had become imbedded in his senses.

"Were you serious about playing for fun?" she said at last.

Not really, but he knew that coaxing her into the game had been his motivation earlier. Still, he couldn't tell her how important winning was to him. "Yes, why?"

"Good." She nibbled her lower lip and he watched. He thought she said something about not caring if they didn't win, but all he could do was watch her teeth and tongue and her sexy lips and wonder how they'd taste under his. Would she react with the passion he sensed was bottled up inside of her? Or would she be cool like her outer surface image?

"I think we have a good shot at winning," he said at last.

"What if we didn't?" she asked.

He realized she was trying to tell him something without saying the words. "I'm not making the connection here, darling. Just tell me what you're trying to say."

She shrugged. "I don't think I should beat my boss."

"Paul doesn't care if we win. I've played him lots of times at basketball and golf. I usually win," he said.

"That's different."

"How do you figure?" he asked, leaning closer to her.

She tilted her head to the side and then stood on her tiptoe to whisper in his ear. "You don't work for Paul."

He ignored the jolt of that went through him. "That's right, I don't."

She pulled back and met his gaze evenly. "You work for me, right?"

He arched one eyebrow. "We both know I do."

She grimaced at him. "I'd like to see you lose when you do that eyebrow thing."

"Oh, does it bother you?"

"You can be so annoying when you try."

"I know. It's a gift."

"I don't like it, Rand."

"I'll try to remember that."

"Good. Remember what else I said."

"You didn't say anything."

"Then I'll say it now. I'd rather not win."

"Do you have a plan to lose? Because Paul will notice if we suddenly start missing the ball."

"You'll just have to pretend to be distracted," she said.

"How am I supposed to do that?"

"You're a smart man. You'll think of something."

Several seconds passed before Rand replied to her rather provocative words. "Will you be distracting me?" he asked. There was something very masculine in his tone that made everything feminine in her stir. She wanted to run from Rand and the male gleam in his eyes but she was made of stronger stuff.

The cowardly part of her doubted that. But she was determined to stay where she was. "How?"

Her world was very narrow and she'd never had to distract a man before. Manipulate them a time or two in a business situation to get the results she wanted, but never distract. Her mind was going wild trying to figure out what he had in mind.

He muttered something under his breath. She tugged at the hem of the jogging shorts that Angelica had loaned her. They were shorter than she was used to, but otherwise fit well.

"What'd you say?" she asked.

"Nothing. You just stand there and I'll be distracted," he said.

It was the closest thing she'd ever had to a compliment from a man. Usually she froze them out before they could work up the nerve to say anything personal to her. She'd learned a long time ago that life was simpler without interpersonal relationships.

But there was something about Rand that made her not want to freeze him out. That made her want to try to bring him closer to her. That made her…just want him.

"Really?" she asked without thinking.

He gave her one of those lord-of-the-manor looks and she wished she'd kept her mouth closed. But it was too late. Besides, he was too arrogant for his own good.

"Don't pretend you don't know that you are an attractive woman," he said.

Scooting a few feet away from him, she glanced objectively down at her body. She spent some time working out so she wasn't overweight, but when she looked in the mirror all she saw was a rather average-looking woman. Now wasn't the time to argue the point with him, but she knew he was mistaken.

A change of subject was needed. "What if I just talk to you?"

"You haven't been quiet the entire game and that hasn't affected my playing," he said.

He was right. She didn't really know how to play the game and had been calling questions to him. He'd been really good and he was hard to distract. One time she'd yelled at him to watch out when he'd dived for the ball and he'd still managed to hit it over the net.

He was a superb athlete. He wore only surf shorts,

leaving his chest bare. He was tanned and his muscles were firm and delineated. She knew why she wanted to believe he found her attractive—he was the kind of man that she'd always secretly drooled over.

Actually, she should probably be the one to act distracted by him. Of course, it wouldn't be an act. She hadn't been able to keep her mind on work all day. Instead of being the key to her next promotion, Rand seemed more like her Achilles' heel.

"What if you think you see someone you know on the beach?" she said. This game needed to end, and soon. She wanted—no, needed—to be back at her small house spending another Saturday evening working on her computer or watching *The Scarlet Pimpernel* on video. No more time in the presence of this man.

"Corrine, if we have to explain what happened it'll look rigged. Trust me—if we win, Paul will still respect you."

"I don't want to do anything to jeopardize my position at Tarron," she said.

"How will this game affect your role there?" he asked.

Now that she had to explain it she felt a little silly. But the truth was there were people who looked down on her because she'd been Paul's secretary before being promoted to manager of operations. And telling Rand didn't devalue her. It only gave validity to the circumstances at work. "I have to be careful about the job, that's all."

"Why?"

"You know I was Paul's administrative assistant." He nodded.

"Some people think he gave me the job because I was displaced from being his secretary when he was promoted. He kept Tom's secretary, Jane."

"Then they don't know Paul or you. He'd never give you a job you couldn't do. And you'd never take one."

She wondered how he knew that about her. It was the nicest thing anyone had ever said about her. She wanted to hug him and hold his words close to her. "Thank you."

"You're welcome. What do you say we let fate decide this match?"

She was about to ask his opinion again, but then remembered that she steered the course to her destiny. And Rand was right. Any boss who'd be upset over losing a game of volleyball wasn't someone she'd be able to respect, and she'd always had the utmost respect for Paul Sterling.

"Okay," she said softly.

"Attagirl!" Rand said, chucking her under the chin.

"Could you try not to sound so patronizing?"

"I don't patronize you."

"*Attagirl?* You make me sound like a five-year-old."

"Baby, I definitely don't think of you as a kid. Stop being so defensive."

"I'm not." As soon as the words left her mouth she realized she sounded like a grade-schooler arguing.

"Are you two going to huddle all day?" Angelica called.

"No," Corrine said. Thankful for the distraction, she returned to her spot near the net.

"Ready, Cori?" Rand asked.

She nodded. Damn the man, he knew he was getting under her skin. She took her position, ready to play her best, and determined to keep Rand Pearson at arm's length no matter how much her instincts might want to draw him closer.

Rand knew he should back off, let Corrine set the tone for the last minutes of the game, but he didn't. Paul was watching the two of them and Rand knew what the other man was thinking. That somehow over the course of the game Corrine had become personal to him. Dammit. No woman got personal. He prided himself on it. His survival depended on it.

And they were winning the game—to hell with what she wanted. He wasn't her lapdog. The agreement they'd signed was one where he escorted her to social functions. This game was not inclusive. Paul had invited *him* to play.

But when he set up to serve and Corrine glanced over her shoulder at him, he knew she was nervous. She nibbled on her lower lip and he felt his resolve crumble. Maybe those feelings went back to when his twin, Charles, had asked Rand to get in the car with him when they'd been sixteen. Maybe it went back to his first summer job at his dad's firm. He hated to disappoint anyone. Maybe it had to do with cheating death more than once and that feeling in his gut that if he didn't live right he might not get another chance.

He just couldn't do it.

So he served the ball straight to Angelica, knowing

she'd be able to lob it easily back over the net, which she did, right at Corrine. He'd left the game in her hands. She broke eye contact with him and jumped for the ball.

He knew she'd probably miss it. She hadn't hit all that many balls today and it would be a believable loss, but instead she tapped it on the outside and it came right at him.

Time seemed to move in slow-motion as the ball came toward him and Corrine's eyes met his. In them he read the same exhilaration he felt at the end of a close game. In them he read the determination to win. In them he saw a reflection of the woman who'd confessed to never being good at sports and wanting to be, this one time.

He leapt into the air and hit the ball with restrained power, this time sailing it over Angelica's head. Paul dove for the ball and barely missed it.

There was total silence. Rand wasn't sure he'd read the signs correctly. Did Corrine want to win? He'd done it for her, but would she believe that? He was almost afraid to look at Corrine and see whatever lurked in her eyes.

Women complicated a man's life, he acknowledged. And though the thrill he'd gotten watching her lithe body move on the sand had been nice, it wasn't worth this type of difficulty. He should have learned his lesson a long time ago and never agreed to this co-ed game. Men were more predictable about sports and winning.

He crossed slowly toward her. Angelica was grinning at Paul, who was covered in dirt and sweat. He was aware on a peripheral level that Angelica was comforting her husband on losing. But his main focus was the blond woman staring at him.

"We won," she said, her voice barely a whisper. She'd pushed her sunglasses back on her head and her gray eyes sparkled in the waning twilight. Eyes were supposed to be the windows to the soul but hers were guard posts, and he thought they did their job too well. He couldn't read a damned thing in them.

"We did," he said. He rarely lost and never tired of winning.

"I've never won at a sport."

"How's it feel?" he asked, still not able to gauge her mood.

She smiled then and his troubles should have melted away, but instead he felt a sense of doom. Because that smile was sweet and innocent and cut past the layers he used to keep others at bay. That smile made him want to always be her champion and he knew he wasn't going to be Corrine's.

"It feels incredible," she said.

"Good game," Paul said as he and Angelica ducked under the net to join them. Rand shook hands with the other man and hugged Angelica. Corrine did the same.

"Thanks." He tried to see if she was nervous but couldn't read her. Which was no surprise—she kept her true self carefully hidden.

"We got lucky there at the end." Though he knew it wasn't true. That last play had involved skill and precision. Maybe Paul wouldn't notice.

"Is that why you always win?" asked Paul.

"Not usually," Rand said wryly.

"Then I don't think luck deserves the credit. We're

going to clean up on the boat. See you at work on Monday, Corrine.''

Paul and Angelica walked away and Rand watched them go. ''Sorry I couldn't convince Paul it was luck that brought us victory.''

''That's okay.''

The beach wasn't too crowded this late in the afternoon. Corrine moved away from him to the low wall that separated the court from the parking lot and sat on the ledge. He wondered what was going through her head.

''You okay?''

''Yes. It felt good to win.''

''I never tire of it,'' he said, crossing to her. Sometimes he thought his interest in sports was the only thing keeping him sanc. He stood a few feet from her and looked at her. She swung those long, shapely legs of hers back and forth. He could almost feel something in the air pulling him toward her.

''I might want to do it again.''

Don't flirt, he warned himself, but his mind refused to listen. ''With me?'' he asked.

She shrugged. ''Maybe.''

''Maybe?''

''Maybe,'' she said again.

She was sassing him again and he liked it too much to walk away. ''Ah, I see. I give you your first taste and you're going to leave me behind to sample it again.''

''Would that bother you?'' she asked.

He closed the gap between them, standing between her legs. She stopped swinging them and tilted her head back to look at him.

"If I said it did, would that matter to you?" he asked, not wanting to reveal too much to her.

He wondered if the rise in endorphins could be blamed on the flush of victory. But he knew that it was her close proximity that was responsible for the blood pooling in his groin and hardening him.

"Say it and see," she said. She licked her lips, and he knew that he wasn't standing there to flirt with her. He acknowledged that he'd moved in to taste those lips of hers. To feel that supple body of hers pressed to his.

He lowered his head slowly in case he'd read her wrong, but she didn't pull away. Instead, she cupped the back of his head and rose to meet him. Nothing had ever tasted sweeter than her mouth when it met his.

Nothing had ever tasted more forbidden, either, because her embrace was filled with both a woman's passion and a sweet shyness that could only be Corrine.

Four

Rand's body pressed against hers, surrounding her with his heat. He smelled earthy and sweaty, like a primal man calling to all the instincts she carefully hid beneath her wall of aloofness.

Shivers spread down her arms from where he held her. She opened her mouth wider, inviting him deeper. He thrust his tongue into her mouth with a surety that told her he knew his way around a woman's body. Later that might bother her, but right now she thanked God for it.

Her breasts felt heavy and full and she leaned forward until her torso rested against his. Her nipples started to tighten and she rotated her shoulder blades, brushing her aroused flesh against the rock-hard planes of his chest.

Rand groaned deep in his throat, his thumb idly caressing her neck as if he had all day to get to know her mouth. As if he'd stay where he was until he'd uncovered all the secrets there. As if he'd wait for her to be ready for more.

And for the first time in three years, Corrine was ready for more. *Much more.* She tugged him closer between her spread thighs.

She wasn't a virgin; she'd had sex before and occasionally enjoyed it, but Rand was shattering her illusions about what she wanted. Lust wasn't in her program.

She was focused on her job. Her career path had become more important to her than all those other relationships, but as he slid his hands down her back, cupping her backside and sliding her forward on the low wall until he rested at the notch of her thighs, she realized she didn't care.

All that mattered was this moment. Rand's large hands slipping over her back and under the hem of her shirt. The roughness of his calluses as he slid his hands down her spine. His long fingers dipping beneath the waistband of her shorts, caressing the furrow between her buttocks. She moaned in the back of her throat, realizing that she was never going to be able to get her guard up around him again.

His kisses were like a drug, making her crave them more and more. She ran her hands over his chest and pecs. Damn, he was in really good shape. His hips were wedged between her thighs and she felt as if she were on the cusp of something.

A piercing wolf whistle made Rand raise his head. Some beach bum was ogling them. His mouth was still wet from hers and she reached up, rubbing her thumb over his bottom lip. He nipped at her finger and tucked her head against his chest, holding her in a hug that made her realize there was more between them than a business contract and lust.

That thing felt scarily like caring. *Oh, God, don't let it be caring.* Caring was the one thing she'd always avoided. Or tried to avoid. She kept her feelings to herself, because every time she'd ventured out of her shell she'd been hurt badly. She wasn't taking that chance again. She had a plan for the future and she was going to work that plan and that plan only.

"That almost got out of hand," he said after a few minutes. He dropped a soft kiss against her temple and continued holding her in his protective embrace. No one had ever tried to protect her. She wasn't sure she liked it. Because she realized he knew she had vulnerabilities.

He was still hot and hard between her legs, and she regretted he'd kissed her in such a public place. They could have followed things to their natural conclusion if they'd been some place private. She could no longer pretend the attraction between them didn't exist.

Corrine regretted that.

"Yes, it did. Why?" she asked.

He leaned back and gave her one of his lord-of-the-manor looks. She flushed.

"Hey, I'm blond. I think I'm allowed the occasionally ditzy comment."

"You know you're leaving yourself open to all kinds of jokes now."

"Isn't that a little too easy for you?" she asked. He smiled at her, and she realized that she liked the way he teased her.

"Where you're concerned there's no such thing as easy." There was a seriousness to his tone that belied the light moment. She realized that for all that she was trying to protect herself from getting hurt, Rand might be doing the same thing.

"If I'm that much trouble, why do you bother?" she asked. No one had ever thought she was worth the trouble. Not her mother or father, not the series of foster parents she grown up with, not the men she'd dated. Was Rand serious?

Grasping her face in his big hands, he tilted her head back and then kissed her. This time his restraint was marked, but fire still zipped through her body, making her nipples tighten and the flesh between her legs throb. He stepped back and lifted her down from the wall she was sitting on.

"You're worth it," he said, dropping his hands and walking away.

Corrine watched him go, aware that he'd crossed a line. And she realized as she slowly started after him toward the clubhouse to change that she didn't regret his boldness. In fact, she hoped he'd do it again... soon.

That thought scared her, because it meant that

she'd already started to drop her guard. There was a darkness in Rand's eyes that mirrored the one in her soul. And she didn't think "casual" was in the cards for them.

Rand emerged from the washroom to find Corrine waiting. The tepid shower he'd just taken had gone a long way to cooling him down, but one look at her and his blood immediately heated and the unresolved desire returned. He wanted her like he'd wanted no woman in the past.

And if she were a different kind of woman, he would take her. They had the weekend—normally that would be enough to assuage him. But he sensed with Corrine he'd want more. He'd need more. He'd never be pleased with anything less than the total annihilation of her cool outer facade.

And he also knew there was no way he'd be able to remain uninvolved if he slipped the leash of his control. Already the tension that was his daily companion was intensifying, making him shake with a weakness he refused to acknowledge.

Corrine Martin was dangerous. He didn't know why she made him react the way she did, only that she did. And he didn't like it. He wanted to blast through her icy exterior and make her the vulnerable one, not him—never again.

She looked fetching, standing there backlit from the setting sun, which streamed in the plate-glass windows. *Fetching* wasn't a word he usually used, but there was something about Corrine that brought out his old-fashioned notions of courting. Hell, she brought out the most old-fashioned thing between a man and a woman in him—lust.

It wasn't only that he'd tasted her mouth and felt the passion she kept tightly under control. She'd left her hair down. Damp from her shower but starting to dry, it brushed her shoulder and curled with a slight wave. He regretted he hadn't taken the time to touch her hair earlier. It looked like silk with the sun illuminating it, and he clenched his hands to keep from crossing to her and taking her head in his grip.

But he knew caressing her velvety hair wasn't going to be enough. He'd soon be tipping her head back and exploring her mouth until she rose to meet him. Until she became as overcome as he. Until nothing less than total completion would satisfy either one of them.

Yeah, he should've felt her hair earlier, but frankly, his body had been focused on much more responsive areas of hers. He'd been on overdrive and needed to arouse in her the same passion that had been flowing through his veins.

"Hi," she said softly. Her voice brushed over him like the hot sun had earlier, making him feel heavy and lethargic. His groin tightened a little more and he shifted his bag so that she wouldn't notice.

He nodded at her, unsure if he could talk right now. He was used to playing and winning, even with women. Winning made him feel in control and sure of himself. And there was a vulnerability in Corrine's eyes that warned this wasn't a game. Or at least not one that would leave behind a victor.

"Hi, yourself," he said, trying for a casualness he didn't feel.

His beast had slipped the civilized reins of his upbringing and the veneer of sophistication was a memory. Winning always brought him a rush, but holding a woman in his arms had never affected him the way Corrine had. Her taste was still on his lips, the feel of her skin, soft and smooth, was still under his fingertips, and the feel of her tightened nipples still abraded his chest.

He hardened more, undoing the effects of the shower. *Damn.* He hadn't counted on this. Hadn't counted on her or the way she made him forget the things about himself he'd always taken for granted. He'd had success with women for one reason and one reason only. He wasn't playing for keeps, so it was easy to play to win. Easy to put their needs first and make them feel as if they were the center of his world.

He knew with gut-deep sureness that if he made Corrine the center of his world—with her wide, unguarded eyes and her shy smile—he'd never want to let her out of his life. And he wouldn't ask anyone to share the shadowy world that was his reality. He might have the world fooled into believing he was the easygoing owner of a successful business, but deep in the night, under the cover of darkness, he knew the truth.

"Ready to leave?" he asked, starting for the door.

Maybe if he could make it to the car and concentrate on driving, this would go away. *Yeah, right.*

"Um…Rand?"

He glanced over his shoulder at her. She hadn't moved. Her straw bag was still over her shoulder, but her hands were crossed around her waist in the most defensive position he'd ever seen.

She wrinkled her nose. "Thanks."

"For what?"

"Winning."

"No problem," he said.

"It isn't for you, but for me it usually is."

"Like you said, winning isn't everything."

"Maybe it's the adrenaline from taking a risk."

"Why risk?"

"I was unsure of Paul's reaction."

"Paul's a nice guy," Rand said. Why the hell were they talking about Paul?

"Yes, he is…nice."

Where was this inane conversation going? He dropped his bag and strode back to her, aware there was more she wanted from him than just a rehash of something that had happened earlier.

"What's with all this niceness?" he asked, barely an inch of space separating them.

"You don't think Paul is nice?"

"Cori, I'm hanging on to my control by a thread. At this moment Paul is the last person on my mind."

"Who's on your mind?"

"Do you really not know?"

She shrugged. "I don't know myself around you. I feel achy and I don't like it."

He framed her face in his hands and bent his head, taking her sweet mouth with his. She dropped her bag and wrapped her hands around his shoulders, holding him to her. He wasn't going anywhere. Not now. Not until he'd appeased the hunger deep inside him.

But not here, he thought. He needed to get them someplace with total privacy. And he needed to think. He lifted his head, rubbed his thumb across her lower lip. Her mouth was wide and full and meant to be under his. Rand dropped a few small, teasing caresses on her face and then stepped away, glancing at his watch.

He saw the uncertainty in her eyes and knew that if he didn't encourage her she'd retreat back behind that coolness she used to keep the world at bay. Deep inside he was touched. Hell, more than touched that she'd dropped her guard for him.

But he knew fate well. Knew that a man wasn't meant to have it all. A long time ago, Rand had decided wealth was enough for him. It wasn't as risky as emotion.

"Well, that was *nice*," he said.

"I'm ready to go home," she said, grabbing her straw bag and walking out of the clubhouse without another word. But each tattoo of her sandals echoed in the room, saying to Rand, "Bastard."

There wasn't anger in her steps, only disappointment, and he wasn't used to inspiring that kind of reaction in women.

* * *

Corrine prided herself on being a smart woman. She rarely had to be shown or told how to do something more than once. In fact, she'd received recognition at work for her quick thinking. So as she sat next to Rand, driving back to her house, she knew with absolute certainty that she would never again attempt to step outside her box.

She thought about pulling out her laptop and escaping into her work but knew that this time work wouldn't be the escape she needed. She had a slight sunburn from being outside, but that sensation didn't bother her as much as what had happened with Rand. Was it his reaction that made her feel this way or the fact that she'd wanted something more from him?

Something physical and deep. Something that wouldn't go away. Because even though she knew he didn't want her, because no one ever really had—but she still wanted him. Her pulse beat languidly and her skin was sensitized. She still felt him pressed along her body, and there was a part of her that wouldn't be content until he was touching her again.

But he didn't want to. He'd made it abundantly clear in one fell swoop. Had he glimpsed the thing that made her unlovable? She wrapped her arms around her waist, chilled at the thought that her vulnerability was so easily visible to this man. The one man who made her want to reach out to him saw her for the incomplete woman she was.

"Cold?" he asked.

She shook her head. Huddling deeper in her seat,

she glanced out the window at the passing landscape. She'd lived her entire life in Florida…carved out a safe niche for herself. And only today had she realized how cold and lonely her place in the sun was. The future suddenly took on a new meaning, and her career, which had been her focus for so long, paled when she thought of her elderly years spent alone with only her mind for company.

"Sure?" he asked after a few miles.

"Yes," she said firmly. It felt as if he was offering her an olive branch. Why the hell didn't she just take it?

But she couldn't. She'd spent her entire adult life keeping everyone at bay, and the one time she wanted to let someone closer—not just anyone, but Rand— he didn't want to come.

He fiddled with the radio, tuning into a hard-rock station. Music blared from the speakers and she wondered if he was trying to quiet his mind with the music. It wasn't working for her. His words echoed over and over in her mind, like a hunter circling his prey…*that was nice.*

Their embrace had shaken her moorings, making her question things in her life that she'd always taken for granted. The very fabric of who she was had ripped in half, and she realized she didn't know herself with this man. Why him?

What was it about Rand that made her sit up and take notice? Suddenly she couldn't wait another minute. She flicked off the radio and he turned to her. He glanced at her from beneath the dark rims of his sunglasses, but his eyes were not visible to her.

He raised one eyebrow at her in question. Unable to help herself she mimicked the action back to him. He cracked a grin but didn't say anything. She liked him, dammit. Why was it when she finally found a man she thought she could connect with he was all wrong for her?

"Did you want something?" he asked after a few minutes of silence.

"Yes." She wanted him. Even if it was only for a short-term affair. But how did you ask a man who you'd bought for business to suddenly make the arrangement personal?

"Why?" she asked at last.

"Why what?"

"I guess I meant, why not? Since the moment we met you've been flirting with me, and when I finally take you up on it…" She couldn't say it out loud. Even though she'd known her entire life that she was not a keeper she didn't want him to realize it. Except he already had.

It had started with her birth parents and followed her throughout her entire life. Quick learner that she was, you'd think she'd have caught on by now. But there was always a feeling of hope deep in her soul that maybe this time someone would want to keep her.

He cursed savagely under his breath, slowed the car and pulled off on the shoulder. He didn't look at her, but instead stared out of the windshield. Not saying a word to her, he rubbed his forehead.

"I got the feeling you didn't want more from me," he said at last.

He had her. Why was it she never seemed to realize how important a person was to her until he'd moved on? "Well, I didn't."

He shifted the car into Park and turned toward her in the seat. He laid his arm behind her, and though he didn't touch her she felt the heat of him. Something deep inside her let loose and she realized that even if she made a fool of herself, this man was important to her and she couldn't let him go without a fight. "So what's the problem?"

"I don't know. It's just that…"

"What?" he asked. He removed his sunglasses and those green eyes of his bore into her. She felt as if he was seeing past the conversation she was using to protect herself.

"It's been a long time since a man kissed me like you did," she said.

"Really?" he asked, his voice dropping to a low, husky growl. His hand moved to the back of her neck, rubbing in a slow, sensuous circle.

"God, I should've known better than to say that to you, ego man." His touch made it hard for her to think, but she didn't want him to stop. God, why was this man the one to bring her to aching attention? Why did he call to all that was feminine in her?

"It's not ego. You're a hard woman to read."

"I've lived a hard life," she said quietly. There

was no use hiding it from Rand. She wasn't the woman she tried to present to the outer world. Though she knew she'd keep up the image around him, he had to know there was more underneath the surface.

"I don't want to hurt you," he said, glancing away from her and taking his hand from her neck.

She wondered if she might already matter to him a little bit. It would be so easy to sink back into silence and let this conversation die, but she wasn't about to miss out on Rand. Something about him called to the wild, untamed part of her soul that she'd hidden forever. Taking his hand in hers, she said, "I won't let you."

"Nothing can stop fate." He turned his hand in her grasp so that he was the one holding her hand. His fingers were large, engulfing hers completely. His thumb rubbed over her knuckles and she knew he meant nothing sexual by his touch, but that didn't stop shivers from spreading up her arm.

"What do you mean?" she asked.

"Just that happiness is a delicate balancing act, and what we feel for each other is too explosive not to blow up in our faces."

She studied him for a moment. "Where does this leave us?"

"With a handful of firecrackers," he said.

She just waited, sensing that he had more to say. He sighed, brought her hand to his lips and kissed her. She felt like a maiden of old receiving a knight's colors. And for the first time since she met him she realized that Rand wasn't wearing shining armor and riding a grand steed. He was weary and riding a horse that had seen too much battle.

That glimpse shook her. There was more to this flirty playboy than she'd imagined. Sensing she wasn't the only one who could get hurt, she wanted to pull back, but he smiled at her.

"How about we start with dinner?" he asked.

Even though she knew better, knew that there was no way she was going to be able to keep this man at arm's length, she smiled and nodded. He drove them to Tasty Thai, where they ordered takeout, and then went to her house to eat it. All the while Corrine knew that she had taken a step that would change her life forever.

Five

Two hours later, Rand still wasn't sure he'd made the best decision, but he couldn't regret spending the evening with Corrine. Her house was neat and homey. Not what he'd expected from her all-business persona. He could tell that she'd created a sort of sanctuary for herself. The only thing missing were family photos. In fact, there were no photographs in the entire house. He'd taken a tour while she'd brewed some iced tea for them.

She'd offered him a beer with dinner, and for the first time in a long time, he'd been tempted to take it and drink it. Corrine made him feel things and he preferred to live in the safety of numbness. At social functions he usually held a glass in his hand and didn't taste it because one taste was never enough.

But tonight his control was shaky, and even smelling alcohol was something he didn't want to attempt. He hoped once he'd had Corrine in his bed, once he'd exorcised the passion she wrought effortlessly from him, he might be able to find his equilibrium again.

Her living room was a homage to the cinema, and it was clear to him that her secret passion was movies. Her bookshelves were crammed full of script versions of films and biographies of movie stars. She had a state-of-the-art home theater system that rivaled his own. As the evening had progressed he'd realized that Corrine might freeze everyone out at work and be a top-notch businesswoman, but the real woman underneath was a bit of an innocent.

There was a part of him that wanted to uncover all of her secrets. She'd teased and flirted with him throughout dinner, and now that they were in the living room enjoying coffee and the sounds of mellow jazz on her Bose speaker system, he should be relaxing.

But she was close to him on the couch. Her pheromones were doing too good a job at attracting him, and he felt as if he might fall on her like a hungry dog unless he distracted himself. No matter that she'd all but asked him to spend the night in her bed. He needed to remember that he'd made a vow to stop hurting the innocents of the world a long time ago.

"I can't believe you don't like period movies. *Emma* was one of the best I've ever seen."

"It's a girlie movie."

"Girlie movie? *Thelma and Louise* is a girlie movie."

"Point taken. Why did you think I'd like that?"

"You just seem different from other men," she said.

He wasn't sure how to take that. He was different and had been for a long time. "You think I'm girlie."

She swatted his shoulder. "Don't be obtuse."

"I'm not."

She gave him a very serious look, but there was a sparkle in her eyes. And he knew that she was teasing him. Suddenly it became very important that he handle her carefully. Because he realized that she was slowly blossoming here tonight. She'd started earlier at the beach when her focus had widened off of work, and then over dinner it had continued.

Normally he'd be happy that a woman he wanted showed signs of wanting him with the same intensity, but tonight, with the full moon shining in through her bay window and the sensual music pouring through the speakers, seduction no longer seemed the order of the day. Seduction, in fact, seemed a violation of the trust that was slowly building between them.

A trust that Rand knew to be false because he was hiding the truth of who he was from her.

"What's your favorite movie?" she asked.

"*Star Wars.*"

"Good choice. The mythical story structure and impact on cinema alone make it a good choice."

"I was thinking of Princess Leia in her bondage outfit."

"You're into bondage?"

"Only if it excites you," he said. He'd like nothing better than to tie her to his bed.

She wrinkled her nose. "I don't think I'd like it."

"I promise you would," he said.

"Get that gleam out of your eyes. I was teasing you."

"I know," he said. He'd lived a decadent life in part because he'd been running from his image as the good son and also because when you had everything, life got boring. But he'd long ago given up on jading innocents.

There was a brief lull in the conversation and Corrine leaned her head back with her eyes closed. "You're the first person I've had to the house for dinner."

"Should I feel special?" he asked.

She turned her head and her bright gray eyes made him feel as if he were being measured. "Yes."

Oh, Corrine, he thought, don't feel too much. Unable to wait another minute, he reached out and touched her cheek. She shivered under his touch. And he knew that the electricity that he felt whenever they were together wasn't one-sided.

"Why do you keep people at arm's length?" he asked.

She shrugged. "It's just easier."

"Why?"

"Don't laugh," she said.

He tugged her close and hugged her tight. "Never."

"Everyone always leaves."

The words were spoken so softly he could barely hear them. And he wasn't sure he understood. But then he remembered her comment on the drive to the beach about her parents abandoning her.

"Like your parents?"

Her fingers nervously kneaded the fabric of his shorts where they covered his thigh. He knew she meant the touch to be impersonal, but he found it arousing just the same. He also knew now wasn't the time for lust.

"Yes," she said.

"How do you know they left you?"

"My foster mother told me."

"How old were you?"

"When she told me the truth?" He nodded. "Six."

"Why did she tell you?"

"I kept crying for my real parents every night, hoping they'd come and take me from the home."

He heard all she didn't say. That those words had cut her more deeply than any others could. He tightened his arms around her. Holding her closer, wishing he could go back in time and protect her.

But he'd never been any good at protecting anyone other than Angelica. This time, he vowed he would be. This time it was extremely important that he keep her safe. The tension that always rode him sharpened and he shivered under the pressure it presented. He should get up and leave. Now. Before this thing went any further and he lost the little bit of sense he had.

But he stayed all the same.

* * *

She'd suggested a movie and they'd watched *The Sixth Sense*. He knew he should have left earlier, but he'd been unable to make himself go.

"This is nice."

"Nice" again. He knew what she was doing. Creating a barrier between them so that she'd didn't feel too much. He knew that he had no business being here with this woman. He was going to hurt her no matter what he did. And hurting her wasn't something he could live with.

He wanted more from her. He didn't question why, only knew that he did. "It's getting late. Should I be heading home?"

She sat bolt upright and looked at him with those wide gray eyes. She was trying to shutter them as she usually did, but there was no real chance for her to do so. Good job, old man. Go right for the jugular every time.

"I'm sorry. I guess that wasn't subtle."

"No, it wasn't."

"If we're going to get to know each other…" He let the sentence trail off, unwilling to be even more of a hypocrite than he was. He wanted to know every intimate detail of her life to figure out what had shaped her into the woman she was today, but he'd never share those same things about himself with her.

"Rand, we work together."

"Unless I've lost my touch we're going to do more than work together."

"Well…"

"I'm not a heartless seducer," he said.

"I wouldn't mind if you were," she said.

"You lost me, sweetheart."

"I'm not looking for anything long-term here. My career is finally on track, and if I play my cards right I could be a VP in the next year or so."

"What does that have to do with me?" he asked, not sure he liked being set up as her stud.

"Everything. I can't afford to get involved with a man."

"What does that make me?" he asked. He definitely didn't like this setup.

"You're a man but you're also one of those guys who has a new girl with him every month."

"I see." It bothered him to realize that she had noticed his predilection. Maybe this was her way of protecting herself.

"Do you really understand?" she asked.

"No."

She took his hand in hers. "I...oh, God, this is harder than I thought it would be."

"Just spit it out."

"Well, I thought you weren't a long-term kind of guy."

"Usually I'm not." Rand had learned a long time ago that leading a charmed life extended only to the outer perception.

She wrinkled her nose, something he noticed she did when she wasn't sure of herself. It might be endearing if he wasn't listening to her say she wasn't as deeply affected by him as he was by her.

"At this point in my life I can't have more than an affair with you," she said in a rush.

He leaned back. *An affair.* The purely masculine part of him said so be it. He wanted her in his bed, and he didn't have to make any kind of emotional connection to her. But his soul—that wounded sixteen-year-old boy deep inside—warned it was too late. That not getting involved with his woman physically was the only way to escape unscathed.

He wasn't the kind of man who should be involved with someone who threatened his self-control. He was more comfortable in complete control. And Corrine had other needs. She needed the kind of man who could give her the family she'd never had growing up. The kind of man who didn't have problems of his own.

Rand put his arm around her and tugged her to him until she rested right next to him. He tilted her head back and took her mouth in a deep, searing kiss. He tried to tell himself it was an experiment to see if she could still say she was objective at the end of it. He tried to tell himself it was to prove a point to her. He tried to keep it purely physical, but he couldn't.

She moaned deep in her throat and her mouth opened for his, her tongue curling around his and making teasing forays into his mouth. Her hands clutched his shoulders, fingernails biting through the thin barrier of his shirt. She shifted on the couch until she was straddling his lap, and her hands left his shoulders to hold his face. Her mouth was as much a participant as his. In fact, if he'd let her, he knew she'd take control of the embrace.

He didn't let her. He'd learned long ago that surrendering any type of control wasn't a good idea. He slid his hands down her back, tugging down the zipper of her dress as he went. She wasn't wearing a bra under the sundress, and he contented himself with caressing her spine and the sides of her breasts for long minutes. Until she thrust her hips against his. Settling her mound right over his aching erection.

He took her buttocks in his hands and pressed her down against him. She felt so damned good. He held her to him and thrust slowly. She lifted her mouth from his and stared down at him, her eyes wide and questioning. He thrust against her again.

"It'll kill me to stop but I need to know that an affair is okay with you."

He thought about it. Knowing himself and his weaknesses, he should get up and leave. But he was rock hard and holding a lapful of woman who excited him more than any had before. And frankly, leaving wasn't an option. "At this point I'd agree to anything."

"I know," she said.

He took a deep breath. He didn't want to stop. He couldn't stop. And her attitude seemed to be the best one—for him. If she wanted a red-hot affair he could give her that. "Okay."

She smiled and shrugged her shoulders until the bodice of her dress fell around her waist. And then she leaned toward him. Her naked breasts pillowed on his chest, her mouth lowering toward his.

She kissed him the way he liked it, hot and deep. He focused solely on the physical. If all she wanted was this, he'd make it the best either of them had ever had. Rand Pearson didn't do things by half measure and he always played to win.

Though she was in the dominant position she knew she wasn't in charge. She hadn't been in charge of herself or anyone else since she'd gotten in the car with him earlier today. This entire episode marked a departure from the person she'd always believed herself to be. And she was glad to see this new woman emerging tonight.

Rand wasn't her kind of guy. She usually preferred men who were bland and ordinary. No, that wasn't right. Just being with him made the others seem bland.

Rand made her feel things too sharply for her to really be able to control them. She'd decided on an affair as the only safe way to burn out the fire that raged between them and to protect herself. Her mind said she'd made the wrong choice, but her body rejoiced in that decision.

She felt flooded with sensations that were generated by the man underneath her. Her center was dewy and wet, and though he wasn't touching her—only watching her—she felt like he was caressing her skin.

He palmed her breasts, plumping them up and staring at her closely. She'd always felt too small in the chest department, but the look in his eyes said he found her just right.

"You're so pretty here," he said, dropping soft kisses on the globes of her breasts.

A feeling of voluptuousness assailed her. She thrust her shoulders back, hoping to entice him closer. He murmured his approval. One of his hands burrowed through her hair and urged her to arch her back even farther.

"That's it, baby."

But he didn't move any closer to her aching flesh. Instead, he kept about an inch of space between his mouth and her nipple. Each exhalation of breath brushed over her, like a silk scarf. Bringing her aroused body to rigid attention.

She tried to move her hands to his head, to force his mouth onto her flesh, but he grasped both of her wrists in one of his big hands. She tried to shift to bring them closer together but he controlled her easily.

"Why?" she asked when it became apparent he wasn't going to move until he was ready.

He brought his mouth to her collarbone and whispered the words against her skin. She shivered. The sensation made her feel so acutely aware of herself as a woman. His woman.

"Because waiting makes the pleasure more exquisite," he said.

He was right, but she didn't want him to crash through any more barriers. They were just having sex.

It wasn't supposed to feel like this. "I can't take much more."

"Oh, yes you can."

He gave her a wicked grin. This time he scraped his teeth from the base of her neck down her chest, stopping at the globes of her breasts. He repeated the caress until every part of her body was on fire. She was unable to keep her hips from rolling against him.

"Rand," she moaned.

"Want more?" he asked, breathing right over her nipple this time. His mouth was so close, she felt the humidity of his words.

"I'll get even," she said, hardly recognizing the breathy voice as her own.

"Give me your breast," he said.

She shifted her shoulders, and this time he supported her back and finally she felt his lips close over her nipple. Again he waited. Not sucking on her but letting her hardened nipple fill his mouth. She needed more. The ache between her legs was growing stronger. Rocking against his erection no longer satisfied it, but intensified it. She wished they were both naked.

Needed them both to be naked. She tugged her wrists free of his grip. She unbuttoned his shirt and caressed the rock-hard planes of his chest. He began to suckle at her breast. His hands roamed over her back down to her waist, then slid underneath the barrier of her clothing to cup her buttocks again.

He bit lightly on her nipple and thrust his hips up

toward hers at the same time. The sensation was incredible. She shuddered and moaned his name.

"Like that?" he asked, moving to her other breast.

"*Like* is too tame a word."

He suckled her other nipple until she felt that she'd explode. He pulled back just short of that. "Rand, please."

"Not yet. Will you strip for me?"

She didn't know if she could do it. Her first instinct was to open his pants, free him and take him. But Rand had made her feel more during foreplay than most of the men she dated. And she wanted to please him.

"Okay."

She climbed off his lap and pushed her dress and panties off in one swift movement and then returned to him.

"That was the quickest striptease in history."

"You wanted a show?"

"Hell, yeah."

"I might be persuaded to do a little more for you, but you're going to have to lose your clothes."

"Happy to oblige."

He shrugged out of his shirt and then stood to remove his shorts and boxers with a quickness that belied his need to go slowly. There was a fine line of hair that tapered down his belly to his groin. He was...bigger than she'd expected him to be. He noticed her staring and held his hand out to her.

"Enough waiting?" he asked, with a gentleness she hadn't realized he had.

"Oh, yes."

He hugged her to him. And she nestled against his chest. Her blood pounded through her veins and the scent of him surrounded her. His heart beat a steady tattoo under her cheek. He settled back on the couch, pulling her over him and taking her mouth in one of those deep kisses of his that made her question why this had to only be temporary.

While his mouth consumed hers, his hands swept over her body. She settled over him. Felt his erection probing at her entrance. He pulled back.

"Are you on the pill?"

"Yes," she said. No way would she ever bring an unwanted child into the world.

"I'm clean. Gave blood last month," he said.

"Me, too," she said. In fact, she'd seen him at the blood drive.

"Ready?"

"Almost," she said.

His roaming hands found the aching flesh between her legs, seeking out the center of her desire and caressing her lightly. His other hand stayed at the small of her back, urging her hips to rock against him. She felt everything inside her start to tighten, and knew that the end was near. She wanted him inside her.

Reaching between their bodies, she took him in her hand and guided him to her entrance. He held her hips in both of his hands and lifted his mouth from hers.

"Ride me," he said.

She did. She felt too full at first and had to wait for her body to adjust to him. Then she started moving on him. Braced her hands on his shoulders and tilted her head back because the expression in those deep green eyes of his made her feel things too intensely.

She kept the pace steady until everything inside of her tightened and her climax washed over her. Rand's hands on her hips changed from guiding to controlling. He held her still for his thrusts. He suckled strongly on her breast and surged up into her three times before he came with a shout of release that echoed in her mind.

He hugged her to him, letting the sweat dry on their bodies. And Corrine could only think that Rand was never going to be a temporary man in her life. She would be remembering him and this moment until the day she died.

Six

"That was nice," Corrine said long minutes later.

"Nice, huh?"

"Oh, yeah. I never knew that I could share something so profound with a man."

Profound? He didn't do profound. In fact, she'd insisted it was just a red-hot affair. Why then had it felt like soul sex? The kind of physical bonding that he'd always dismissed as bragging by other men, and fantasy by the women they'd shared it with.

He'd isolated himself from the world a long time ago. He worked hard to give the impression that he was open and gregarious, but the truth was he felt safest by himself. Felt most comfortable when he was in his dark cave. Why then did he have the urge to drag Corrine back there with him?

There were maybe three moments in his life that he'd felt this intensely since he'd given up the bottle. The first had been when Roger had died. The second had been when he'd joined Angelica to create Corporate Spouses. And tonight with Corrine in his arms he felt it again.

Something deep inside him shuddered and he wasn't sure he was going to be able to stay here. He needed to get away from her. To get away from this place where he felt too vulnerable. And there was no escape. She was murmuring something soft against his chest and he didn't want to separate their bodies and leave.

But he had to. He lifted her from him and she smiled shyly at him. The tension, always his constant companion, tightened the back of his neck. He stood abruptly, tugging on his pants and zipping them.

Her smile faded and she grabbed a blanket from the back of one of the end chairs and wrapped it around herself. She looked incredibly small standing there, her thick blond hair hanging around her shoulders, her gray eyes not frozen for once but alive with questions and a lingering desire. Her mouth was still swollen from his kisses. And there was a flush on her skin from the climax she'd just had.

Leaving now was the last thing he wanted. His recently satiated body still craved more. He needed to make her his again and again until he'd made her his completely. Until all her secrets had been found.

Inside his head a war raged. He wanted to stay. Hell, his body screamed he had to stay. He longed to

scoop her into his arms and carry her down the hall
to her bed. Then he would take her in every way he'd
ever taken a woman.

He felt the man he was expected to be colliding
with the man he really was. He gritted his teeth and
clenched his fists.

"Rand?" Something in her voice revealed the vulnerability he'd never expected her to experience.

He glanced up at her. Why did he always seem to
hurt those he wanted to protect? How many times was
he going to have to fail at this before he learned the
lesson?

"Are you okay?" she asked.

No. He'd never been okay. He'd been running all
his life, and for the first time had met someone who
made him want to stop. But he couldn't—wouldn't—
stop now and bring her into his world. She deserved
better. In fact, she wanted a better man—from him.
She only demanded sex from him.

"I'm fine."

"You seem—"

"I'm okay. Listen, I've got to go." He walked
around her living room, grabbing his clothing, shoving his boxers, socks and tie into his pockets and
shrugging into his shirt.

"You don't have to leave."

"Yes. I do."

She trailed behind him to the door, and he knew
that this wasn't what she'd had in mind. His body
urged him to stay, as well. Stay through the night and

twist with her on her bed. But he knew himself well enough that he had to leave now.

"I'll call you," he said.

"Don't bother."

"You're the one who wanted an affair."

"I know. But I didn't want it to feel like a one-night stand."

He pivoted to face her. He could tell she was trying to put on her office face, cool and calm, but instead she was wary. Watching him as if he were a dangerous animal. Hell, he felt dangerous and out of control. God, he needed something to numb him to this feeling.

"This isn't a one-night stand."

"You're right. It feels more like a quickie."

"Don't push me, woman. I'm trying to do what you asked."

"When did I ask for you to make me feel as if I'd just discovered fire and then to walk away?"

He dropped his jacket and moved toward her, then caged her face in his hands and tilted her head back so that she was defenseless to him. Bending his head, he took her mouth in a ruthless kiss. He expected her to be passive or rebuff him, but instead her hands grabbed his head and she gave him back the same kiss.

Damn, she was his equal on too many levels. He pulled back. Her mouth was full, lips wet and glistening from his kiss. His erection throbbed against his inseam and he knew that he wasn't in for a comfortable night. But comfort had walked out the door the day he'd met Corrine Martin.

"Next time we'll take all night," he said.

"Maybe there won't be a next time."

"Dammit, Corrine."

"Yes, dammit, Rand. I didn't sign up to be your plaything."

"But you expected me to be yours?"

"I didn't hear you objecting," she said.

"Show me a man who'd object when he has a willing woman on his lap."

She flushed. He knew he'd gone too far, but he was feeling trapped and his instincts always said to come out fighting.

"Goodbye, Rand," she said.

He grabbed his stuff and walked out the door. He heard it close quietly behind him.

Corrine knew a brush-off when she got one. She hoped she'd come out the winner of her last confrontation with Rand, but she knew deep inside there had been no winner. Just two losers.

Which was why she'd never let herself become involved with men she had to work with. Sure, there had been that incredible heat between them, but now all she could do was regret it. And she hated regrets because they were a useless waste of energy.

She'd been unable to sleep after he left so she'd spent the night doing new projections for the coming quarter. She worked through the rest of the weekend, telling herself that it didn't matter that he hadn't called. She didn't want to talk to him again.

But inside she felt the same way she had when she'd been six and Mrs. Tanner had told her she'd been found in a trash can. And that *no one* wanted her. Even though she'd said she only wanted an affair, she'd expected—okay, hoped for—more from Rand.

That was in the past. Today was Monday and she was ready for a busy week, dressed to the nines in a severe black Donna Karan suit that she'd purchased when she'd first been promoted. She loved the suit. It made her feel invincible.

She walked into Tarron and wanted to groan inside. Rand was standing in the lobby chatting with one of the security guards. She walked straight past him, not even glancing in his direction. Keep breathing, she reminded herself as she waited for the elevator doors to close.

They started to shut and she let her guard start to drop, but then a large, masculine hand blocked them and Rand stepped inside. He hit the button for her floor and then the button to close the doors.

"Good morning, Corrine," he said.

She nodded at him. Not really wanting to start an inane conversation that would mask what she really wanted to say, which was something mean and sarcastic. But she wasn't going to let him see how deeply he'd wounded her.

"Not talking to me today?" he asked, moving closer to her in the elevator.

"That would be childish," she said.

Her gut told her to step away from him, but she refused to give even the appearance of backing down. So she stood her ground, even though now she could see that he didn't look as well put together as he usually did. His tie was knotted perfectly, his suit neat and clean, but there was something different about him today.

"And neither of us are children," he said, facing her.

"What do you want from me?" she asked. She knew it was abrupt, but she didn't really know how to play games with men. She knew how to keep them at bay with an icy glare or a few well-phrased barbs, but shoving a man back outside her inner wall after she'd let him in…that was one thing she'd never attempted before.

He sighed. "A few minutes of your time."

"Why?" she asked, realizing he looked different today because of his eyes. He seemed tired. No, more like exhausted. She linked her fingers together to keep from reaching out and soothing the tension she could read in his face.

"I don't like this awkwardness between us," he said. This was more than she'd anticipated. There was a genuineness to him that she hadn't expected.

"Me, neither. I mean, we have to continue working together on the training project. And Paul would notice if I never claimed my other two dates."

"I wasn't talking about our business relationship."

"That's the only one we have, Rand." An affair was all she'd wanted. But after making love with

Rand one time she'd realized an affair would never be enough. That she wanted more from him than she'd ever be comfortable asking him for. Because if she did ask him to stay she'd have to open all of her vulnerabilities to him. And she'd learned an important lesson the other night: Rand Pearson wasn't a man she wanted to know her weaknesses.

"I disagree."

She swallowed, unsure what to say to him. She was swamped with emotions that eroded her confidence and made her feel inadequate, and she was a grown woman for God's sake. She wasn't going to let him make her feel that.

"Please, Cori. Just give me a chance to explain."

"Why should I?"

"I haven't slept since I left your place. I can't close my eyes without seeing you."

Why did he have to say things like that? He made her believe that maybe her instincts had been correct when she'd decided to make love with him.

"I asked Adam to give me fifteen minutes alone with you this morning."

"Why?" she asked.

"I thought the office would be the best place for us to talk."

She nodded. It would be a safe place. Neither of them would ever do anything to jeopardize their professional images.

Silence descended and then the doors opened on her floor. Adam, her assistant, was sitting behind his desk. "Hello, Adam. Any schedule changes for today?"

"Just Mr. Pearson. I left you a voice mail with all your updates."

"Thank you, Adam."

"Will you be with Mr. Pearson all morning?" Adam asked.

"No. Just fifteen minutes."

"I might need longer. I don't like to rush," Rand said.

She remembered the fierce look in his eyes when he'd left on Saturday night. For her own sake, she needed to get him in and out of her office as quickly as possible. But if she treated him any differently than she normally did she'd subject herself to gossip. And she didn't want to let that happen.

"I don't want to keep you," she said.

"I won't let you," he said.

She stepped into her office. Rand followed her. He smelled good—better than a man who'd left her should smell. She knew better than to let things go further between them. But her heart sometimes didn't listen to her mind. And this was one of those times.

Rand had no real plan in mind when he'd followed Corrine into her office. He only knew things couldn't continue the way they had been. He'd spent last night in a dark place he hadn't visited since his brother Charles's death so long ago.

A sealed bottle of Cutty Sark had been his only companion there. He hadn't broken the seal even though his hands had sweated and he'd reached for the bottle too many times to count.

Something had to be resolved with Corrine. And it had to be done today. He wasn't sure how much longer he could battle his need for a drink and his need for Corrine. He needed some kind of semblance of normalcy in his life.

He glanced around her office. He'd been in here twice before and he'd never noticed how cold it was. Only seeing her home had given him a glimpse of the real woman behind her corporate suits. And now he realized how well she hid herself. He knew the price for doing just that, because for years he'd been doing the same thing.

"What did you want to discuss?" she asked, seating herself behind her desk.

Her hands were primly folded on the surface, and he realized she was treating him the same way she treated all the other men she interacted with. She tucked a strand of hair back into the bun at her nape and then straightened her blotter.

"I'm not going to let you do it," he said, walking around her desk and propping one hip against the side.

"Do what?" she asked, tilting her head to meet his gaze.

Though he was in the dominant position, he felt the way he always did around her, that she held the power. Maybe that was part of what drew him to her. He only knew that he'd been raised to win, and whatever it took, he'd find a way to manage Corrine Martin. "Relegate me back to the role of stranger."

She shrugged and looked away. "Don't be ridiculous. I'd never do that."

"And I wouldn't let you. We've been too much to each other."

"Too much?" she asked, her voice a husky whisper.

"Lovers," he said, brushing his finger down the side of her face. She had the softest damned skin he'd ever touched. Whenever she was near him he wanted—no, needed—to touch her. His fingers actually tingled with the urge to feel her.

Her pupils dilated and he knew she was remembering their one time together. It wasn't enough. Would a million times be enough to get his fill of her? Would becoming so familiar with her lithe body appease the hunger that ran deep in his veins? He doubted it.

Nothing short of her complete surrender would satisfy him. And he knew damn well that wasn't in either of their best interests.

He had to touch her. Grabbing the arms of her chair, he swung it toward him. Sliding his legs along the side of the chair, he caged her.

She looked up at him, awareness in her eyes. A flush of arousal faintly tinted her cheeks. No longer was he a man to be kept at a safe distance.

"I thought I knew what I wanted from you, Rand. But I was wrong."

''What do you want?'' he asked, knowing on one level they both had the same objective.

''I'm not sure. I only know that I can't handle a repeat of the other night.''

Honesty was important now because he was keeping other secrets he'd *never* share. ''Me, neither.''

''I'm not looking for happily ever after,'' she said quietly. ''Frankly, I've seen enough of life to doubt it exists, but there is something about you that makes me want to believe it. And I know that's a dangerous thing.''

''Why is that a dangerous thing?'' he asked, because it was easier than facing the truth that her words struck a chord deep inside of him. They'd both been shaped by a hard life, although he knew she'd never guess that he'd suffered as she had, albeit in a different way.

But how hard was it really? He'd been given every luxury and sent to the finest schools. When had he turned into such a whiner?

''I don't know. I've forced myself not to form attachments, and you're a playboy, so it should be easier with you than with any other man.''

''I'm not a playboy.''

''Please. You've had more women than James Bond.''

''Does that excite you?''

''I don't know. But the thought of all the experience you have...all the things you've done that I haven't...it makes me feel inadequate.''

''You're not.''

"Usually I'm confident of myself in any arena, but you're used to dealing with upper executives and I'm still middle management."

"Corrine, don't belittle yourself. None of the women you've seen me with hold a candle to you."

She bit her lip nervously. He knew she wanted to ask more questions, saw it in her eyes, but she didn't. "What I meant before was that I'm trying to keep you from being more than a temporary affair, but it's not working. Even when I was saying I wanted something temporary with you, my body was saying 'no way, girl—this isn't a temporary thing.'"

Taking her shoulders in both of his hands, he urged her to stand. Pulling her close to his body, he held her. "I wish I could make you promises."

"Why can't you?"

"Because you can't have everything."

Their eyes met and she took a deep breath before she said, "I don't want everything, Rand…just you."

Seven

Corrine wasn't sure when she'd decided to ask for what she wanted in her personal life. It had started when she'd watched Rand drive away on Saturday night. It had grown all day Sunday when she'd realized that hedging her bets hadn't protected her from feeling washed-up and used. It had solidified when he'd said he couldn't close his eyes without seeing her.

She knew that she meant more to him than the temporary easing of some sexual ache. He held her closely, carefully. Made her feel like she was the most precious woman in the world. And she'd always dreamed of feeling that way.

Snuggling closer in his arms, she realized this wasn't the first time he'd held her so. There was a part of Rand that was as unsure as she was in this situation. She felt it in the way he watched her when they were alone.

She slid her arms around his waist under his jacket. Even in the trappings of corporate America he stood out. His suit was by a top designer, his scent totally male and his body rock hard. He wasn't a man who found his way to the top and was content to stay there. He kept climbing up when most people would be content to stop and enjoy the fruits of their labor.

He ran his hands up and down her spine, and she wished she'd gone to his house yesterday so they could have made love. But she knew this moment couldn't have come any sooner. It took her a while to puzzle things out in her head, and she knew she needed some reassurance from Rand that he still wanted her.

That reassurance was nudging at her belly. She slid her hands down his back to his buttocks and he groaned deep in his throat. She loved the way he reacted to her touch. She glanced up at him and he smiled ruefully.

"I know I'm at work, but my body doesn't care."

"We could…" There was a need deep inside her to cement the tentative bond they'd formed. To make him realize how deeply he needed her. She wasn't sure that he could ever really want her in any way that wasn't sexual, but she wanted to probe into their new relationship and find something that proved she wasn't the only one involved.

He tipped her chin up, brushed a featherlight kiss

against her mouth and then all across her face. She leaned up and found his mouth with hers. Tilting her head, she kissed him with all the pent-up longing that flooded her body. His hands on her face changed, supporting her head for the demands he made of her. He thrust his tongue deep inside her mouth, seeking out her secrets. Tasting her so completely that her entire body was sensitized to him.

She reached for his tie, started to loosen it, then unfastened the button underneath. He took her wrists in one hand, bit her lower lip gently and lifted his head.

"We can't. I'd never be happy with the five minutes we have left here. And neither would you."

"You're right," she said. She wanted to explore him, and she promised herself the next time she had this man naked she was going to find out all the places he liked to be touched.

"I know."

"Smart-ass."

He just grinned at her, and she couldn't help herself from smiling. He set her back in her chair and walked around her desk. She wished the desk and office made her feel more professional, but for once they didn't. Even her career goals paled while he sat in her office. All she wanted was him. That thought scared her, shook her to her core. Who was she if she wasn't an executive?

"I'd like to take you to dinner tonight," he said.

"Sure," she said, knowing that they should take the time to get to know each other. Maybe even slow things down. Yeah, right. Who was she kidding? She'd never be satisfied with anything less than a full-out naked affair with this man.

He took his PalmPilot from his pocket and consulted his schedule. "I'm working until eight. How does nine sound?"

She wasn't sure she could do what Rand did. He worked all day teaching classes in business manners and etiquette and then spent all night at various corporate functions. Being "on" that often wasn't something she'd ever be comfortable with. "Do you really want to go to a restaurant?"

"No, I want to see you."

"Why don't you come to my place and I'll fix us dinner?"

"I'm not sure I'll be able to eat," he said.

"I'll make something that can be reheated."

"I'll bring dessert."

"I was thinking you were dessert," she said with a grin.

He straightened his tie and then stood, walking toward the door.

"Rand?"

"Yes?"

"Why did you leave the other night?"

He walked back toward her. "I'm used to being in control."

"So?"

"You make my control disappear, and that's not a comfortable place to be," he said.

"You do the same to me."

"I'm not like other guys, Cori."

"I don't think you're all that different," she said.

"You're right. Maybe it's ego or wishful thinking."

"I don't think it's ego," she said.

"Why not?"

"There's something solid about you, Rand."

He waggled his eyebrows at her and she knew he was trying to tease her into leaving off this conversation. "I hoped you'd notice."

She let him change the subject but promised herself she'd dig deeper later. "It's hard not to."

"Come over her and kiss me before I leave."

"Why?"

"Because it'll make the day shorter." She was helpless to deny him. And after she'd kissed him and he walked away, she worried that she was losing herself. Not so much because her goals no longer seemed important, but because for the first time it didn't matter if they weren't.

Rand was late. Traffic on I-4 was a bitch and unless he missed his guess it was going to be more like eleven when he got to Corrine's place. He'd had Kelly, his secretary, call Corrine and tell her he wasn't going to be able to make it. So why was he still heading for Kaley Street and her house?

He knew the answer. Despite the fact that he'd never been good at interpersonal relationships, there was a part of him that liked being near her. Even if he could just hold her and listen to her breathing he'd be content.

Twenty minutes later he parallel parked in front of her house and sat there. The same tension that always rode him was there, but being closer to Corrine tamed it—most of the time. Her lights were off and he knew he should just go home. But instead he grabbed his cell phone and dialed her number.

She answered on the first ring. Her voice was softer than it was in the office and he wondered what she was wearing. He'd noticed she changed her attitude with her clothing. "It's Rand."

"Hey," she said. Her voice was dreamy and sleepy. And he knew he should just put the car in Drive and go home.

"Did I wake you?" he asked. If he had, he'd leave. It'd kill him to go home to his dark, empty house in Winter Park, but he'd do it, dammit. He wasn't a cad. He was a Pearson. A gentleman through and through. No matter how high the cost, no one had ever seen him behave as anything but a gentleman. Corrine wasn't going to be the first.

"No. I'm reading. Long day?" she asked. He heard the springs of her bed creak as she changed positions. Or maybe it was only his imagination. He doubted it. He knew she was in bed…imagined her there wearing something slim-fitting and sexy.

"The longest." Made longer by the ache in his soul to claim this woman again. To make love to her until exhaustion took them both and he could no longer think.

"I'm sorry. I missed you at dinner."

Her words were a salve for his soul, for that weary part of himself that had been alone too long. She called to a part of his soul he'd walled off long ago and made him wish he was a better man. "Good."

She chuckled. "That's one of the things I like about you."

"What?" he asked.

"That self-confidence. I wish I had an eighth of it."

Would she still like him if she realized it was all a role he'd written for himself to play? He wasn't sure she would. He'd long ago decided he liked himself better when he was pretending to be the good son.

"Speaking of self-confidence…" Despite his training in manners and deportment he knew there wasn't a right way to invite yourself for a sleepover.

"Yes."

"Would you let me in if I showed up on your front door?" he asked.

"Maybe."

Damn, she kept him on his toes. "What would it take to make it a yes?"

He heard her sigh, then the sound of the bedsprings creaking again. If she turned him away he knew he was going to spend the night with the most lurid fantasies of her twisting beneath him on a creaking bed, with only the sounds of her moans and the bed filling the room.

"You did promise me dessert."

"I did, didn't I?" There had been no time to stop

at a bakery. But he had something for her that was just as satisfying as a chocolate dessert but with none of the calories.

"Mmm, hmm," Corrine said.

She was teasing him. He liked it. He thought this might be the problem with Corrine. He plain liked too much about her and he knew from experience and life that things he wanted the most were the ones he never got to keep. "You won't be disappointed. I guarantee it."

"Is that an ironclad, money-back guarantee?" she asked, her voice dropping a notch.

"Oh, yeah." He was getting hard, sitting in front of her house and talking to her. He wanted to be in there with her, to let her tease him while they were cuddled close to each other. So he could let things develop to their natural conclusion and then he'd make her forget all about teasing him.

"Where are you?" she asked.

"Parked outside your house."

"What if my answer is no?"

"Then I'll drive home and take a cold shower."

"Really?"

"Really," he said.

"I don't want to be responsible for that. Why don't you come in?"

He switched off the phone and tossed it on the seat. He didn't want to appear too eager, but hell, he'd just invited himself over. She had all the power in this situation. He didn't ring the bell since she knew he was out there.

She didn't turn on the lights, just opened the front door and stepped back. There was a faint light at the end of the hallway and he could barely make out her face. She wore a voluminous gown that flowed around her when she turned and walked back up the hall. Though not the slim-fitting one of his imagination—still sexy as hell. He closed and locked the door. And then followed her.

Her bedroom was large and had a sitting area off to one side. At first all he could do was stare at her bed. It wasn't overly large but had a wrought-iron bedstead that he immediately pictured her wrists tied to.

He should have guessed with all that creaking earlier that she'd have a bed made for sex. There was a mound of pillows at the head and he could still see the faint indentation from her body.

He glanced around the room. She'd set up a cold supper on the coffee table in the sitting area. He realized she'd been waiting up for him.

"What if I hadn't come by?" he asked, unsure of himself suddenly.

"I'd have been disappointed."

He was humbled.

"Come and eat. Then we can talk."

He knew he shouldn't let himself be so comfortable with her, but for once he silenced the voice inside his head. Shrugging out of his jacket, he sat on the love seat. Corrine curled up next to him as he ate. The tension that was always his companion grew a little tighter deep inside.

* * *

Despite the long day he'd put in, a kind of kinetic energy buzzed around Rand. He talked a little about his job and ate in a way that only a man could. She'd thought she'd kept out too much food, but he finished it all in rather little time.

A nervous excitement bubbled inside her. Rand made her feel alive in a dangerous and exciting way. A part of it was the way he watched her and made her aware of him as a man. The other part was…well… purely sexual.

She'd made her plans for the night very carefully. There were things she'd always wanted to try but she'd never trusted a man enough before. But things were different with Rand and with her. After watching him leave the last time, after being so totally at his mercy, she'd decided she'd be a full participant or none at all.

When he was done he turned to her with that white-hot gleam in his eyes. "Well?"

"Has your hunger been satisfied?" she asked. Having made her decision to see this thing between them through to the end, she felt free. It was as if she'd cast aside whatever inhibitions she had. She was going to enjoy every second of her time with Rand.

"One of them."

She stood, removing her white silk robe. His breath hissed in through his teeth and his eyes narrowed as he saw the white teddy and thigh-high hose she wore underneath. She'd never owned a piece of fancy lingerie before. Her drawers were stuffed with cotton bras and panties that were utilitarian. "Let's see what we can do about the other one."

Taking him by the hand, she led him to her bed. With a slight shove she forced him to sit on the edge of the mattress. "Take off your shoes and socks."

"Are you in charge tonight?" he asked.

"I did just feed you."

"You have a point."

He bent and removed his socks and shoes, then removed his belt and tie, as well. "That's enough."

He raised one eyebrow at her in that manner of his that now just excited her rather than annoyed her. "I'm all yours."

"Lean back on the bed."

He did. She knew it was now or never. Be gutsy. Starting at his neck she undid the buttons of his shirt and pushed it from his shoulders. When the shirt was at his elbows, she stopped pushing it off and tied the sleeves together very neatly. Trapping his arms.

He raised one eyebrow at her in question.

"You mentioned bondage," she said.

"I didn't imagine I'd be the one tied up."

"I did," she said with a grin.

"Go for it," he said.

"I intend to."

His chest had enticed her since she'd seen him bare it on the beach. And the last time they'd had sex she'd been too caught up in her own feelings to really learn what he liked. Tonight was her chance.

She scraped her nail lightly over his pectorals. The muscle jumped under her finger. She leaned down and blew gently on his nipple. It tightened and the surrounding flesh was covered with goose bumps. "Like that?"

"Hell, yes."

She lowered her head. Bracing her hands on his shoulders, she dropped butterfly kisses all over his chest. He tensed his arms, straining against his shirt as she neared his nipple. First she licked the flat brown flesh and then when he moaned, she bit very lightly. His hips lifted from the bed and he groaned deep in his throat.

The sound sent shock waves through her. She felt her own body growing heavy as she touched him. She trailed her mouth down his skin, licking and biting at his rock-hard abs and stomach. When she reached the barrier of his waistband, she settled back on her haunches and toyed with the button.

"Don't tease me."

"I thought you liked anticipation."

"Sweetheart, I'm going to explode in another minute."

"Good."

She bent and took the tab between her teeth, pulling it slowly down. Then she slid her hand inside the placket and fondled him through his underwear. His breath hissed through his teeth and his hands were fisted.

She knew he was reaching the breaking point. So was she. The flesh between her legs was moist and ready to be filled by him. She tugged his pants down, stopping again before they were completely off, leaving the fabric just below his knees.

She caressed the corded tendons in his thighs. Damn, he had nice muscles. And then traced the line of hair from his chest to his groin. His penis was hard and red. She tiptoed her fingers around him. Watched as he grew even larger at her touch. Bending, she dropped kisses on his thighs and the bottom of his abdomen, letting her hair brush over his erection.

"Now," he said.

Until that moment she hadn't realized that position had nothing to do with power. Just hearing his voice was enough to make her want to respond. But it was her show. She unfastened the snaps between her legs that held the teddy closed and then slid up over him.

The first touch of their naked loins made each of them sigh. She reached between their bodies and positioned him before sinking down on him.

She heard the fabric of his shirt rip a second before his hands came up. Fondling her breasts through the lace of her teddy. One hand snaked around her back and nudged her shoulders forward until her breasts dangled within reach of his hungry mouth. He suckled her and his hands caressed her legs and buttocks.

She gripped his shoulders as exquisite sensation flooded her. She was so close to the edge. She tipped her head back and tightened herself around his flesh and felt the first contraction sweep through her. He felt it, too, as he grabbed her hips and pulled her down into his thrusts. She moaned his name as her climax rushed through her. He released her nipple and thrust into her three more times before roaring his completion.

She sank down onto him and closed her eyes. Reality said this couldn't last, but she couldn't regret the time they spent together. She knew he'd leave her one day, but didn't dwell on that. Instead, she held him tightly in her arms and enjoyed his strength and warmth.

Eight

Rand kicked off his pants and threw aside the remains of his shirt. She watched him warily, as if not sure how he'd react to her bondage play. And he wanted to keep her guessing.

If only for a few more minutes. The woman was too sexy for her own good. Fulfilling fantasies he'd only admitted to having to himself.

She held all the cards in this thing between them. She'd surprised him this evening. He'd have expected her, the women he'd come to know after a year of working together, to have refused to let him come into her home. But this was a new Corrine.

The soft Corrine, with her hair down and her sexy lingerie, touched the tender part of his soul. The part that had stopped growing the night Charles had died in the car.

The need for her was so all-consuming that it washed away his longing for the bottle. At least temporarily. He pushed those thoughts away and concentrated on the lovely blonde who was all his.

"Your turn," he said. He was having an X-rated fantasy involving her hose binding her wrists to the wrought-iron headboard. He wanted to hear the springs on the bed creak as he thrust into her hips. He wanted to love her slowly and for a long time.

One time wasn't enough. Hell, twice wasn't enough. There was a part of him that feared he'd never get his fill of her. And he already had one thirst that could never be quenched, he didn't need another one.

"What did you have in mind?" she asked.

He knew she meant the words to sound flirty but they came out worried. "You should have thought of the consequences of your actions. You know I play to win."

She scooted back on the bed, reaching around for her robe. That white silk that made her look untouchable.

"You liked it, don't deny it," she said.

"I loved every second of it. But that doesn't mean I don't want my chance to be in charge."

"You're always in charge. I'm not sure I can surrender my control."

"I did it."

"Your will kept you my captive. You broke the bonds easily."

"Do you honestly believe I'd do anything to hurt you?"

"No," she said, the word barely a whisper.

He expected more of the teasing play that they'd fallen into. But instead her eyes were very serious and he knew he'd stumbled into one of the secrets she was keeping. It was funny how they both had things they didn't want to discuss. Was this a healthy relationship? He doubted it. But then he'd never really had a healthy one.

He crawled up next to her. Propped two pillows against the headboard and then tugged her down until she was in his arms, her head resting right over his heart. She made him feel bigger and stronger than he was. For her he'd fight battles. For her he wanted to be better than he was and that scared him.

"What are you afraid of?" he asked.

She swallowed and looked away. "I don't want to talk about that."

"Tell me," he said, tipping her head back so their gazes met.

She walked her fingers over his chest. He sensed her intent was not to arouse him but to distract him, yet his body couldn't tell the difference and he felt himself start to harden. It was too soon, he thought. He shouldn't want her again—not yet.

"Promise not to laugh."

"Promise," he said. What had he done to convince her that he'd ridicule whatever she'd reveal to him?

He knew then that he couldn't just want to be better than he'd been before. He *had* to be better. Or he'd wind up hurting Corrine in ways he didn't want to.

"I'm not sure where you fit in my world."

"I think I fit nicely right here," he said, tightening his arms around her.

"I don't have a personal life. Just work, and the lines don't blur…or they haven't until you."

"Corrine, I'm not getting it."

"You know I was an orphan. Well, I created a picture-perfect image in my head of what my home life should be. I've created that here. It's a nice, safe world that I don't have to worry about losing."

"What does this have to do with me?"

"You don't fit here."

Her words cut him and he couldn't help it; he stiffened and pulled away.

But she cupped his jaw and gave him the most exquisite kiss. It was deep and carnal but at the same time touched something emotional inside that he was uncomfortable admitting he felt.

"I never put another person in this equation and I'm flying blind here."

"I'd say you did pretty well tonight."

"Well, I've always wanted to try some different things but never trusted a man enough to do it."

He rubbed her arm and felt that tension deep inside him squeeze tighter. "I don't know that I fit in your world here. But I think I could provide you with a place to experiment."

"I'm not just talking about sex."

"Of course you aren't."

"I mean sex is a part of it, too, but not just the only thing I want from you."

"What else do you want to do? Find your parents?" he asked, wanting to understand.

"No."

"Why not? It might give you some closure." Closure was something that had given him some peace. He still had to visit Charles's grave on the anniversary of his death. He still had to celebrate his brother on their birthday. Closure for him had come with remembering that just because a person died didn't mean they'd never lived.

"They threw me in a trash can, Rand. They wanted nothing to do with me."

A shiver walked across his spine, and he held Corrine tighter until he had a leash on his rage against the people who'd tossed her aside with little thought for how that would affect the child they'd brought into the world.

Then he made slow, sweet love to her, removing every stitch of her clothing first. Then kissing her from head to heels and back again. Her hands alternately returned his caresses and clutched at him as if she was afraid he'd leave her. He cherished every inch of her with his mouth, and when they both couldn't stand another minute of separation, he slid into her body.

Only when he was buried deep inside her body and she was moaning her climax did he let loose the feelings pouring through him. Finding his own satisfaction with this woman who was too vulnerable for a man whose greatest accomplishment was that he hadn't had a drink in almost ten years since he and Angelica had started working together.

He didn't think that would be enough. Because he knew that Corrine needed more and he also was sure she'd never ask for anything more from him. Someone who'd been left time and again was used to being disappointed. And he had only just realized that he'd rather die than disappoint her.

Corrine woke up in the middle of the night with a feeling that all was right in her world. It scared her. She'd spent so much time protecting herself that Rand had slipped under her guard. Not unnoticed, of course, but his presence was shocking all the same.

It was funny, really, but she liked having him there. For so long she'd been lonely on a very intimate level. She'd had lovers before, but they'd never made her feel anything near as transcendental as Rand had made her feel. Even the memories of what they'd shared were more shattering than actual consummation with other men.

Lying on her side, she felt Rand curled against her back. He held her with a fierce tenderness that made her hope she affected him as deeply as he affected her. She was surrounded by him. And in the middle of the night with no one around to witness it, she wrapped her fingers around his wrist, snuggling back against him. She felt safe.

It was a new feeling and one that frightened her.

Rand would leave, she knew this and she would mourn that loss. Because for the first time since she was six years old she really felt as if she'd found the seeds of a home.

Even just a temporary home would be fine with her. She knew he wouldn't stay forever. From what she'd observed, few people did last longer than five to ten years together. She'd take whatever time she was given with Rand because tonight was the first time she felt as if another person really cared about her.

When she'd tied his arms and had her wicked way with him, she realized that fun was an important part of relationships and she'd never relaxed enough in the past to actually enjoy anything close to what she'd found with Rand.

Finally she understood her power as a woman. It wasn't to dominate men, though it had been heady to have Rand under her and at her mercy. It was something different. Maybe just the knowledge that she had some power. That she didn't have to wait for life to happen to her. She could go out and make it happen.

Rand moved restlessly behind her and she turned to face him. Touching his face gently, she felt the wild pumping of his pulse. He kicked the covers off the bed and he jerked and groaned. Then a scream was ripped from his throat.

"Wake up, Rand," she said, leaning over him and stroking her hands down his torso. "You're here with me. Everything's okay," she said, repeating the words until his eyes opened.

Sweat covered his body and tension gripped his wiry frame. He sat up and rubbed his eyes with the heels of his hands. She was powerless to do anything to help him.

What did he dream about? Why hadn't she realized he had his own demons? That a man who wanted something temporary wasn't sometimes just looking for sex. Sometimes he was running from circumstances just as powerful as the ones that had shaped her.

"Are you okay?" she asked. Even to her ears the question sounded inane, but she didn't know what else to say. She was dealing with too many things right now. Her own feelings of need and now her knowledge that she'd overlooked a very important part of this man who'd become so significant to her.

He pushed her hands away. "Yeah, fine. Sorry about that."

She laced her fingers together and stared at the pillow, not his face. He was awake, but the feelings engendered by his dream still seemed to be with him.

"No problem. Do you want to talk about it?" she asked.

"No."

"Sure?" Why couldn't she just let it be? She didn't know, but she hated seeing him this way. She wanted to pull him into her arms and comfort him. To soothe his troubles and promise him that everything would be okay, even though she knew such promises to be false. Rand made her want to vow she'd do everything in her power to protect him.

"Corrine," he said. Just her name. A warning, she guessed, to back off.

She needed to do something. Her arms felt empty from not holding him the way he'd held her earlier when she'd confessed her dark, ugly secret. But she knew he wouldn't welcome that embrace.

"Want me to get you some water?" she asked.

He nodded. "I'll be fine in a minute."

She slipped her robe on and went into the bathroom, and returned, bringing him back the drink. He'd put his pants on in the short time it had taken her to get the water. She wondered if his dream had left him feeling vulnerable.

Of course it had. She'd felt the same way when she'd brought him into her room and let him see she'd been waiting for him. "Here you go."

"Thanks," he said, stalking to the window and staring out at the world covered in shadows. He tipped his head back and drained the glass in one long swallow.

"I don't think I'm going to be able to sleep anymore tonight."

She thought talking about whatever had woken him would be best, but it was clear he didn't want to. She wasn't sure what else to do until her eyes lit upon the thigh-high hose she'd had on earlier. She didn't want him to leave. Didn't want him to be alone now and didn't want to be alone herself.

"Come back to bed, Rand," she said, holding out her hand.

"You need to sleep. I shouldn't have come here tonight."

"Yes, you should have. I don't pretend to know what's going on between us, but we need each other. Now, come over here."

He still hesitated.

"I need you," she said.

Still he didn't move.

"Earlier I let you calm me."

"That was different."

"Why, because I'm a woman?"

He shrugged. She knew she'd struck close to the truth. She just waited.

"I don't want comfort from you, Corrine."

"What do you want?"

"Solace."

She understood. She let her robe drop from her body and opened her arms to him. He took two steps toward her and stopped.

"That's not fair to you."

"Let me decide what's fair."

He closed the gap between them and picked her up, settling her in the middle of the bed. There was no slow-building seduction this time. Rand suckled her breast and his hands went straight to her sweet spots, arousing her to the flash point quickly.

He made her feel everything too intensely, but she was aware for the first time that there was a part of himself he was keeping in check. She tugged his face down to hers and kissed him, but he pulled back. And when their eyes met she saw the struggle inside him.

He rolled her over onto her stomach, kissed the length of her spine and then took the pillows from the head of the bed and piled them beneath her hips. He slid into her from behind, his hands gripping hers and his body covering hers completely. His breath rasped in her ear, hot and desperate, as he drove them both toward the pinnacle.

She came once and felt him still hard inside her. He pulled out of her body and turned her over, tossing the pillows on the floor. Then lowered his head once more to her breast. He entered her again and moved with slow thrusts until she started to rise to meet him again. Then he increased the pace until they both climaxed with shattering intensity.

She closed her eyes and curled her arms around him. She held him tightly to her, never wanting to let him go.

Rand liked his office and enjoyed the fact that Corporate Spouses was the one place where he felt totally in control. Angelica was predictable, even though she'd started to get a little more emotional with her pregnancy hormones. Still, he knew how to handle her. Kelly, their secretary, could be counted on to be irreverent and sassy.

"Hey, boss man, Corrine is on line one for you," Kelly said through the open office door. Despite being only twenty-two, the secretary kept the office running smoothly and the mood light, even when they were having a crazy day.

Rand reached for the handset. It had been two

weeks since that night in Corrine's bed when he'd awakened from a nightmare of twisted metal and bloody regrets.

Frankly, he wasn't sure what to say to her. But she'd called at the office and this was one time he couldn't dodge her call as he'd been doing.

"Hello, Corrine."

"I know this is short notice, but I need to use our second date from the package I bought—tonight," she said, all business.

"The timing is bad." He had three classes this afternoon and he'd just fired one of only three of the men Corporate Spouses employed. There were more and more women executives who needed escorts to functions.

"I'm sorry for the short notice. Paul just gave me the Cortell account and mentioned the dinner. I could go alone, but this is really important to my career."

"I know how important your career is."

"So is yours," she said.

"What time?" he asked. He wasn't going to let her go alone. Even if he wasn't sure of his own control, he knew that he still couldn't willingly disappoint her.

"Eight at the Samba Room. It's over near Metro West."

"I've been there before. Want me to pick you up?" he asked.

He liked the Latin-flavored restaurant. He knew that Corrine would, too. It was just the kind of place that he should have invited her to. Would have invited her to on some semblance of a normal date if she hadn't seen him sweating in the middle of the night.

But she had, and it didn't matter that *he* knew where *she* was most vulnerable. He had to deal with her knowing his weakness, though he didn't want anyone to know he wasn't invincible. Especially not Corrine.

"Pick me up at my house. Angelica's been to dinner with the Cortells before so she can brief you on them. Jeff Cortell just sold us his yacht-building company. I e-mailed the information I have on it to Kelly."

"We're set, then," he said.

"I guess so."

Silence buzzed on the line. He wanted to say something but felt inadequate to the task. He didn't know what to say to reassure her and still protect himself. He hadn't slept any better by himself than he had in her bed that night two long weeks ago.

"You still there?" she said.

"Yes," he said curtly. He clicked on his e-mail icon and opened up his in-box. He needed a distraction. She wanted to talk about their relationship and he still wasn't sure what had happened the other night. Was it Corrine who'd brought back the dream? He hadn't had that one in almost ten years.

"I…"

He waited. He should make it easier for her. That's what a gentleman would do. But hell, he knew the truth. Underneath his breeding he was a real beast. So he let her stammer her way through the conversation even though he wanted to put her at ease. Anything to keep himself safe.

"I've missed you."

God, he'd missed her, too. His body craved her more than it ever had alcohol. He'd caught glimpses of her at Tarron when he'd been in the building to teach his training class. But he'd avoided her. She was a new weakness, and the only way he'd ever managed his weaknesses was to avoid them altogether.

"I guess I shouldn't have said that."

"I'm not good with this kind of thing," he said at last. Her voice was usually cool and well modulated, but when she spoke to him he heard the nuances of her emotions. And it only happened when they were alone.

She'd kept so much of herself locked away he felt as if he'd been chosen for the grand prize that she'd selected him to let her guard down with. Yet at the same time he didn't want the prize. The price he had to pay was too damned high.

"What kind of thing?" she asked.

What could he say? He knew men were supposed to be enlightened and more in touch with their emotions these days, but the plain truth was he felt better when he was just reacting. "Talking about how I feel."

"I'm not asking you to talk," she said.

But she was. He didn't call her on it. More silence on the line and then she sighed.

"I'll see you later."

"Corrine?

"Me, too," he said.

She sighed. "Was admitting you missed me so hard?"

"Yes."

"Then I'll have to reward you."

"That sounds interesting."

"You did say I could experiment with you."

"Yes, I did."

"Somehow I thought we'd be spending more time together," she said.

He wanted her. Each night he went home and fought between his twin desires—that damned unopened bottle of Cutty Sark and his physical need for this woman who made him feel like the soft underbelly of a turtle. The rest of the world didn't realize he had that vulnerability.

He hadn't been sleeping well because when he closed his eyes he was plagued with dreams of her soft, sexy body, welcoming his. And he knew she wouldn't turn him away if he showed up at her door in the middle of the night. But he couldn't use her that way. Wouldn't add more pain to a life that had already been filled with it.

"Work has been crazy," he said.

"I know," she said.

"Hell, that's an excuse."

She said nothing. He wished he were in the same room with her so he could see her. So he could touch her and put an end to this conversation he didn't want to have.

"I wouldn't hurt you for anything," she said quietly.

"I'm used to being the strong one," he confessed.

"Oh, Rand. You still are the strong one. Sometimes you need someone to stand beside you."

She hung up the phone and he realized the truth of her words. But standing shoulder to shoulder meant being equal to the task, and he never knew when his own demons would spring out and render him incapable.

Nine

Corrine was nervous. And she didn't like it. She'd worked hard to get respect from her boss and here she was about to blow it. It was ten till seven. Rand should be at her place any minute, and instead of running stats in her head about the Cortell yacht company, she was debating if she should wear her silver or gold jewelry with the Ann Taylor pantsuit she'd purchased on her way home from work.

And it wasn't Jeff Cortell she was worried about impressing. Biting back a scream of frustration, she shoved her silver hoops in her ears and left the bedroom. She wasn't getting changed again. Snap out of it, girl. It's time to be an executive, not a woman.

Her perfect world was changing and she wasn't sure she liked it. She knew there was little she could do to stop the change. Well, there was one thing she could do, but not seeing Rand wasn't something she was willing to do. She liked him. She wanted him in her bed and in her life for as long as fate would let them be together.

She'd missed him the last few weeks they'd been apart. Especially late at night.

The doorbell rang and she collected her purse. She checked her appearance again in the mirror. Damn, did she have time to go back and get the gold earrings? Instead, she opened the door.

Rand looked like a cover model for *GQ* as usual. His tie was the same striking green as his eyes and perfectly knotted. He looked as if he'd effortlessly put himself together. She'd bet he hadn't stood in front of the mirror debating his appearance. She envied him that self-confidence.

"Hello. Traffic is heavy tonight so we'd better go."

"I'm ready. Did you get a chance to read the info I sent over on Cortell?"

"Before we talk business…"

"Yes."

He put his hands on her face and kissed her deeply and thoroughly. She was breathing heavily when he pulled away. He hadn't touched her hair or her clothing so she knew she was still presentable, but inside she felt rumpled and wished they didn't have to be anywhere.

"Nice outfit," he said, taking her key from her hand and locking the front door.

"You think so? What about the earrings?" she asked before she could stop herself. What was she, sixteen?

But she hadn't dated when she was sixteen. In fact, the men she'd had relationships with in the past had been more like ships passing in the night. One of the men had been an E.R. doctor who'd worked weird hours. The other one a traveling salesman who was only in Orlando two days each month.

This was a new type of relationship for her, she told herself. It was okay to be insecure. Except that Rand didn't make her insecure—he made her want to be more womanly than she'd been before. And she'd never been sure of what that entailed.

"Your earrings are fine."

"Just fine?" she asked. What the hell was wrong with her? She was about to have a panic attack over clothes. She couldn't believe this.

It was more than wanting to be Rand's equal. She knew that. It was more than wanting to impress Jeff Cortell for Paul, who was counting on her. Her job didn't hang in the balance of this one dinner. It was...oh, damn, she thought it might be that her world was changing and she wasn't ready for it.

"Nice?" Rand waggled his eyebrows at her. She knew he was teasing.

"*Nice?*"

"Cori, what's up with you?" he asked.

I'm having a mental breakdown because I've only just realized that you mean more to me than my job. And no person had ever meant that much to her.

That's not true—her birth parents had meant that much until she'd turned six and had her illusions shattered.

It wasn't the earrings, she realized. It was her. She'd never felt like this before. Rand stared at her as if she were going to freak out at any second. *Pull it together.* "Nothing. I knew I should have worn the gold earrings."

He led her to the car, then went around to climb in, but when he sat down he didn't start the engine. He turned to face her, one arm resting on the back of her seat.

"We're not leaving until you tell me what's wrong," he said.

The sincerity in his tone touched her. He cared about her, but then she'd already guessed that. There was something different about Rand when they were together. And maybe that was the thing that scared her so deeply.

"I don't know. I've never had any problem picking out clothing, but tonight I changed three times. I'm sure I'm wearing the wrong earrings, and for the first time *ever* I'm not thinking about my career."

"Sweetheart, you are gorgeous in whatever you wear, and earrings on your ears only enhance that image." He rubbed her neck while he spoke.

She knew he meant the touch to be soothing, but instead he was starting a fire throughout her body. It had been too long since they'd touched. Too long since he'd lifted one eyebrow at her in that lord-of-the-manor way of his. Too long since she'd touched him.

"Is that a line?" she asked.

"Is it working?"

She laughed and nodded. "Thanks."

"Nervous about the Cortells?" he asked.

"This is my first big account. I don't want to blow it."

"You won't."

"I wish I had your confidence."

"You do," he said.

He started the car and drove them to the Samba Room. The entire way she let his faith in her flow over her. It was heady to know that for once she had someone else on her side.

The Cortells were as affable as Angelica had said they were. Despite Corrine's worries in the car, she was effervescent, easily charming both Jeff and Alice. Corrine knew her job, and as Rand watched her interact with her clients he had a glimpse of what the future could hold for her. Tarron wasn't like other Fortune 500 companies in which women faced a glass ceiling. Paul Sterling was well aware of what the opposite sex could do and would promote on merit regardless of sex.

Rand was a little awed to realize that Corrine would probably be a VP in six months when Ross Chambers retired. Corrine had worked hard for her success, and he realized as he watched her work the table that she deserved a man who could share that with her. A man who brought to the relationship the skills needed to be successful in life.

Could he be that man?

They'd ordered wine with dinner. An expensive label from California and the smell of the alcohol had overwhelmed him. The lure of it was almost too much temptation. He had a glass sitting in front of him. He drained his water glass about five times but still he was thirsty.

The tension that had been getting stronger these past weeks without Corrine tightened even more and he felt that he wasn't going to escape it. He reached for his wine glass. Just one sip and he'd be okay. One sip and he'd— Hell. He stood abruptly. He needed a hell of a lot more than one damned sip of some wimpy wine.

''Rand?''

''Please excuse me,'' he said. With all the damned water he drank, let them think he was going to the bathroom.

He stalked out of the restaurant and found company with the smokers. Ha, his fellow addicts condemned by society to hang out in the front of establishments and puff away.

A guy in an Armani suit offered him a smoke but Rand declined. Smoking had never been his vice.

''My wife thinks cigarettes are gauche. Yours?'' he asked.

''I'm not married.''

''Even though I've been relegated outside I don't regret marrying her.''

Paul Sterling had shared a similar sentiment with Rand. Seemed happily married men didn't mind making sacrifices for the women they loved. Rand didn't expect to ever be in their crowd. Being happily married would require him to talk about the things he held most private, and he couldn't imagine having that conversation with any woman, especially Corrine.

The Armani-suit guy left. Rand stared out at the parking lot and the busy cars on Sand Lake Road. He usually handled the presence of liquor better than he was doing tonight. For some reason his defenses were down and he thought he understood why. Corrine.

"Rand?"

He glanced over his shoulder to see Corrine standing there. She looked like salvation, with the restaurant lights shining behind her. Illuminating her as if she'd come from heaven to rescue him. But he'd found out long ago that no one was coming to rescue him. He would have to be the one to rescue himself.

"Yeah?" he asked. One time he'd like to be able to face his demon and feel as if he'd come out the winner. One time he'd like to be able to feel like the strong man he knew everyone expected him to be. One time he wanted…hell he wanted to feel normal.

"You okay?" she asked.

He nodded. Somehow saying no would make him feel like a wimp. "Just needed a breath of fresh air."

She crossed to him, standing so close he could smell her perfume. Damn, if she wasn't the sexiest woman he'd ever met. She was still in business mode, so it wasn't as if she were trying to seduce him, yet he was seduced. Her scent, her looks, her touch on his wrist. Soft and warm, reminding him that for tonight at least he wasn't alone. "Long day?"

Lying seemed like a sin in this moment. And since she was looking like his angel he knew better than to commit another sin. He wanted to touch her. Needed to feel her skin under his fingers so that he'd know, really know he wasn't alone. But he didn't want to turn her into his latest addiction. Didn't want to make her into his salvation because then they'd never be equals.

"Not really."

"Oh. Then what's up? Jeff and Alice thought you were in the men's room but I saw you come out here."

"I just needed some fresh air."

"You already said that."

"I'm saying it again."

"Well, it doesn't ring true."

"Sometimes I need to get away. You were handling things."

"Are you claustrophobic?" she asked.

"No. Not that." He rubbed the bridge of his nose. Silence fell between them. "Jeff and Alice are moving into the cigar room. They invited us to join them for cognac and cigars."

He nodded. *Of course.* Cognac was never his favorite drink, but the urge tonight was almost inescapable. He breathed deeply and clenched his hands. He would master this. The same way he'd mastered it countless times before. He was just tired tonight, his guard lowered by Corrine.

She took his hand. He didn't feel so alone anymore. She rubbed her finger along his knuckles and then dropped a kiss on his hand. ''Come on. Whatever is bothering you we'll work out later.''

He followed her back into the restaurant. Into the cigar room where four snifters sat. It had been a long time since he'd had anyone by his side. In fact, the last time he hadn't felt alone had been before Charles had died. He wasn't sure he trusted Corrine to stay.

He pushed the cognac aside and lit a cigar with hands that shook. Deep inside a voice whispered that one sip wouldn't hurt him. But Rand resisted, instead taking a long pull on the Cuban-style cigar.

Hell, he knew enough about fate to know she wouldn't, but in this moment he needed the lifeline she provided with her soft touch and understanding eyes. He knew he was going to have to tell her something of his past. Knew he needed to tell her before too much time had passed, but he also knew that once he did tell her, things between them would never be the same.

''Want to come in for a drink?'' Corrine asked. Rand had been quiet all the way home. And though it was after midnight, the last thing she felt like was sleeping.

She was too up from dinner. Rand had put on a Steely Dan CD on the ride home. The mellow, jazzy sounds of ''Babylon Sister'' still played in her ears, enhancing her mood. She felt the sensuous strains of the music deep inside her.

Rand pulled into her driveway and let the car idle. He'd been in a strange mood all the way home. She wasn't sure what was going on with him.

When she'd stepped outside the restaurant earlier and found him standing there—she couldn't be sure but he seemed unsure of himself. She'd wanted to wrap him in her arms but knew he wouldn't tolerate that. He hadn't that night he'd woken from a nightmare. Frankly, she had no idea what he needed from her.

She hoped it was more than sex. But he'd been avoiding her and the doubts crept back in. Tonight she was in a weird spot. She felt at the height of her personal power—as a woman, as a businesswoman, as a lover.

Angelica had explained her relationship with Paul to Corrine one night when they'd met for margaritas. Angelica said she believed all relationships were yin and yang. Tonight she'd felt at the pinnacle of her spiritual self. Did that mean that Rand had to be at the bottom of his?

She wasn't sure.

But she sensed that sending him home alone wasn't a good idea. Besides, she wanted him to stay. She'd realized that she needed him in her life.

Even though he'd been physically avoiding her he'd called her every night to make sure she got home okay. He'd left little messages on her voice mail. It made her feel less alone in the world. And she was afraid to trust that sensation and afraid not to.

"I'll come in," Rand said. He turned off the car and walked around to open her door.

She could have gotten out of the car without him, but it was a nice gesture and one she noticed he liked to do. He put his hand on her elbow as they walked toward the house. It sounded silly even when she said it to herself, but he made her feel cherished. After a lifetime of being abandoned that was a potent feeling.

However, making her feel cherished was not all he did for her. After a mere second there was a distinctly sexual buzz in the air. Her blood started to flow more heavily through her veins and her entire body felt sensitized by his touch.

Her breasts were fuller and her breaths shorter. The scent of him surrounded her, and she realized she wanted to celebrate her successful dinner meeting in a very physical way.

She fumbled with her key and realized she was nervous tonight. The last time they'd made love he'd left. Why didn't that bother her more? She hadn't thought about it until this moment, but she realized that she expected him to leave. Everyone always did.

It wasn't just the series of foster homes she'd grown up in or the friends she'd made over the years who'd returned north when their jobs in Florida were finished. It was the entire timbre of her life. No one had ever been consistent in her life.

And she very much wanted Rand to be. But until she took the risk of letting him know she wanted him to stay, she'd never be able to get what she secretly wanted. She'd always formed emotional attachments, though she'd never wanted to acknowledge them. She'd hidden those feelings and put on her moving-on face more than once and then cried in the privacy of her own space.

This time she wanted to acknowledge her feelings for Rand. To find out if he felt the same. Then make some plans…for the future.

"The moon is nice tonight," he said. He'd taken his suit jacket off in the car and now he rolled his sleeves up.

"Yes, it is," she said, tipping her head back. The night sky shone with stars and the full moon. "It'd be a perfect night for a shuttle launch."

"I have a great view from my patio. The next time there's a night launch we'll watch it together."

She'd never been to his house. She wondered what it was like. She was still reeling from the thought that she wanted more than something temporary with him. She wanted to make a commitment to him and have him make one to her. Oh, God, what was she thinking?

"Will we still be together?" she asked. Damn, she was usually a lot better at screening her thoughts before she spoke.

He didn't say anything for a few minutes. He moved to the porch railing and leaned back against it. Despite his casual pose there was a tension in the air. "I don't know."

"Sorry. I don't know where that came from," she

said. But she did know. It came from her heart. She'd spent a lifetime ignoring her emotional impulses, but suddenly she couldn't anymore. Suddenly it seemed more important to react and feel everything that she could with Rand before he was gone.

"Don't you?" he asked. He didn't sound removed. He sounded as moved by these emotions as she was.

"I just said I didn't," she said, because she wasn't about to trust…him, she realized. She wasn't ready to lay her soul on the line on the off chance that he might be feeling something that was nearly as intense as what she was. She wouldn't let herself be that vulnerable to him. Not now. Maybe not ever.

He sighed. "I know."

She opened the front door. Her house smelled of the lilac potpourri she kept in the foyer. It welcomed her and made her feel more secure than she had only a moment before. She glanced over her shoulder. "Coming?"

"Still want me to?" he asked. She knew he needed reassurance, but she had her hands full taking care of her own battered self.

She didn't answer that. She just entered her house, set her purse and keys on the hall table and left the door open. She heard the door close but no footsteps. Damn, she was afraid to turn around to see if he was still there.

She closed her eyes and pivoted around, but didn't open them. She listened as hard as she could, tempted to open her eyes, but she didn't want to be disappointed again.

Especially not by Rand. Not this man she'd come to put all her trust in. This man whom she'd come to realize was more than a temporary lover. This man she'd come to love.

Oh, God, did she really love him?

She felt the humid warmth of his breath against her cheek and then his hands on her shoulders. Still she didn't open her eyes. Not wanting to see in his eyes pity or simple lust. In her mind she could supply the caring and affection she wanted from him. The kind of reaction that she'd give her career to elicit from him. But that she was afraid she'd never see there.

Ten

The basketball hoop behind the Corporate Spouses offices had seen more than its fair share of grudge matches. But today Rand played alone. The tension he'd always felt had grown stronger in the last month. The closer he got to Corrine the more he felt a sense of rightness. Yet at the same time he felt a sense that she was going to be his ultimate destruction.

"Telephone call, Rand," Kelly said from the doorway.

"Take a message."

"It's Corrine. This is the third time she's called."

Damn. He glanced over his shoulder at his secretary, who was wearing a skintight leather miniskirt and matching black leather bustier. Her hair was slicked back in a severe ponytail and she had long earrings dangling from her lobes. Her legs were encased in black hose and she had a pair of low boots with stiletto heels. She looked ready for an S and M club instead of the office.

"I'll be right there. Kel?"

"Yes?"

"Did Angelica talk to you about the dress code?"

She rolled her eyes. "Yes."

"Then I won't say anything else."

"You better not, boss man, or I'll have to crack my whip," Kelly said before walking back inside the building.

He laughed and watched her walk away. Why couldn't he have been attracted to someone like Kelly? She was fun and sexy and she didn't cause a quaking deep inside him.

Rand walked slowly back to the building. He couldn't escape the feeling that his life was falling apart. He'd never blown off a business call before, yet he'd been willing to do it just a few minutes ago.

"Rand, I need to see you," Angelica said as he passed her office.

"I've got a call, then I'll be in."

"Thanks."

"No problem, kiddo." Angelica's pregnancy was starting to show just the tiniest bit, but that hadn't stopped her from wearing maternity clothes.

He entered his office and tossed the basketball in the corner. He was sweaty so he didn't sit in his chair but merely propped his hip against the desk and lifted the handset. His hand was shaking as he reached for the receiver.

He needed to do something about Corrine. Either give her a place of permanence in his crazy life or stop seeing her. She was making him realize some things about his life that made him uncomfortable.

"This is Rand," he said.

"Hi, Rand. Sorry to bother you at work," she said, her voice brushing over his overheated senses. He wished she were in his office so he didn't have to think and could just react. Kiss her lush mouth and caress her lean body.

"It's not a bother," he said, and meant it. She was always a welcome diversion.

"Are we going out tonight?" she asked.

"I thought so." Why was she calling? She sounded nervous, and they'd done too much together for her to be acting this way. Rand wondered if she'd picked up on his problem. Did she suspect he had drinking issues? It was way beyond the time when he should have mentioned it to her. A lot of women—smart women—didn't want to get involved with someone who had an addiction.

"Good. Just wanted to make sure. There's a new foreign film at the Enzian, want to catch it?"

"Yes. I'll pick you up."

"I'll fix dinner for us."

"You can cook?" He was surprised, because Corrine was a workaholic with little time or interest in anything that wouldn't further her career. He couldn't imagine her taking time to learn to fix food.

"Well, no, not really. But I thought I'd give it a try."

She sounded abashed and that hadn't been his intent. As always when he cared about someone, he bumbled around, unintentionally hurting them. "You don't have to. I'll pick up some sushi on my way over. We can eat in the park before going to the movie."

"Are you sure?" she asked.

"I wouldn't have said so if I wasn't."

"Sorry about that," she said with a little laugh. But it wasn't her normal one.

"What's up with you, Cori?"

Silence grew between them, and he thought she might have hung up before he heard her sigh.

"Nothing. I just want things to be right between us."

Uh-oh. This didn't sound good. "Is there some reason why they aren't?"

"Do you think they aren't?" she asked.

"I have no idea what you are asking me," he said. The only relationships he'd had with women before Corrine had been short-term, red-hot affairs. This was a totally different experience and he had no idea how to handle her in this mood.

"I guess…I've never had a relationship with someone like you."

"What's that mean?" he asked. Had she suspected he had problems that made him inadequate?

"Just that I don't want to sabotage things the way I sometimes do."

"How do you do that?" he asked. What he really wanted to know was how could *he* keep from doing that?

"I'm not sure how I do it. Just that I usually do."

"Does it have to do with your parents?" he asked.

"Maybe," she said. He heard her chair creak. "I've just never wanted anyone to stay around for a while."

"I've never wanted to stay," he admitted.

"Really?"

She needed something from him, and the tension inside him tautened to the breaking point. Could he promise her something he wasn't sure he could deliver?

"I've got to go. We can talk later."

"'Bye, Rand."

Corrine seemed to be acting strangely. Having never been in this kind of intense relationship before he wasn't sure what the hell was going on. But he hoped to God he would find out.

The movie had been really good, but then Corrine enjoyed seeing angst on the screen. Sitcoms felt foreign to her; she was a woman traveling through life on her own creating a quasifamily wherever she went.

Corrine put the coffee cups on a tray and carried it into the living room. As she did she noticed for the first time that her house—her sanctuary—was not a sitcom version of home. She'd created a place of solace for herself.

"Ready to talk?" she asked as she came into the

room. It had seemed to her earlier on the phone that they had turned a corner in their relationship. Realizing she loved Rand had made her want to put down roots.

But she'd been unable to trust herself and him enough to do that. Until now. She was ready to take the risk. Ready to jump off the cliff and hope that the water would be there. Okay, that was a cliché but it made her feel better to repeat it in her head.

Rand was standing by her wall of DVDs, scanning the titles. She wondered if he'd stumbled on her secret addiction—black-and-white romantic comedies from the forties. She stored them on the bottom shelf because one of the men she'd dated had called them corny. That might be, but she loved them.

"Sure," he said.

She set the tray on the table and then seated herself on the couch. Rand paced around the room, prowling it like a caged tiger. Okay, maybe tonight wasn't the night to take her leap.

"What's wrong?" she asked. Had she timed it wrong? Were cookies and coffee not the right thing to be serving a man when you wanted to ask him to hang around for longer than the spring?

"I'm restless. Sorry, it's a family trait," he said.

She realized she knew little of where Rand came from. Angelica had mentioned one time that his family was wealthy and Rand had mentioned a brother, but other than that she knew nothing of who he was. Where had he come from, this man she loved?

"Do you miss your family?" she asked. *Real sub-*

tle. Was it any wonder she'd never had any lasting relationships? Her skills at this type of thing were rusty at best. And of course, she'd never wanted a person to stay as much as she wanted Rand to.

"No," he said, arching one eyebrow at her. "Should I?"

She shrugged her shoulder and tugged a strand of hair behind her ear. Now would be a good time for that water to appear, she thought. "We've never talked about your family."

"What do you want to know about them?" he asked. The intensity in his green eyes unnerved her for a moment. He stopped pacing and stood near her state-of-the-art television.

"Do you like them?"

He smiled wryly. "Most of the time."

"Is it a large family?" she asked.

"I'm one of six kids. My father is one of six. My mother, one of two. Her brother is Lord Ashford, a British Peer."

She felt kind of small. She didn't know her ancestry—never would—and she'd told herself it didn't matter. Only now did she realize she'd been lying to herself. She wanted what he had. She wanted to know where she came from so that some day if she ever had children of her own they wouldn't feel so adrift in the world. They'd have an anchor linking them to past generations. An anchor that she'd never had.

"What's the matter?" he asked.

No way was she going to point out all the reasons why he shouldn't be involved with her. Corrine had learned long ago how to ignore the unpleasant parts of her life. The ones that she wanted to stay hidden. Then she focused on the parts she could control. The parts that didn't give her nightmares.

"Nothing," she said, taking a sip of her coffee and burning her tongue.

"No more questions?" he asked, sinking down next to her on the couch. Memories of the first time they'd made love assailed her. She shifted a little in her seat as lust settled heavily in her veins. Her blood seemed to run heavier and her pulse beat a little faster.

He slid his arm along the back of the couch, his fingertips caressing the back of her neck with a delicacy that made her shiver.

"Uh.. I can't think when you touch me."

"Good," he said, leaning over and nibbling on her neck.

He caressed her through the thin layer of her rayon shirt and silk bra, his big hand encompassing her entire breast, rubbing with a lazy movement that made her believe he'd be happy to spend all evening on the couch petting her. She shifted, pressing her thighs together as an ache started deep inside her.

It felt as if it had been forever since he'd been joined with her. And she'd missed him. She needed to reassure herself that despite the differences in their backgrounds, Rand and she shared something very right.

"Do you really want coffee?" he asked.

She trembled with awareness and let him take her coffee mug from her hand. He hooked his free arm around her and pulled her to him. His eyes narrowed and she sensed that he was trying to distract her. But she didn't care.

When Rand touched her, the world glowed with a brightness that her dull gray life had rarely experienced. He made her feel as if there was such a thing as happily ever after and that he could be her Prince Charming.

Perhaps that was why she loved him. She didn't know. She only knew that when they were in each other's arms she forgot that she'd been abandoned too many times to believe that a man—this man—would stay with her forever. She only knew that Rand made her want to forget the lessons she'd learned early on and believe once more in dreams she'd long since stopped having.

The evening had been too intense. Actually, since that fateful February night when she'd bid on him, Rand's life had been spinning out of control. The tension inside him was wound so tight he had no reprieve from it.

Except when he was buried hilt-deep in Corrine's body. And he knew it was a crutch. A dependence he shouldn't be forming, but he was a weak man. Never before had one person affected him this deeply. Deep inside, where he hid his fears from the world, he worried that some day she'd be taken from him and his life would be nothing.

He should get in his car and head home, but he needed Corrine. Her full, luscious mouth was parted and she was sitting so trustingly in his arms. Her scent—that damned spring flower smell—assailed his senses and he knew he wasn't going anywhere on his own tonight.

He didn't question it, just lifted her in his arms and carried her down the dark hallway to her bedroom. He liked her house, felt more at home here than he did at any other place. He'd worked hard to make sure that he didn't become too connected to any place.

Here he felt comfortable for once with the illusions of who he was. He felt there was a good chance he could be the man he wanted to be when he was with her, even if he was only doing something as mundane as eating or watching television.

But tonight comfort was the last thing on his mind. He'd seen Corrine effervescent in the restaurant a few nights ago, clearly an up-and-comer in the business world. He'd seen her strong when he was weak, struggling with something she didn't understand but still offering her support. And he'd seen her when they'd discussed his family, unsure of herself.

She'd given him so much he wanted to guarantee that she would never again doubt her worth.

He set her carefully in the middle of her bed and turned on only one light—a soft one on her dresser. He opened the shades on her windows so the moonlight streamed into the room, as well.

He needed the shadows now because he wasn't sure what he felt for Corrine, but it was tearing him in two and he didn't want her to catch a glimpse of that conflict inside him. He wanted to be her hero, he realized, unable to be vanquished in her eyes.

She shifted on the bed, kicking her shoes off and stretching her arms above her head with a voluptuousness that made him harden. She'd been acting strangely since her call earlier this afternoon. Unsure of himself in this mood of hers, he knew he needed to be in control. Needed to control not only the hunger deep inside him but also the reactions of the woman who was soliciting this reaction from him.

"Where are those stockings you had on the other night?" he asked. Since he'd seen her in them and felt the lace rubbing against his skin as they'd made love, he'd had an incredible urge to use them to bind her to the bed.

"Which ones?" she asked.

"The thigh-high ones you wore that night you tied me up," he said.

"In the top right-hand drawer. Why?" she asked. She sat up on the bed and watched him.

He shrugged at her. "I'm ready for it to be my turn."

"Your turn at what?" she asked. He hid a smile as he turned and rummaged through her dresser. Corrine liked to be in control of everything and she was damned good at it. Sometimes he thought she did it too well.

"Being the master."

"The *master?*" she asked.

He arched one eyebrow at her. "What would you call it?"

"I don't know. I wish you wouldn't say it like that," she said, sounding more surly than argumentative.

"Do you object?" he asked, finding the hose in her lingerie drawer. There were several colorful scarves in the drawer as well and he removed an especially soft silk one.

"No," she said.

He sank down to the bed beside her and started to unbutton her blouse. He slid it from her body, then tossed it aside. She wore an ice-blue silk-and-lace bra. The color made her skin seem even creamier than usual. He lowered his head and tongued her nipple through the material. He teased her other nipple with his fingers, pinching it until it, too, hardened.

He leaned back to look at her. He'd never get tired of the way she looked with the red flush of desire spreading over her body. Her breaths came rapidly, her breasts strained against her bra. He removed the garment, leaving her naked from the waist up.

He wanted to touch and taste her turgid nipples again but waited for now, teasing himself with what would come. He burrowed his hands into her hair and spread the silky blond mass out on her pillows. Then, taking one of the silk hose, he gathered her wrists together and bound them. He looped the free end through the headboard, tugging to make sure the knot was secure.

"Is that comfortable?" he asked.

"No."

He checked the bond at her wrists. "Too tight?"

"No. I just feel so helpless," she said.

"Want me to untie you?" he asked. Though, see-ing her bound and waiting for him had hardened him even more. He felt full and stronger. Bigger than he'd ever been before, and he wasn't sure he could take his time with her as had been his intent.

His blood was pounding in his veins, demanding he take her. Now. Instead, he took the colorful scarf in both of his hands and rubbed it back and forth across her nipples. She moaned deep in her throat and twisted again on the sheets.

She was so responsive to his every touch and there was a part of him that felt they were made to be together. Especially in the dimly lit room with the creaking bedsprings.

"Hurry up."

He chuckled and stood to remove her pants and panties at the same time. Seemed Corrine felt the same way. Knowing she needed him with the same urgency enabled him to slow his pace. He wanted to draw it out, to make this experience one she'd always remember.

She twisted on the bed, her legs moving restlessly. She looked so wanton in that moment. Her nipples standing proud and tight, begging for his touch. Her eyes glazed with sensuality.

He bent and suckled at her breast. At the same time, he slid his hands all over her body, caressing her stomach and belly button.

She called his name and he nibbled his way up her torso to her mouth. Thrusting his tongue past the barrier of her teeth, he tasted her deeply. He tilted her head back and took her mouth, not letting her reciprocate because he wanted this time to be about her. This time was for her, her pleasure first. Her pleasure above his.

She moaned deep in her throat, her hips moving restlessly against his lower body. Reaching between their bodies, he found the center of her desire and caressed her gently. She tore her mouth from his. In her eyes he saw a million words that she'd never say. Knew that the rawness he felt was mirrored in her.

"Take off your clothes," she said.

"Not yet."

"Rand, I can't wait much longer."

"Then don't," he said.

Taking her ankles in both of his hands, he pushed her legs back toward her body until she was totally exposed to his gaze.

"You're so beautiful here," he said, leaning toward her. He let his breath brush over her first. Inhaled deeply the scent of Corrine. Then lowered his head and tasted her.

She screamed. Her humid warmth welcomed him as he worshiped her with his mouth, until he felt her body gripping him, heard the sounds she made when she came echoing in the room. Then he slid up her body and kissed her deeply.

He was rock hard and needed release, but he waited until her body had calmed and started to build her again to the pinnacle. He removed his shirt and rubbed his chest against her breasts. He removed his pants and briefs and let their naked loins rub together until at last he had to plunge deep into her. Their eyes met as he thrust into her with a rhythm that drove them both to the edge.

Something deep passed between them and Rand knew he'd never be the same.

Eleven

Corrine couldn't catch her breath; she felt as if her soul had been taken from her body and it wasn't back yet. Rand untied her hands and cradled her close to him, holding her with a desperation she felt deep inside.

She knew that what they had could never last. Or could it?

Why couldn't they both stay together? Despite his wealthy family Rand seemed like the perfect man for her. He knew what it was like to be alone and she thought together they could find happiness. The kind of happiness that had always eluded her.

He made her feel everything more intensely, and though she'd never admit it out loud, she'd spent the majority of her life hiding from her feelings because she didn't want to be hurt again. But Rand had always made her feel things even when she didn't want to.

That was the reason why she'd bid on him. Why she'd taken the risk of starting an affair with him. Why she was going to take an even bigger risk… trusting him with her heart.

She'd been tired of living alone for a long time but had never found one person she wanted to share her space with until Rand. Every time he left, the house seemed too quiet. Not that he was loud or gregarious. Despite the ease with which he mingled with others, when they were alone he was happy to spend the time sitting quietly or making love.

She caught their reflection in the mirror over her dresser. He was bigger than she was and more tanned. But wrapped around her as he was, she felt he needed her as much as she needed him. Her heart was full and her mind heavy with all the thoughts that kept buzzing back and forth.

The sweat on her body was drying and she rubbed her hands up and down his spine. She loved the strength of him. Loved that he had the confidence to let her take control and didn't feel threatened by her drive or her intelligence.

The silence between them wasn't uncomfortable at all, but she needed to talk. To find a way to ask him to stay. Not just for a night but forever. And words, always her ally, deserted her.

Rand stirred against her, strafing her nipple with his fingertip. Though she'd been thoroughly satisfied, she felt the beginning twinges of desire. Before they made love again she needed to find out if he felt as deeply as she did.

"Okay, you are definitely the master," she said.

"Did you really think I wouldn't be? I'm very good at physical things," he said.

He was very good at them and she worried this was just one of the many things he had to win at. "Is sex just a sport to you?" she asked.

She didn't think so, but she needed to know now before she revealed herself to him.

Cupping her face with both of his hands, he lowered his mouth to hers and kissed her. "I'm not playing with you, Corrine."

"I'm not playing, either. In fact, I want to ask you something." She loved his green eyes, filled with satisfaction as he teased her.

"What? Want to tie me up again?" he asked. Sex had unwound him, but she remembered a few days earlier outside the restaurant when he'd been so tense. There was more to Rand then he let the world see. Maybe because she loved him she was able to see past his facade, but she suspected it was only because of their mutual feelings that she could.

As much as she'd love to spend the entire evening twisting on the sheets with him, she needed to settle some things before they went any further. She'd survived her upbringing only because she'd protected her heart. And she needed to know now if Rand was going to break her heart or help her find the kind of happiness she'd stopped believing in a long time ago.

"Rand, we need to talk."

"Maybe later. This is, um…important."

Rand said nothing, but rather lowered his head to her neck and suckled against her skin. She buried her fingers in his hair and held him to her. She loved that he seemed not to be able to get enough of her. But at the same time she recognized his actions for what they were. A diversion.

She knew that he was going to pull away again, to back away from her. She wasn't sure she could take it. She shifted away from him on the pillow.

"Rand?" He lifted his head, watching her warily. "I want to talk."

"Can't it wait until morning?" he asked, caressing her with an intent.

"No."

He sighed, then shifted around, piling pillows against the headboard and leaning against them. He crossed his arms across his chest and gave her an aggrieved look. "Okay, talk."

"Why are you so surly?" she asked.

He gestured to his erection. "One guess."

She was tempted to give up trying to talk to him and just let the moment lead them to ecstasy again. "I'll make it up to you, I promise."

"I'll hold you to it."

She cleared her throat. Now that she had his attention she was nervous. "I'm not sure how to say this."

"Just say it."

She twisted her fingers together, then shrugged her shoulders, unable to look at him when she asked him what was on her mind and in her heart. "Will you live with me?"

He jerked upright and she glanced at him. He was staring at her as if she'd suddenly grown a second head. "What? Why?"

Oh, God. Had she misjudged things? But he didn't seem disgusted; instead he seemed…afraid. But that couldn't be right. "I know we'd decided on a temporary affair, but I…I care for you and I'm tired of living alone."

He cursed savagely under his breath and stood, pacing around the room. There was a leashed violence in his movements that took her by surprise. "Maybe you should get a pet," he said.

"I don't want a pet. I've never wanted a pet. Listen, just forget this," she said, standing and grabbing his shirt to cover her nakedness. "I think you should leave."

"Ah, hell. I don't want to leave."

"Well, you don't want to stay, either." She sensed his reluctance very clearly. She knew then that he'd finally noticed whatever it was that made people leave her. He'd found that flaw, and she wanted to ask him what it was so maybe she'd stop doing it and just once someone would stay with her.

"I want to. Too damned much."

"I don't understand," she said, facing him.

"Come here."

She crossed to the bed and sank down next to him. "There are things about my life I haven't shared with you. Things that make me less than desirable."

"Rand, please. I know you're not just the fun-loving sports enthusiast that you like the world to believe you are."

"Do you?" he asked.

"Of course I do. I love you."

"Don't do that, sweetheart. I'm not the right guy for you."

"Yes, you are. I've never said those words to another person and I don't say them lightly now. But my soul recognizes you and I need you. Asking you to live with me is a big, scary step. But I think we're meant to be together."

"Corrine, you don't know what you are asking," he said.

"Yes, I do. Will you live with me?"

Deep inside Rand a part of him died. He was tempted by her in the same way that alcohol had lured him before. Not even a case of Cutty Sark could numb this feeling. His tension gripped him tighter and he fought the urge to go to her kitchen, where he knew she had brandy, and drink straight from the bottle.

In that moment, he realized he was a fraud. He'd never learned to deal with his drinking, only how to hide from it and cope with it. And Corrine had torn that safe facade away and made him face the truth of who he was.

That truth meant he could never live with Corrine. She made everything more vivid, more alive, and if she were taken from him the world would be a dull, gray place. And he'd always believed he wasn't meant to be happy. There had to be a reason why he'd been spared death. The more he thought about it, he'd come to the conclusion that his life was a penance for those he'd lost.

Happiness wasn't meant for those in purgatory. There was no way he could face his own fear that he would fail. No way that a real man would ever put a woman he loved in jeopardy. And that's exactly where she'd be. Because every day was a juggling act for him. He balanced work with an extensive amount of physical activity because it kept him busy, so he didn't have time to dwell on matters that had led him to his addiction.

He wasn't one of those people who blithely drifted through life. Each day was a struggle. A struggle not to think, a struggle not to remember and a struggle to survive. That wasn't something you invited a woman you cared about to share.

But her words touched him deep inside and he knew he'd keep them close for a long time. He thought about the long, lonely road ahead of him and knew that he would always have the memory of Corrine to warm him.

The cowardly part of him was glad she'd forced his hand now before he'd confessed his deep, dark sin. His eternal weakness that no matter how old he got he couldn't escape. No matter how much money he made on his own he couldn't buy his way out of it. No matter how often he drove home sober he couldn't forget that one lethal drunken ride.

"I can't live with you," he said at last, when he realized too much time had passed. What the hell was she thinking? He couldn't read her face; she again resembled the ice queen her co-workers knew her to be.

"Why not?"

"Some people aren't meant to have it all."

"That's bullshit."

"I wish it were."

"Are you saying that I'm not meant to be happy?"

"No. You deserve a great guy who loves you and will give you kids."

"But you're not that guy?"

"No. I'm not."

"It's me, isn't it?" she asked.

He hated that she doubted herself. Hadn't she realized anything when he'd made love to her? He'd never be able to say the words he knew she needed to hear, but he'd shown her in the only way he could how important she was to him.

"No, it's not you," he said, running his hand through his hair.

"Tell me, Rand. I can take it. I know there is something about me that makes people not want to stay. Is it the insecurity that I try hard to hide, but people see anyway?"

"No," he said. Her words cut him like tiny blades. He felt as if he was bleeding inside and knew from the pain on her face that she was bleeding, too. There was no way to make this right. No way for him to come back from the edge where he'd pushed her and himself. No safe place for him to hide anymore.

The thing was, no living person knew about his struggle. He'd hidden it for so long that he'd never really had to talk about it. Roger had known; but he'd guessed, so Rand had never had to say the words out loud. And he didn't know if he could. Even to stop Corrine from hurting, he didn't know if he could say what needed to be said.

"Is it my abandonment issues? I'm trying to get over it."

The sheen of tears glistening in her eyes made him feel like a coward. "No, baby. Stop it. It's not you."

He cradled her close, holding her with a fierceness he denied even to himself. The people who had hurt this woman deserved to pay and he could only hope they were miserable, unhappy people.

He was coming to realize what a risk she'd taken by asking him to stay. She'd said herself that no one ever had. And it humbled him that she'd taken such a risk and knew that her love for him had enabled her to do so.

Rand wished he loved her in that moment. He wished he was able to let himself feel safe enough to admit out loud that he cared for this complex, beautiful woman who'd made a place for herself in his life without him noticing.

"It's not you. God, you humble me with your bravery."

"How am I brave? I've spent my entire life hiding."

"You don't know what hiding is," he said, knowing escape wasn't going to work for him. He owed her more than a casual brush-off. He owed her the truth so she'd understand that the problem was him.

"Then tell me so I can understand."

"I need a glass of water."

"Okay."

He left her in the bedroom and walked into her bathroom. The room was neat and cheery, very much like the woman who owned it. He gulped down two glasses of water before looking at himself in the mirror. He took a deep breath and returned to Corrine.

Shutting off the lights, he left the room bathed only in moonlight. He sat on the edge of the bed with his back facing her.

"You asked earlier about my family."

"Yes."

"I need to tell you about my brother Charles for you to understand why we can never live together."

She said nothing, but he felt her shift on the bed. Felt the warmth of her body as she scooted closer to him. In his weakness he wanted to turn to her and hold her to him. To whisper his words against her sunny-colored hair so that he didn't have to hear them echoing in the silence of the room.

"Charles was my twin. We went everywhere together. Played pranks and got into trouble. We did the normal teenage things—partying, drinking, driving too fast. One night when we were sixteen, we combined all three of them and I woke up six weeks later in the hospital with a feeling deep inside me that something was gone. Charles had died instantly in the accident.''

"Oh, Rand. You were little more than a boy.'' She touched his back and he flinched away from her touch, knowing he still had more to tell her.

"That's no excuse. I was a Pearson and I knew what my duty was. After I was out of the hospital I returned to school. But life was different. Ah, hell, I started drinking to numb the pain and never stopped.

"I'm an alcoholic, Corrine. Since that party I've never had a drink in public because I was aware of the danger involved. But it didn't stop me from drinking,'' he said. He didn't tell her how he'd spent the evenings at home alone with Charles's class ring in one hand and the bottle of Cutty Sark in the other. He didn't tell her how he'd fought a battle with God and with the world. Why had Charles died?

He couldn't ask that question now. He still didn't understand why he'd survived the crash when everyone said he should have died. And the pressure of living when he knew that death should have been his had left him feeling like an empty shell. And the only thing to ever fill the void had been the booze.

"Have you been drunk since we've been together?'' she asked. She still sat close to him, but she was no longer leaning toward him.

Hell, he couldn't blame her. If she'd confessed to being an animal with the scent of prey in its nostrils he would think twice about staying near her. And in effect that was all he was. He'd hidden his addiction from the world, but that didn't mean he didn't struggle with it every day, and Corrine was a very smart woman. She, more than anyone else, understood that some things never left a person.

"No. I haven't had a drink since six months after Roger died."

"Roger?" she asked. Sitting up, she crossed her legs and watched him in the dimly lit room. His shirt was draped over her, keeping her warm when he wanted to do it. This confession would be so much easier with her support. Knowing he wasn't alone. But he didn't want to make things easier on himself.

"Angelica's first husband. He was my best friend. He died in a waterskiing accident on his honeymoon." He still missed Roger. They'd spent a lot of time together even after Roger had fallen in love with Angelica. And Roger had been the only person who'd realized Rand drank. Roger never said anything but had just started involving Rand in sports and challenging him to stay sober.

"He convinced me to stop drinking in college," Rand said at last.

"You started again after he died?" Corrine asked.

He couldn't really explain it to her, but there had been that feeling of "why me" again. Why had he lived when he'd done nothing with his life? Why had he survived when he didn't have a wife? Why had he remained? "Yes."

She scooted closer to him, kneeling next to him and touching his shoulder with just the tips of her fingers. He wanted to drag her to him and cling tightly to the warmth in her, because he felt so cold inside.

"Does Angelica know?"

"No," he said, remembering that he hadn't seen her after the funeral for six months and then she'd shown up on his doorstep. Tired of living with people who thought she needed to be cosseted, she'd presented him with a proposition to combine their backgrounds and knowledge. And Rand had found a way to repay his friend for years of support and friendship by helping his widow stand on her own.

Corrine was quiet for so long that Rand was afraid to look at her—but she hadn't stopped touching him.

"I admire your strength," she said at last.

He snorted. "There is no strength in me. Every day I have to struggle with the urge to open the bottle."

She caressed his shoulder with a tender touch that made him feel exposed. More exposed than his confession had. Did she realize how much he'd come to need her?

"We all struggle with things," she said. He knew her struggle. It was in her living room lined with movies about families. It was in her cozy kitchen and her house in a family neighborhood. It was in the real Corrine that few people were ever allowed to glimpse.

"Yeah, but if you give in to your struggle you don't have the potential to harm someone," he said.

She slid down next to him on the bed, lying on her side and wrapping her arms around him. He shuddered at her touch and gave in to the urge to hold her.

"I can't see you doing that," she said.

"Sometimes I can." He slipped his hands under her shirt and traced the line of her spine.

"Rand, you've faced something that would have brought most people to their knees. The fact that you're surviving it is remarkable."

The emotion shining in her eyes humbled him but still he knew he couldn't risk it.

She'd never expected that a man as strong and in control as Rand would have something so uncontrollable in his makeup. It only fit with who he was when she looked closer at the man she'd come to know. Then on an odd level it made sense. She sensed, though he hadn't said it, that there was something he never talked about.

Her heart ached at the thought of a sixteen-year-old Rand waking up to realize his twin was dead. Her heart ached to think of how he'd struggled to fill a void deep inside. Her heart ached with the thought that her love might not be enough for him to take a chance on caring again.

She tugged him down on the bed next to her, holding him closely, needing to feel him next to her so that she'd still believe he was real. And to remind him that he was here with her in the present. He held himself stiffly and she realized now she was in danger of losing him. Before she'd only been focused on herself and her own shortcomings, ones that Rand didn't seem to see in her. It was strangely reassuring.

However, his critical eye was turned toward himself and she could do little to control what he saw.

"Is your brother's accident what you dreamed about?" she asked.

"Sort of."

Still holding himself stiff, he wouldn't look at her. "Tell me."

"I…I was driving the car, which was different because Charles had insisted on driving the night he was killed. And the car spun out of control, only this time I wasn't in the car with my brother."

"Who was with you?" she asked, though a part of her felt sure of the answer.

"You."

She shuddered. "I trust you, Rand."

"I don't."

"I still want you to stay," she said, unable to think of anything else.

Rand cupped her face in his hands. He traced the line of her eyebrows, her cheekbones and her lips with his forefinger. She held still as their eyes connected.

She felt her pulse beating a little faster. He always made her feel so feminine, so womanly, especially when she'd spent her entire life hiding that part of herself. Because that was where she'd always been the most vulnerable.

"Losing you, Corrine, would put me over the edge," he said, his voice husky and deep.

Tears burned the back of her eyes. She'd waited so long to love someone and when she did… She had no idea what to say to make him stay. But she had to try something. She started to speak, but he covered her mouth with one finger.

"Let me finish. Since Roger's death I've made sure not to form any lasting friendships. I've kept my distance from my family because there are a million little ups and downs in their lives that seem like tragedies that, if I took them to heart, might drive me to drink."

"What about Angelica?" Corrine asked, because she knew he and his partner shared a deep bond.

"She's an extension of Roger. And we struggled together to move on after Roger died. It was a difficult time for her. I had to be the strong one."

Corrine understood. Roger, because he had helped Rand, had created a bond that nothing would ever erase. And that bond extended to Roger's widow. "You're always the strong one."

"I just pretend to be." He believed what he'd said, which scared her.

"What about me?" she asked.

"You slipped past my guard while I wasn't looking."

She wasn't sure that sounded good.

He pulled her closer, tugging her head against his shoulder and leaning down, then whispered in her ear, "I care about you."

Those words lit a fire deep inside her. No matter his denials, she'd known she'd finally found a man who'd stay forever. She pulled back and took his face in both of her hands.

"You've done the same to me. All my life I've tried hard not to care and then suddenly there you were, ignoring my no-trespassing signs and making me care. Making me love you.''

''I never could resist a challenge,'' he said.

''Me, neither,'' she said, kissing him softly. ''I think we can find happiness together. Please say you'll live with me.''

He was going to say no. She saw it in his eyes. So she threw caution to the wind. She kissed him with all the pent-up desire and passion she had inside of her. ''I dare you to.''

Rand looked down at her and she clearly saw the torment in his eyes. She knew he didn't expect what they had to last, yet she accepted his simple answer. ''Okay.''

Twelve

The three weeks Rand had spent living with Corrine were at once the best of his life and the worst. The thirst for that damned unopened bottle of Cutty Sark had grown, and he woke every night in a sweat with the image of Corrine crushed in the metal hull of a car. The temptation to leave was so strong that he'd actually left her house and sat in his car twice. But both times he'd returned to her.

The pull she had over him was stronger than the need to leave. Other nights, he'd pace around her room unable to escape the portrait of horror in his head, until Corrine awoke and beckoned him back to bed. Then he'd make love to her with a desperation he only felt comfortable showing with Corrine, in the deep, dark hours of the night.

Only then could he find an escape from the feelings that dogged him. But that surcease was only a temporary one, and was soon as they were apart he'd feel again the tension from which there was no escape.

Because he couldn't go on like he was, he'd decided to try to find some closure to the past. He'd decided to fly to Chicago to visit his family. And Charles's grave. He didn't know what he'd been hoping for; maybe some sort of blessing that said it was okay to start living again—not just existing as he had been. He really wanted to make Corrine his wife, but he wasn't sure he'd ever feel comfortable enough to do it.

He'd left late Friday evening and after spending all day Saturday with the family, Rand had decided to cut his time in Chicago short. The visit had been strained. He'd found himself working harder to keep alive the illusion that he was the perfect Pearson son.

So Sunday morning, he'd kissed his mom goodbye, shaken hands with his dad and left for the airport about five hours earlier than scheduled, needing to get back to Florida and to Corrine. Being away from her had reinforced the fact that she soothed him.

O'Hare was busy as always, and the increased security was a pain, but he didn't really mind. For the first time since Charles died he felt like he belonged somewhere. And he knew that he belonged with Corrine.

It was midafternoon, but his flight didn't leave until six. He reached for his cell phone and called her. He wished he'd brought her with him to Chicago. He'd needed to be able to talk to someone, and though he and his dad had made a stab at it, in the end there were too many words to say.

"Hey, Rand," she said, most likely knowing it was him by the caller ID on her phone. "I didn't expect to hear from you until you were in Orlando. Are you?"

"No, I'm hanging out in the lounge, waiting for my flight."

"How'd it go with your family?" she asked. Corrine had thought he should mention his alcoholism to his family, but Rand had taken one look at the Lake Shore mansion and known that talking about his addiction wasn't going to happen this trip. Maybe next time. Maybe with Corrine by his side the words would come more easily.

"Same as always," he said. "What are you doing?" he asked. She sounded breathless.

"Missing you."

"Yeah?" He still wasn't used to the way she made him feel. Since asking him to move in she hadn't hesitated to tell him her feelings all the time. She was more relaxed than she'd ever been.

"Yeah," she said.

"Good."

She laughed and he let the sound roll over him. "I'm meeting Paul and Angelica for an early dinner in about an hour. Paul mentioned he wants a rematch at volleyball. Do you feel like driving over to the coast next weekend?"

"That'd be fun. He must think he can take us. We'll have to practice your moves."

"What's wrong with my moves?" she asked, laughing.

"Nothing. But practicing should be fun."

"When does your flight get in?"

"Late."

"Want me to come pick you up?"

"No. I want you in bed, waiting for me."

"I'll be here. I have some plans for you."

"Do they involve those hose of yours?"

"What do you think?" she asked, her voice husky.

"I wish I was home now."

"Me, too. I love you," she said, and disconnected the call.

She'd done that a few times. Hung up before he had the chance to say the words. Frankly, he didn't know if he'd ever be able to say them out loud to her. But in his heart he felt the words every time he thought of her. It was unnerving.

Thirty minutes later his cell phone rang and he thought this time he'd tell her how he felt. But it was Paul calling, not Corrine.

"Corrine's been in an accident."

He felt like the blood had drained from his body and his hand shook. "How bad?"

"I don't know. They airlifted her to Orlando Regional Medical Center. She's listed in critical condition. We won't know anything for a few hours."

"I'll be there as soon as I can."

Paul hung up and Rand sat down. At first he felt

overwhelmed by everything exploding inside him, but then he shoved all those emotions away and found the calm he'd always wielded as a shield in trying times.

Taking a deep breath he went to the desk and asked for an earlier flight, explaining there was a medical emergency. By some quirk of fate he got a seat on a flight leaving in twenty minutes.

Rand spent the entire flight to Orlando trying to ignore the fact that he'd been right. His gut had said he couldn't have it all. And he'd learned long ago that his gut sensed things his mind didn't.

On one level he wasn't even that surprised that Corrine's life was in danger; he'd been having dreams about it since the first night he'd spent at her place. This time he wasn't a boy facing a loss he couldn't understand, but a man with a lot at stake. He closed his eyes and whispered a fervent prayer that Corrine would be okay. Asking for help, even from God, was something he'd never been able to do, but Corrine meant more to him than anything else, even pride.

Rand arrived at the hospital just before 10:00 p.m. He was surprised to see Paul and Angelica in the waiting room. Knowing Corrine had no family, he'd been afraid she'd wake up alone. Angelica hurried to him and gave him a hug. Paul shook his hand and told him everything they knew. Corrine had a lacerated liver. They'd operated on her and now had to wait and see.

''We've been in to see her once. I don't know if

they'll let you go in or not,'' Paul said. Paul had an arm around Angelica. Angelica had a soft heart and he knew that she and Corrine had become good friends over the past year and half.

''I'll go check,'' Rand said. Rand found the nurses' station and told them he was Corrine's significant other. He was glad she'd nagged him into getting the address on his driver's license changed, otherwise he'd have had a hard time validating that claim. He realized while her life hung in jeopardy that he'd made some mistakes with Corrine.

He should have cemented his bond with her a long time ago. Regardless of what he struggled with, he was stronger with her by his side. The nurse agreed that he could visit for ten minutes, and he stalked past Angelica and Paul to enter the room.

Corrine was small and pale on the bed, her vivid eyes closed, her breath rasping in and out slowly. He bent over her, lightly touched her face, caressing her eyebrows, the line of her cheeks and lastly her lips.

She stirred but her eyes didn't open. Inside he felt a few of his emotions escaping and he was weakened by what he felt for her. He'd never told her how important she was to him. He'd never told her that he loved her. And he wanted the chance. He needed the chance, too.

He leaned over her and whispered the words that had been echoing in his head since he'd heard the news of her accident. ''I love you.''

Then he stood and walked out of the room. A million feelings roiled inside him and he needed to do something to get rid of the energy. He thought about putting his fist through the wall but knew in his logical mind that wasn't the solution.

When he came back out of the room only Angelica was sitting there. She watched him as he approached as if she'd never seen him before. He struggled to hide what he was feeling, running his hands through his hair.

Rand wanted to escape. To find an all-night liquor store and drink away the feelings rolling through him like a hurricane in the Atlantic. Angelica patted the seat next to her.

Rand struggled as he always did to keep his game face on. For the first time he felt it was nearly impossible to do it. Angelica held his hand tightly and didn't say anything. But he felt the love and friendship she had for him flowing over him.

He realized for the first time that although he'd thought he was keeping a wall between himself and the world, he'd created a little family in Orlando for himself.

"I never told her how I felt, kiddo," Rand said.

"Women know," Angelica replied.

"You didn't know how Paul felt."

"You're right, but I think Corrine knew. She's different with you."

"I hope so."

They sat quietly, each caught up in their own thoughts. Paul returned with coffee for everyone. When Angelica left for a few minutes to go to the ladies' room, Paul turned to him.

"You okay?"

Rand didn't know what to say. Just cocked one eyebrow at the man who'd become a friend.

"Don't let this drive you away," Paul said.

He looked at the other man and realized Paul was trying to tell him something important. "I won't."

"I almost lost my Angel because I thought life was safer if you didn't love."

Rand nodded. Angelica returned, saving him from saying anything else. Rand hadn't realized until that moment that, despite his belief to the contrary, he'd never been alone. He'd been surrounded by people who cared about him all this time.

There was a commotion in the hall and Kelly came hustling in the room. "Rand, what's the matter with you?"

"What?"

"You look unkempt. Tuck your shirt in, man. Comb your hair."

"Kel, leave the man alone, the woman he loves is in fighting for her life," Angelica said.

"Sorry. Love, eh?" Kelly asked.

Rand wasn't sure he liked everyone knowing how he felt, but he was past the point of denying it. He nodded.

"All right, boss man. I was so worried when I got that message."

She enveloped him in a hug. She continued talking a mile a minute and Rand's heart felt a little lighter. He'd never realized that families could come in so many different shapes. This one, his unexpected family, was more comfort to him than his blood relatives ever could be.

They all settled in to wait. Hours later, Kelly went out for food and drinks. Angelica and Paul left after midnight because Angelica's pregnancy was making her tired. Corrine was moved to a private room early in the morning and finally Kelly went home.

The nurse allowed Rand to sit in Corrine's room. The chair was uncomfortable, but he scooted it close to her bed and held tightly to her hand, knowing only that he needed her touch to comfort him. He hoped maybe even on an unconscious level she'd realize he was there for her. And once she woke up he planned to let her know.

Corrine woke up disoriented. The last thing she remembered was being on I-4, slowing for traffic and being rear-ended. She had a vague memory—or was it a wish?—of Rand touching her face, and she thought she remembered hearing Angelica and Paul.

She was incredibly thirsty and in a fair amount of pain. She stirred, looking for the nurse call button but stopped when she saw Rand sleeping in the chair next to the bed.

"Rand?" she asked. She was incredibly tired and was afraid she was dreaming.

He stood in a rush, knocking the chair back, and stared down at her. "Everything okay? Do you need something?"

"I'm thirsty," she said.

He checked with the nurse and then when she

okayed it poured her a glass of water. She closed her eyes again, opening them when she felt the cup against her lips. She took a swallow, then reached up to touch his dear face, so glad that he was here with her. Things must be okay if Rand was here. She closed her eyes and drifted back to sleep.

When she opened her eyes again she glanced around for Rand. The room was empty and the clock on the wall read 7:00 p.m. What day was it?

She must have dreamed that Rand had been in her room. But then the door swung open and Rand entered.

"Damn. Have you been awake long?"

"No. What day is it?"

"Monday evening. Do you remember what happened?"

"Car accident," she said.

"Yes. You had a lacerated liver. You'll be sore for a while but are on the road to recovery."

"Good."

He arched one eyebrow at her in the way she'd come to love.

"About the recovery," she said.

"Want to sit up?"

"Yes, please."

Rand adjusted the bed for her, so she was sitting. She had a moment to take in Rand's appearance. He didn't look like himself. His hair was rumpled, his shirt half untucked. She'd never seen him when he wasn't put together and she was a little worried.

Though his eyes seemed clear and aware she wondered if her accident had driven him to drink.

"What?" he asked.

She realized she'd been staring at him. "Uh... nothing. Is everything okay with you?"

"Yes." She could read nothing in his tone. She wondered if he'd stayed out of pity. She'd had her appendix out when she was twenty-three and had been alone in the hospital for three days. It was the worst experience of her life. Even if Rand was here only because of pity, she was glad.

"I didn't think anyone would be here."

"Why wouldn't I be?"

"Well...we're lovers. And I don't know—I've lived with other families before and they wouldn't have come."

He cupped her face and just looked at her for a long minute. "I thought you loved me."

"I do."

He sighed. "Listen, I'm no good with words."

She nodded.

"That doesn't mean I don't care for you."

"That's very kind of you."

"I'm not being kind," he said. Leaning over the bed, he caged her face in his hands and gave her a kiss that was sweet and gentle. Then he whispered, "I love you."

"Really?"

"Really. I can't live without you."

"Oh, Rand. I never dared to dream I'd find my own Prince Charming."

"Well, if you want to get technical, you didn't exactly find me."

"I didn't?"

"No, you bought me off the auction block."

"Lucky me," she said.

"No, lucky me. I'd been playing at living and never realized what I was missing. You've brought more to me than you'll ever know."

"You did the same for me. I love you."

"I love you, too. I'm so glad I have you. You have a family, too."

"What family?"

"Us," said Angelica from the doorway. She entered the room carrying a large bouquet of balloons.

Paul followed her with a floral arrangement, and Kelly brought up the rear with a basket of bagels.

"You have a family now, Corrine."

He smiled at her. She'd never seen such a tender expression on his face before.

"*We* have a family now."

Their family stayed for a few hours and they talked and laughed. Corrine knew that Rand was stronger because of her love and realized that his love made her stronger. She had never felt a part of the community until now, and she savored every moment. And when Angelica, Paul and Kelly left, she was also glad to have quiet time with Rand. He sat on the edge of her bed, holding her hand. They talked about the future and their dreams. Both realized that life would be full of ups and downs and only together could they weather the storm.

Epilogue

Two months later Rand couldn't believe the differences in his life and in Corrine. She'd fully recovered from her injuries and had been promoted at work two weeks later. She was now a vice president. Her job was more demanding than ever, but Rand had found that he had the power to break her single-minded focus.

He'd like to say he'd lost the urge to drink and for the most part he had. But sometimes he still felt the temptation to have just one drink, but he'd resisted. And it was easier to resist with Corrine by his side. She made him want to be better than he was.

Rand's family had visited from Chicago. He'd had a few quiet moments with his family and, with Corrine by his side, had been able to talk about the problems he had. The ones that had started long ago with Charles's death.

His father had told him that the perfect Pearson son was the man Rand had become. The words had humbled him and given him a confidence he hadn't been aware he'd been lacking. The confidence he needed to ask Corrine to be his wife.

Which he planned to do as soon as she got home from work. He'd planned every detail. Soft jazz music played in the background, the scent of fresh-cut gardenias filled the room and on the table candles flickered. He'd ordered dinner from a French restaurant in Winter Park. He had a marquis-cut diamond ring in his pocket. But that wasn't the only piece of jewelry he had for Corrine.

He had a locket with the words *Love is home* engraved on it. Inside he'd put a picture of the two of them. He paced around the room straightening the napkins and fiddling with silverware until he heard her car in the driveway.

"Rand? I'm home."

"I've got dinner ready," he said.

She entered the dining room. And he couldn't speak. Could only stare at this angel who'd come into his life when he'd least expected it.

"What?"

"You're beautiful."

She flushed. He held the chair for her. "Thanks." She noticed the jeweler's box and toyed with it.

"Open it up," he said.

"What is it?"

"A gift."

"I haven't done anything to deserve a gift."

"I'll be the judge of that," he said.

She opened the box and pulled the necklace out. She fingered it carefully and then lifted it the read the inscription. Tears clouded her eyes. She opened the locket and saw the picture of the two of them.

"Oh, Rand. Thank you."

"No, Corrine, thank you for giving me a home to call my own.

"I have something to ask you," he said.

He cleared his throat and dropped to one knee next to her. "Will you marry me?"

She smiled down at him. He felt ten feet tall when she looked at him like that. She stood and then tugged him to his feet and wrapped her arms around him. He kissed her, putting all the emotion he'd suppressed for so long into the embrace. When he lifted his head her lips were full, her face flushed and her eyes sparkling.

"Yes."

Rand let out a whoop of joy and swung her around before kissing her again. For the first time in his life he was living for himself and for the woman he loved. A woman he'd thought he'd never find.

"Good thing I'm so smart," Corrine said.

"How do you figure?"

"If I hadn't bought you we'd both still be alone."

"Bought me?"

"Really, Rand, how often do we have to cover this?"

"Just one more time so I'll know what to tell our grandkids," he said.

"Grandkids?"

"I figure we'll have at least four kids, so we should get some grandkids out of them."

"Four?"

"Will you mind?"

"No. I've always wanted a big family."

"I plan to give you one."

"I think we'll give each other one."

She was right. But then the woman he loved often was.

*   *   *   *   *

SLEEPING WITH THE PLAYBOY
by
Julianne MacLean

JULIANNE MACLEAN

Before embarking on the wonderful challenge of writing romance, Julianne earned degrees in both English literature and business administration. She spent some time as a financial statement auditor, but is now wildly happy to be a full-time mum and romance writer. She lives in Nova Scotia, Canada, with her husband and five-year-old daughter. Julianne loves to hear from readers, and invites you to visit her website at www.juliannemaclean.com.

A thousand thank-yous to a writer's dream editor,
Melissa Endlich.

One

Here we go—trotting into someone else's world again. Jocelyn Mackenzie followed her client out of the mahogany-paneled elevator and across the marble vestibule, to the double doors of the ritzy Chicago penthouse. She glanced up at the crystal chandelier overhead and the modern steel sculpture against the side wall, and felt the familiar onslaught of awe.

Not that she hadn't seen her share of fancy penthouses and stone mansions. To be honest, that's where she usually took assignments as a bodyguard, because quite simply, the average Joe couldn't afford her.

It was for reasons of her own, however, that she would never choose this kind of lavish, pretentious lifestyle for herself.

The elevator doors slid closed behind them, and Dr. Reeves knocked on the door. Jocelyn waited beside him, hands clasped at her back, curious as to how her potential "principal" would answer. Would he open the door without asking who it was, or would he use the optical viewer?

The crystal knob turned, and the door swung open. She'd have to educate her client about that.

Before she could give that another thought, however, Jocelyn found herself gazing up at a handsome, golden-haired gentleman dressed in a tuxedo, his starched, white shirt unbuttoned at the neck, his black bow tie undone and dangling in front. Slender and strong, tall and confident, with just the right mixture of arrogance and appeal, he was alarmingly, heart-stoppingly gorgeous.

This was a man who belonged on the cover of *GQ* magazine—a man who made Jocelyn's breath stop and twirl around in her throat. Before she realized it, she'd taken a stupefied step back.

Good God, what was wrong with her? This was a business call.

Sweeping her feminine instincts out of her head and summoning more professional ones, she surmised that this wealthy doctor undoubtedly had his share of obsessed lovers. Potential stalkers were probably where she should begin if his case was typical.

The man's green eyes warmed at the sight of Dr. Reeves, then his gaze moved leisurely to Jocelyn and settled on her face.

"Mark, what are you doing here?" he asked, looking at Jocelyn, not Mark. His voice was calm, but there was an underlying sensuality as he watched Jocelyn, a tone that warned her right off that he was a flirt.

Why wouldn't he be? Most women would probably fall at his feet for a single moment's pleasure of being the object of that fiery gaze.

She chastised herself again. *He's a client, Jocelyn. Those thoughts should not even be in your brain.*

Still holding the door open, he backed up a step. "Come in."

Dr. Reeves gestured for Jocelyn to enter first. She stepped inside, her loafers hushed by the oriental rug as she took in the style of the penthouse—the marble floors, the Grecian columns and the sheer square-footage and height of the ceilings. Classical music played softly from the living room just ahead of her, where the lighting was dim and restful. A glass of red wine had been placed on the coffee table. An open, hard-covered book lay beside it.

Jocelyn looked up at another enormous crystal chandelier over her head in the center of the foyer, then pulled her gaze down and held out her hand. "Dr. Knight, I'm Jocelyn Mackenzie."

He hesitated a moment, then shook it. "It's a pleasure to meet you." He looked over her shoulder at Dr. Reeves. "What's this all about?"

Jocelyn turned. Dr. Reeves, the man who had retained her to be Dr. Knight's bodyguard for the indeterminable future, fumbled for an answer. The two doctors stared at each other for a second or two.

Oh, no. "He's not expecting us?" she asked Dr. Reeves.

"Should I be?"

Jocelyn felt her temper begin to rise. She didn't like being misled, nor did she wish to work for anyone who wasn't absolutely in need of her help. In *desperate* need. She had been under the impression that Dr. Knight was anxious for her to begin. His friend, Dr. Reeves, had told her about the intruder who'd broken into this penthouse a few nights ago, and the threatening letter that had come the next day.

Hell, she'd already done the advance breakdowns on Dr. Knight's parking garage, the hospital where he worked and his regular route to and from.

"Now, wait a second, let me explain," Dr. Reeves said.

"Explain what?" her principal replied.

Jocelyn shook her head and stared at the man who'd hired her. "He's waiting, Dr. Reeves, and frankly so am I."

"What the hell's going on here?"

Dr. Reeves raised his hands. "Calm down, both of you. Donovan, I wanted you to meet Ms. Mackenzie before you said no."

"Said no to what?" He took in Jocelyn's full appearance, from her starched white shirt and brown blazer, down the length of her pants to her brown leather shoes. "Who are you?"

Jocelyn squared her shoulders. "I've been hired to be your bodyguard, Dr. Knight, but I was under the impression you wanted one."

"A bodyguard? Mark, you had no right—"

"I had every right. You're my partner and I'm not about to lose you and have to cover all our patients while you're laid up or dead. I'd be on call 24-7, and that was never how we intended to run our practice." Dr. Reeves's cheeks colored. "Besides, I'm worried about you, buddy."

The two men stood in silence, as if neither was sure what to say to the other.

"Maybe I should leave," Jocelyn said. "You two

can discuss this, and when you've got it figured out, you can call me, though I can't guarantee I'll be available.'' She turned to go, wishing she had taken Congressman Jenkin's request instead.

Dr. Reeves grabbed her arm as she tried to pass. ''Ms. Mackenzie, please wait.''

Jocelyn glanced down at his hand, tight around her elbow, then sent him a warning look.

He immediately released her.

''Dr. Knight needs your services, and his patients need him. Chicago can't afford to lose its best heart surgeon, nor can I lose a friend.''

She shook her head. ''It's his choice, not yours. I need cooperation from my clients. They have to be willing and eager to work with me and take the situation seriously. Without that kind of commitment from the people I work with, I walk.''

She tried to leave again. Dr. Reeves followed her into the vestibule. Jocelyn pressed the elevator button.

''Please, I'm begging you,'' Dr. Reeves said. ''Stay and check things out. See what you can do for him.''

''Why is it *you're* the one out here begging me, and not him?'' She gestured toward the open door of the penthouse, where Dr. Knight was still standing in the foyer, looking as relaxed as ever, watching.

''I can convince him.'' Dr. Reeves took a desperate step toward his friend. ''Donovan, you need her. You can't put yourself in danger like this. Your patients need you and your penthouse needs a security system. The police don't have time to give your case the attention it needs, and I sure as hell am not going to lose any more sleep worrying about you.''

"I'll change my locks."

"That's not enough. If this attacker is determined, he'll be back. Besides…" Dr. Reeves lowered his voice. "Think of the Counseling Center. You're almost there, buddy, and it means everything to you. You can't take these kinds of risks with your life, nor can you give the project what it needs if you're checking over your shoulder every five minutes. You need to finish what you started."

A long silence ensued. Jocelyn had the impression Dr. Reeves had touched a nerve with that Counseling Center argument, whatever that was about.

Jocelyn pressed the elevator button again, and Dr. Reeves returned to her. "Please, Ms. Mackenzie, don't go."

"You should have discussed this with Dr. Knight before you called me out here and wasted my time. I have a long waiting list of people who need and want my help, and this is not—"

"How long a waiting list?" Dr. Knight asked, moving forward to stand in the open doorway. He leaned a broad shoulder against the doorjamb.

Both Jocelyn and Dr. Reeves faced him in silence.

He had way of halting a conversation just by entering into it, Jocelyn thought as she stared at him in a studious kind of way. She had the most intense desire to know what he was thinking.

God, he was gorgeous.

"Long enough," she replied.

"So you're that good?"

"She's the best," Dr. Reeves replied. "She used to be in the Secret Service. She has a list of references a mile long. Very *impressive* references, Donovan."

Dr. Knight stepped out of the doorway and sauntered leisurely toward her. Jocelyn's senses became acutely alert as he grew closer and closer, and she fought the urge to take another step back.

She fought also to understand that self-preserving urge, for he was in no way threatening. Predatory, yes, in a sexual kind of way, when she suspected he was not trying to be sexual. That particular aspect of his demeanor seemed to come naturally; it was an unconscious part of him.

Maybe that's why she found him threatening.

"Why did you leave the Secret Service?" he asked. "You weren't fired, were you?"

Now he was insulting her. "No, I wasn't fired. The money's better in this racket."

Money, as it happened, was something she needed a great deal of right now.

He nodded. "I take it you know how to use that Glock." He glanced down at the gun she wore inside her jacket.

"I can drop you on your ass with it, Dr. Knight, and that's without pulling the trigger."

He inclined his head at her and said nothing for a long moment. She guessed he was taking his turn at being studious.

The elevator dinged and the doors opened. No one moved. Dr. Knight continued to gaze at her, waiting to see what she would do. For a moment or two, they all stood in the gleaming vestibule while the elevator waited.

Then the doors quietly closed, and the lighted buttons went dark.

Jocelyn sensed Dr. Reeves' heavy sigh of relief.

"I'd like to know how you work," Dr. Knight

said. "Then I'll decide whether or not I can commit."

Jocelyn raised an eyebrow. She almost laughed. "I'm afraid it's going to be the other way around, Dr. Knight. *I'll* be the one to ask the questions, then *I'll* decide if I want to commit."

To her surprise, Dr. Knight smiled at Dr. Reeves. "You've checked out her references?"

"Of course."

"Good, because I think I like her."

Dr. Reeves sighed again. "I figured you would."

Jocelyn leaned forward in the plush, white, overstuffed armchair. "So you think the intruder had a key, Dr. Knight?"

"Yes. He was already inside when I returned home from the opera three nights ago, and the door was locked as usual when I came in. He must have wanted me to think everything was normal, so he'd have the element of surprise on his side."

The doctor crossed one long leg over the other and took a sip of his red wine. Jocelyn had to resist staring at what was obviously a beautiful, muscled thigh under those black tuxedo trousers.

"Possibly." Jocelyn noted the details in her Palm Pilot.

"And call me Donovan."

Jocelyn didn't glance up. She merely nodded. "Is that how you got that mark on your knuckle?"

Donovan looked at the tiny laceration, no more than a quarter of an inch long. "You're very observant, Ms. Mackenzie. Yes. I got in a few good swings before he gave up whatever he was looking for and took off."

"And what do *you* think he was looking for?"

He shrugged. "That night, the police concluded it was a burglary. They said keys can be stolen easily enough, an imprint made in a matter of minutes. I've often left my keys in my lab coat pocket at the hospital while I grab a bite to eat, or misplaced them every so often."

"Doesn't everyone?" Dr. Reeves offered helpfully.

Jocelyn didn't crack a smile. "I don't. And if I take this case, Dr. Knight, the first thing I'm going to do is work on getting you out of habits like those."

Donovan's brow furrowed. "You've *never* lost your keys?"

"Not since I was in high school."

"You've never left your purse anywhere? Forgotten a credit card in a store?"

"Never."

Donovan set his wineglass down on the wrought iron end table. "You must be a detail-oriented person."

"I'm an everything person. I value my security."

"Hence your career choice." He gave her a probing look that told her he wanted to know more about her career choice and why she was what she was.

Jocelyn shrugged. She wasn't about to give him the how's and why's of her life. She had her reasons and they were her own. Besides that, she made it a rule not to divulge personal things about herself that cultivated a familiarity with her clients. She asked *them* the questions. It was entirely a one-way street, and she liked it that way.

That was the "hence" in her career choice.

"Dr. Reeves told me a threatening letter came the next day," she said.

"Yes, the police have it. It said, 'You deserve to die.'"

"Do you have any enemies, Dr. Knight?"

"Donovan. No, not that I can think of."

"Any medical malpractice suits against you? In the past or pending?"

"No."

"And it was definitely a man who attacked you? You're sure of that, even though the intruder wore a ski mask?"

"I'm sure. Why? You look like you don't believe that."

Not the least bit concerned with what he thought she believed or didn't believe, Jocelyn continued to take notes on her Palm Pilot. "I like to ask questions, Dr. Knight. Cover everything."

"Donovan," he repeated more forcefully. "Do you have a problem with first names?"

She stopped her note taking and looked directly at him. Perfection. His face was completely flawless. And damn her eyes for noticing. *Again.* "I don't have any problem with first names, Dr. Knight. Do you have a problem with *last* names?"

He watched her for a moment, then the tension in his face broke, and he smiled—the most sensual, sexy, flirtatious smile she'd ever seen in her life. His eyes flashed and he exuded an almost tangible charisma.

A hot current tingled through Jocelyn's veins. She clenched her jaw and worked hard to throttle the vexing sensation. What was wrong with her tonight? She was a professional. A damn good one.

He took another sip of wine.

Jocelyn turned her attention to Donovan's partner, because she couldn't bear another second of those olive-green eyes moving over her in that disarming way, studying her. She was not an open book, nor did she wish to feel like one. Neither did she appreciate her hormones behaving like she was back in high school. She had thought life experience had taught her to be stronger than that.

"Dr. Reeves, do you know of anyone who would want to hurt Dr. Knight?"

He shook his head. "Could be anyone. Donovan has a lot of…female acquaintances."

Jocelyn nodded, getting the picture. "Perhaps the man was a jealous lover or a husband of one of Dr. Knight's 'acquaintances.'" She turned back to Donovan. "Have you had any threats or meetings with anyone like that?"

"Hey, wait a second here. I don't have *that* many acquaintances, and certainly not ones with husbands, jealous or otherwise. Mark, you're making me out to be some kind of sex addict."

"No, not at all," Dr. Reeves replied, holding up his hands. "I just want to make sure we have all the bases covered."

Jocelyn interrupted and spoke in a professional, detached voice. "I'm not judging you, Dr. Knight. To tell you the truth, I don't really care if you're a sex addict or a gigolo or a Chippendales model on the weekends for that matter. I just want to know who would want to break into your home, and how I can prevent it from happening again. Now, I would appreciate it if you would just answer my questions honestly and stop worrying about what I think of you.''

He set down his wineglass. Looking almost amused, he inclined his head at her. ''I truly believe you *don't* care, Ms. Mackenzie, and that, oddly enough, is what makes me want to hire you.''

What did he mean by that?

He glanced at his friend. ''You chose well, Mark. Even if I didn't ask for your help.''

''I knew you'd see the light,'' Dr. Reeves replied.

Donovan stood. ''I'd like you to start right away, Ms. Mackenzie. Tonight as a matter of fact.''

Jocelyn raised her eyebrow at him again. ''When I start—*if* I start—Dr. Knight, is entirely up to me. I'll take a look around and ask some more questions first, then, and only then, will I consider taking your case. So you might as well sit back down and think back to every woman you've been with in the past six months. Then we'll talk about a retainer.''

Dr. Knight smiled again, and quite agreeably sat down.

She was the rudest, coldest, least friendly woman he had encountered since he'd finished medical school ten years ago. And she was completely irresistible.

After Mark left, Donovan followed Jocelyn into his bedroom while she examined the door that led out onto the rooftop terrace. She tried to stick a finger into the gap between the door and the frame.

''This needs to be reinforced. It should be less than one-sixteenth of an inch, or a pry bar could be slipped in and the door worked open. And you could use some more floodlights on your terrace." She tapped the glass. "Is this shatterproof?"

He nodded, and listened attentively to all her comments and suggestions, all the while thinking about how long it had been since a woman had spoken to him with such disinterest.

Because of his profession and his wealth—a good deal of which was inherited from his parents—women pasted on exaggerated smiles and laughed a little too long at his jokes. They generally dressed to kill, showing off cleavage and wearing spiky heels and glittery lipstick when they were in his company. The women in his life were predictable. They always had that "Maybe I can be the future Mrs. Dr. Knight" look in their eyes. Over the past few years, that kind of social life had begun to grow tiresome.

Jocelyn Mackenzie was different, though. She wore a plain brown suit with flat shoes, and practically no makeup. Not that she needed any. Her face had a natural beauty with healthy, rosy cheeks, full, moist lips and huge dark eyes a man could lose himself in.

She didn't give him that flirtatious look, either, batting her lashes at him. Hell, she barely even noticed him. She was more interested in the nooks and crannies of his penthouse where there were flaws in the security, and figuring out how best to fix those flaws. She didn't want to impress him. She didn't care if she pissed him off.

It was a refreshing change, to be sure.

"So tell me, Ms. Mackenzie, is my penthouse in bad shape security-wise?"

She glanced around the bedroom, her face serious, her gaze going everywhere. She eyed the mahogany, king-size bed and the cream-colored, down-filled duvet, the black-and-white photographs on the wall; she glanced at his dresser with his wallet lying open on top of it, loose change from his pockets scattered all around.

"There's always room for improvement," she replied, still in that disinterested tone. She moved to the door, wiggled the doorknob and tried the lock.

"You're being vague, now. Are you going to transform me, or not?"

She turned around to touch and inspect the doorjamb. "I don't transform people."

"No, but you said you were going to break me of some bad habits. I think I might enjoy that."

She gave him an unimpressed look. "Like leaving your keys places. If you leave the toilet seat up, that's your problem."

He followed her out to the kitchen. She glanced quickly at the stainless steel appliances, the butcher's block in the center and the white custom cabinetry.

He would've given his eyeteeth to know what she was thinking. He could see the wheels turning in her head as she sized up his penthouse before she decided if she wanted to take this case.

"Do you have any hired help?" she asked.

"Yeah, I have a housekeeper who comes in every morning through the week."

She walked down the hall and returned to the foyer, then faced him. She was petite, but there was a strength in her that she emitted like perfume. He wondered what kind of personal life she led. He glanced down at her hands. No wedding ring.

Some deep male instinct in him rejoiced.

"First of all, whether we work together or not,"

she said, "I would recommend updating your alarm system. The one you have is at least fifteen years old. It's a dinosaur."

"Done."

"And you need to *use* the system. Half the people who have them installed can't be bothered punching in the codes, so they leave them inactive."

Donovan smiled. "I'm guilty of that, I'm afraid."

"I figured you were." She moved to the front door to gaze out the peephole. "Are you looking for round-the-clock management and surveillance, Dr. Knight, or just improvements to your home security?"

"I think Mark had a round-the-clock bodyguard in mind."

She faced him. "I asked what *you* wanted, Dr. Knight."

He thought about the baseball bat under his bed, and how he'd stared at the ceiling for six hours last night, then fallen asleep on his lunch hour today.

Then he thought about what his twenty-four-hour-a-day bodyguard would look like in a nightie. If she wore one. Negligee maybe? He could picture her in a red one....

"I think round-the-clock management might be beneficial—at least for the short term."

She nodded, then quietly returned to the living room. Touching a long slender finger to the book he was reading that lay open on the coffee table, she raised her eyebrows as she gazed over the page. "Triathlons."

"You look surprised."

She shrugged. "I was expecting it to be about art history or something." She moved across the room and knelt on the white sofa, to pull the ivory-colored shears back to examine the windows.

Donovan watched her reflection in the clean, dark panes. She flicked a latch.

As she reached up to try a higher latch, her jacket lifted and pulled tight around her shoulder blades, and he could see that she had a shapely behind, trim and firm beneath her loose, wool dress pants. He found himself wondering what kind of panties she wore. He suspected they'd be white. Probably cotton. Maybe silk.

"I'm not much interested in art history," he said distractedly, watching her return to her feet and smooth out her clothes.

She ignored him, and that intrigued him even more. He caught a perfumy whiff of her dark, shoulder-length hair as she strode by him.

A few minutes later, they were back in the foyer and she was reaching into her breast pocket for a business card. She gazed directly into his eyes. "You are *definitely* in need of help."

She handed him the card, and turned to the door.

He glanced down at the card, then followed her out to the elevator. "Wait a second. Does this mean you're taking the job?"

She pushed the button. "Yes."

"But…when will you start?"

The elevator dinged and the doors opened. She stepped inside. "Right away."

"But how do we do this? If you're going to be my bodyguard, shouldn't you be staying here? Where are you going?"

As she pushed the down button inside the elevator, a tiny infectious grin sneaked across her lips. "I liked

the look of those feathery pillows in your guest room,
Dr. Knight, so if you must know, I'm going to get
my toothbrush and jammies.''

The doors closed in front of Donovan's face.

He stood in the vestibule holding her card, feeling
transfixed and suddenly exuberant, and totally surprised by the fact that his cool, reserved bodyguard
actually had a sense of humor.

Things were definitely going to get interesting
around here.

Two

Jocelyn grabbed hold of the brass handrail in the elevator, then tipped her head back and tapped it three times, hard against the oak-paneled wall.

What in God's name had possessed her to say such a stupid, suggestive thing? She was a professional, dammit, and she had a well-deserved reputation for objective, serious behavior and an almost masculine demeanor that demanded respect from the world of executive protection. She *never* smiled at clients. Not unless they made a joke and etiquette required it. Never was *she* the one to make the joke. And certainly not a sexual one!

She reached the bottom floor and stepped off the elevator into the lobby. The uniformed gentleman at the security desk nodded at her as she passed by.

A few minutes later, she was walking down the dark street to where her car was parked, debating whether or not she should have taken this job. She didn't approve of rich, snobby doctors—especially gorgeous ones who wore tuxedos and went to the opera and ballet just to add polish to their appearance, and expected every female within spitting distance to dissolve into a puddle of infatuation at their feet.

It was all so pretentious, and she hated that kind of thing. She had her reasons, of course. And okay, maybe they were personal, but what had happened in her life *happened,* and she'd experienced firsthand the kind of shallow pomposity people like Dr. Knight were capable of.

Besides her father—who had left his own, personal imprint on her as a woman—she'd experienced the social-climbing doctor type. The type who went to medical school just to get a summer home on Rhode Island, a yacht moored at the most prestigious club and a Mercedes parked in a three-car garage.

A Mercedes. All through medical school, Tom had talked about getting one. He'd lovingly referred to his future purchase as "The Merc."

Jocelyn pushed those memories aside and pulled out her cell phone. She called her assistant, Tess, to tell her she'd be taking the assignment. She then retrieved her overnight bag from the trunk of her 1987 Acura Legend, and headed back to Dr. Knight's high-rise, wondering if it wasn't too late to back out, and how she could go about doing that. Because, despite everything she'd just told herself about how much she hated pretentious men who wielded their wealth like swords dipped in liquid aphrodisiac, she had responded to the bold, sexy look in Dr. Knight's eyes. The sheer perfection of his face and the sensual way he'd walked as he'd followed her around his penthouse, so relaxed and casual about everything, had made her feel uncomfortably hot beneath her starchy, cotton blouse. She'd had to work hard to keep her eyes to herself and concentrate on her job, and she wasn't used to distractions like that.

Perhaps she could tell him that her assistant had just called to inform her that her previous principal wanted her to return for another month.

But that would be lying, and she really hated people who lied.

Surely she could handle this.

Deciding to at least give Dr. Knight's case some time—it would be a hefty paycheck after all, and she wanted to cover her sister's university tuition—Jocelyn returned to his building and purposefully didn't stop at the security desk to check in. The guard didn't say a word. Sure, he might have already seen her come and go once, but that wasn't good enough for her. She pulled out her Palm Pilot and made note of it, then while she rode the elevator up, checked the red emergency phone, just to make sure it worked.

Donovan leaned back against the kitchen counter and took a sip of his beer. What had he been thinking, hiring a woman on the spot to move into his place and be his bodyguard? His bodyguard!

He should have given it more thought. He usually didn't make decisions on the spur of the moment, unless they were medical emergencies and circumstances demanded it. When it came to his personal life, he preferred to take three days to mull over a decision, just to make sure he wasn't acting impulsively.

Which in this case, he most certainly was.

Damn Mark for bringing up the Counseling Center. Mark knew Donovan too well—knew he wouldn't be able to say no after that. The Center was, after all, the most important thing in his life these days, and he wanted to see it through to the end. A security expert was definitely a sensible idea.

Sensible indeed. While his "expert" had been wandering around the penthouse poking her nose everywhere, all he'd been able to think about was what she would look like naked.

Unfortunately, that last bit weighed a little too heavily in the decision-making process. What could he say? He was a man, and the idea of sharing his penthouse with an attractive woman who didn't seem to *want* something from him was an appealing notion. It hadn't been entirely about her skill as a security expert, though she certainly seemed competent enough, and as much as he'd initially denied it to Mark, he did feel the need for hired protection.

To give himself credit, though, he supposed his decision was something his gut had played a part in. Somehow he'd sensed that Jocelyn Mackenzie was knowledgeable about security and more than capable, and for reasons he couldn't quite explain, he felt comfortable trusting her—which was a novel concept for Donovan.

The doorbell rang, and he carried his beer with him to answer it.

"That's the second time you did that," Jocelyn said as soon as their eyes met.

"Did what?"

"You opened the door without using the optical viewer."

"The peephole? I knew it was you."

"How?"

"I knew you were coming right back." He stepped aside to invite her in.

"I could have been anybody. And your security guard downstairs isn't a hundred percent reliable, by the way. I'll deal with that tomorrow, after a few more tests."

"Tests? What kind of tests?"

"I'm just going to see how easy it is to get by." With a large, black tote bag slung over her shoulder, she waited in the center of the foyer while Donovan closed the door.

"How do you *know* I didn't use the optical viewer?"

"I know. I heard your footsteps and there wasn't time. Lock that, will you?"

He stared at her a moment, then realized she was right. He hadn't locked his door, and if she hadn't mentioned it, he might not have realized it until he went to bed, when he made a point to routinely check locks.

Her intelligent gaze swept the penthouse again. "One of the first things I do is get a feel for the boundaries with new clients. Some people like their privacy and don't want me to disturb their things, or they want me to stay out of certain rooms. Other people want me anywhere and everywhere, attached to their hip so to speak. What about you, Dr. Knight? Any preferences? Any limits?"

He considered it. Attached at the hip sounded kind of interesting, though he could imagine some other places on her body where he might prefer to be attached.

"No, not really. Go ahead and snoop around, especially if you think it will help you do your job. You can go through my underwear drawer if it turns your crank."

She glared at him, stone-sober. No giggles. No leaping on an opportunity.

This was new territory for sure.

"The guest room is down here," he told her, leading the way down the hall, fully aware that she knew exactly where it was. "You know, I've never done this before and I'm not sure how to treat you. Like a guest, or an employee."

"I'm neither. Mostly, treat me like I'm invisible. I'll take care of myself and try to stay out of your way as much as possible. We'll go over the contract tomorrow, and I can fill you in more on how I work. But it's late now, so..."

Donovan reached the door of the guest bedroom and held out his hand for her to enter first. As her tiny body brushed by his in the doorway, he breathed in the scent of her hair again. It smelled fruity, and the fragrance wafted by him and disappeared all too quickly, leaving him feeling a little parched, so to speak.

She glanced at the bottle of beer in his hand. "What happened to the red wine in the fancy crystal glass?"

"My mood changed. You want one?"

She moved all the way into the room and set her bag on the bed. "No, I never drink on duty. You like Canadian beer?"

He looked down at the label. God, she was observant. "Yeah."

"Me, too. I didn't take you for a beer drinker,

though.'' She unzipped her bag, pulled out a baby monitor and an alarm clock, which she set on the bedside table.

"That's two things then," he said.

"I beg your pardon?"

"Two things that have surprised you about me. Triathlons and beer."

She smiled noncommittally. "Yeah. Two things." She pulled out a laptop and set it on the bed, then unraveled the cord and went looking for an outlet.

Donovan continued to stand in the doorway. "Can I get you anything? Towels? Something to eat? If you don't want a beer, there's orange juice and Perrier and Coke and…I think there's ginger ale—"

"I'm fine. If I want anything, I'll help myself if that's okay."

"Sure." He continued to stand there while she plugged in her computer at the desk.

After a moment, she approached him. "Look, you don't have to baby-sit me. It's my job to baby-sit *you*. I don't sleep much, so I'll be working late on some proposals for improvements to your alarm system, and making sure your place isn't bugged. I've got keen ears, and when I do sleep, I generally do it with one eye open, so you can relax and get a good night's sleep tonight, and not worry so much about being able to reach that baseball bat you've got stowed under your bed."

Donovan slowly blinked. She'd noticed the bat, too. And she wanted him out of her hair. He couldn't remember the last time a woman had told him to go away, and certainly not in a bedroom doorway at this time of the night.

He never imagined rejection could feel so damn good. And so damn frustrating.

Sometime after three in the morning, wearing her tank top and plaid pajama bottoms, Jocelyn e-mailed her assistant, Tess. She gave her instructions to contact the two alarm system companies she trusted for quotes, and to arrange for Dr. Knight's locks to be changed first thing in the morning. She then shut off her computer and rubbed her burning eyes with the heels of her hands.

Dr. Knight seemed to prefer lamps that gave off dim, golden lighting. Relaxing and romantic, yes, but not very practical. She should have had the overhead light on, rather than staring at that bright screen in the semidarkness.

She rose from her chair to take her empty water glass back to the kitchen. After rinsing it out in the spotless, gleaming sink, she still didn't feel much like going to sleep, so she decided to look around the penthouse a bit more. She wandered leisurely around the kitchen.

Dr. Knight certainly had an impressive collection of cookbooks. He had an entire floor-to-ceiling bookcase full of them, and they covered everything from vegetarian cooking to Indian food to chocolate and poultry. Did he like to cook for himself? she wondered, imagining those hands of his stirring chocolate batter, cracking a delicate egg.

She could imagine those hands doing a lot of things—unbuttoning buttons, unzipping zippers, sliding beneath a waistband....

Something inside her tingled pleasurably as her mind meandered around that idea, but when she caught herself veering off the path of professionalism again, she shut her eyes and shook her head. She spent the next few minutes forcing herself to think about the penthouse, instead of the man who inhabited it.

Jocelyn made her way out into the main hall and walked slowly in her bare feet, checking out the paintings on the walls. Most of them were contemporary landscapes, with plenty of seascapes as well. Closer to the front door, there were more framed black-and-white photographs of old abandoned, dilapidated farm houses.

She peeked into Dr. Knight's exercise room and flicked on the light. He had a treadmill, a life cycle and a weight bench, and again, everything was shiny and clean. There wasn't a hint of clutter anywhere. She wondered how anyone could be so perfect all the time.

Where did he keep his junk? Did he even have any?

She crossed the room to check the window latches, even though she had already checked them a couple of hours ago, then realized with some uneasiness that she was overcompensating for something: a personal rather than professional interest in poking around. She had questions about the man down the hall, sleeping soundly in his bed for what must be the first time in days.

An image of Dr. Knight stretched out on that huge bed, his muscular arms and legs sprawled out, his sun-bronzed body tangled in that thick, down duvet, burned suddenly in her brain. Her vision had him sleeping in jockeys, but perhaps he slept in boxers. Or maybe nothing at all.

Damn, she was doing it again. She willed herself to stop, and tried to remember her rule about not permitting herself to entertain any *personal* curiosities about her clients.

Not to mention the fact that Dr. Knight seemed like Tom in every way, and she had no business feeling curious about anyone who resembled her ex— people who derived their joy from living in lavish penthouses, wearing expensive tuxes and being spotted at the opera.

Then again, a few little things had made her wonder if there was more to Dr. Knight than what appeared on the surface. The beer thing had thrown her.

She came to the telephone near the front door, and noticed the high-tech answering machine beside it. Since he'd told her she could go through his underwear drawer if she wanted to, she decided to listen to his messages. One never knew where clues about stalkers could emerge.

She pressed play and reached for the volume control so she could keep the messages from waking her client. The machine clicked as it kicked in.

"Hi, Donovan, it's Eleanor. I had a great time last week. Just wondering how you're doing. Give me a call." *Beep.*

"Donovan, where were you the other night? I missed you, baby. Oh, it's Christine." *Beep.*

"Hi, gorgeous. Where've you been? Call me when you get a chance. I have tickets to *Die Tageszeiten* on Saturday night, and no one to go with." *Beep.*

There was one message from Mark, then four more like the first—more women sounding desperate and needy, wondering why Donovan hadn't returned their calls.

Pitying those poor women, Jocelyn shook her head and slid back into security specialist mode. She returned to her computer to note the names of the women, and decided to ask Dr. Knight about them in the morning.

At 4:45 a.m., the baby monitor that Jocelyn had positioned by the front door woke her instantly. She heard the sound of a key in the lock. She sat up and grabbed her gun.

Slipping out of bed without making a sound, she glided out of the room and made her way down the hall. A woman was sneaking in, quietly closing the door while she made an effort to be quiet. Before she had a chance to turn around, Jocelyn was behind her with the gun pointed at her head. "Hold it!"

The woman screamed and jumped.

"Put your hands on your head!" Jocelyn ordered.

Dr. Knight's bedroom door flew open and he came hurling out. Jocelyn kept her eyes on the intruder. "Get back in your room, Dr. Knight."

"No, no, it's okay!" he said. "This is my housekeeper!"

Only then did Jocelyn feel her own heart racing and the searing sensation of adrenaline coursing through her veins. She lowered her weapon. "I thought you said she came in the morning! It's 4:45 a.m."

"She likes to start early."

Jocelyn's shoulders went slack. "You could've told me! What was I supposed to think when someone sneaks into your penthouse at this hour?"

Dr. Knight moved toward the woman at the door. "I do apologize, Mrs. Meinhard. I'm so sorry. This is Jocelyn Mackenzie. She's a security specialist. I hired her last night. Jocelyn, this is Brunhilde Meinhard.''

Shakily, the older woman turned around. Her gray hair was pulled into a tight bun on top of her head. Her glasses were large with clear, plastic rims—the old-fashioned kind from the eighties.

Jocelyn, feeling guilty for frightening the poor woman, held out her hand and gave her an apologetic smile. ''Hi.''

With trembling fingers and a limp, fishlike grip, Mrs. Meinhard shook Jocelyn's hand.

Suddenly uncomfortable in her skintight tank top and pajama bottoms, Jocelyn nodded politely and pointed toward her bedroom. ''Well, now that I'm up, I'll go get dressed.''

Neither Dr. Knight nor Mrs. Meinhard said a word. Jocelyn turned away from them.

In her bare feet, she padded down the hall, and to her chagrin, all she could think about was one thing: Her client wore pajama bottoms to bed. And Lord, what a chest.

She was in deep trouble.

Three

An hour later, showered and dressed, Jocelyn walked out of her room with her gun holstered under her arm, her blazer buttoned over it. She went to the kitchen to make a pot of coffee, and met Mrs. Meinhard who had already taken care of that and was now polishing the brass knobs on the white cabinetry.

"Good morning, again," Jocelyn said.

Mrs. Meinhard regarded her coolly. "Morning."

Jocelyn poured herself a cup of coffee and watched the housekeeper scrub the hardware. "Look, I'm sorry for what happened earlier. I didn't mean to frighten you, but Dr. Knight hired me to do a job, and that's what I was doing."

Saying nothing, the woman continued to scrub.

"I guess you weren't here when the attack happened," Jocelyn continued, taking a sip of coffee, "but is there anything you noticed that was out of place when you came in the next morning? Anything out of the ordinary that you might not have told the police?''

The woman straightened and folded her cloth. She spoke with a thick, German accent. "I tell police everything.''

"I don't doubt that, ma'am, I'm just asking if there might be something you didn't think of before.''

"No. There is nothing. You work for police?''

Jocelyn carefully studied the woman's face. "No, I'm a private Executive Protection Professional. E.P.P. for short.''

Mrs. Meinhard nodded, but Jocelyn suspected she wasn't completely sure what that meant.

Jocelyn fired out some more questions. "Can you tell me anything about the people who visit Dr. Knight? What about friends or family? Do any of them have keys?''

She shook her head. "Dr. Knight has no family— at least, none that come here.''

"No brothers or sisters?''

"I don't know.''

Jocelyn cleared her throat. How could a house-keeper, who worked in someone's home everyday for four years, not know if her employer had brothers or sisters? Then again, besides one framed picture of a young couple and a baby, there were no photographs of people anywhere, only landscapes and seascapes and old farm houses. Maybe Dr. Knight was at work most of the time when Mrs. Meinhard was here, and she was gone home when he entertained.

Still, it was strange.

"What about friends? Does his partner, Dr.

Reeves, have a key? Or what about any girlfriends, past or present?''

Again, she shook her head. ''No women. He goes out a lot, but there is no one.''

Jocelyn heard Dr. Knight's bedroom door open, and the sound of footsteps approaching. She expected to see him in his work clothes, but instead, he wore a tank and shorts.

Jocelyn felt a sharp tingling of awareness move through her. He looked nothing like he did last night in the tuxedo. In sneakers and a shirt that showed off his broad, muscular shoulders, he looked almost like a regular, everyday guy. Well, not too regular. Not with *that* body.

He passed through the kitchen, apparently on his way to the door. ''Morning.''

Jocelyn set down her cup and followed him. ''Wait a second, we were supposed to go over the contract this morning. Where are you going?''

''For a run.'' He reached the marble foyer and pulled open a small cabinet drawer to retrieve a key in a shoe wallet and fasten it to his sneaker.

''Not without me you're not. Did you forget what you hired me for? I'm not here to guard your penthouse. I'm here to guard *you.*''

He stared at her for a long moment. ''I was wondering how this was going to work.... Do you think you can keep up?''

She gave him a you've-got-to-be-kidding look.

''Of course you can. Sorry.'' He glanced down at her loafers. ''Even with those?''

She glanced down, too. ''Yes, with these, but I'd rather not risk an injury. Wait here and I'll change.''

"You have running gear?" His voice gave away his surprise.

She flipped her hair over her shoulder as she headed to her room. "I have everything. We can discuss the contract while we run."

Jocelyn placed the flat of her hands on the marble, vestibule wall, and leaned in for a calf stretch. She wore black, thigh-length Lycra shorts and a matching Y-back bra top. Her arms, shoulders and stomach were firmly toned, and just as Donovan had imagined last night as he'd watched her flicking window latches in that brown suit, she had a terrific, tight butt and long, suntanned legs to die for.

"Is there anything you *don't* do?" he asked.

She finished the stretch and bent into another one. "Cook."

"No? I love to cook."

"We'll get along well, then. You love to cook, and I love to eat what other people put in front of me."

Her delivery was deadpan, but there was something there that suggested again that she did have a sense of humor, even if she wasn't obvious about it.

Donovan suspected there was a lot more to his bodyguard than what she showed the world. No one could be as indifferent as she seemed to be, every day of their life. This had to be her professional persona, and he found himself wondering quite acutely what she was like around her closest friends. He'd give anything to see her smile or laugh. Maybe he should make that his goal for the day.

Donovan continued to watch her. "Anything else you don't know how to do?"

She pulled her arm across her chest to stretch her triceps. "I don't know how to fix cars. It's on my to-do list."

"Me, neither, but I can't say it's on mine."

"No, you probably hire people to do that kind of menial work."

Donovan grabbed onto his sneaker and lifted his foot for a thigh stretch. "Now, why do you say it like that? Like I'm a snob or something."

"I never said that."

"No, but you implied it with your tone, and it's not the first time."

She said nothing. She just continued to stretch.

"You're not much of a talker, are you?"

"Like I said, I try to be invisible."

"Invisible is one thing. Rude is another."

"I wasn't being rude."

"Yes, you were. I asked you a question, and you ignored me."

She glanced at him only briefly. "I didn't ignore you. I just didn't reply to what wasn't a question in the first place. It was an observation on your part, and you're entitled to your opinions."

Donovan stretched his hamstrings. "My opinions… God, I don't even remember what I said now. Do you always have this effect on men?"

Jocelyn ignored the last part of his question. She finished stretching and pressed the elevator button. "You said I implied you were a snob."

He snickered at her deadpan tone again, as he gazed down at her dainty profile. She was looking up at the lighted numbers over the elevator doors.

"So, did you?" he asked.

"Did I what?"

"Imply that I was a snob? You can't argue that *that* wasn't a question."

The elevator dinged, the brass doors opened and Jocelyn stepped inside. She held him back from entering, looked up at the ceiling, then motioned for him to follow. "If I implied it, I apologize. It's none of my business what kind of person you are."

Donovan pressed the lobby button. "So you don't deny it. You think I'm a snob."

Her mouth curved up in a half smile as she shook her head at him. It was a cute smile. A little on the devilish side, but cute. He'd like to see another one. A looser one. The kind of smile she'd have right after sex.

If she ever had sex. He imagined there'd be a few "walls of inhibition" that would have to come down first. Or be scaled.

He would enjoy that—scaling her walls.

"What does it matter what I think, Dr. Knight? I'm just your bodyguard."

"It matters a great deal. We're going to be in close quarters over the next little while, and call me vain, but I can't stand the idea of a woman not liking me, especially when she doesn't even know me. And why can't you call me Donovan?"

"Because our relationship is a professional one, and keeping those lines firmly drawn is important in my line of work, especially when I'm required to inhabit people's homes."

He nodded. "Ah, that makes sense. You could have said so last night, when the subject came up."

"I hadn't decided whether or not I was going to take the job last night."

The elevator reached the bottom floor, and they

crossed the lobby and passed through the large revolving doors. Once out on the street, they began to
jog alongside each other.

"How'd you get the scar on your left shoulder?"
she asked, never taking her eyes off what was ahead
of her.

"You don't miss a thing, do you? I was in a car
accident a year ago."

"Your fault?"

"No, I was rammed by another driver who ran a
red light. My door caved inward and broke my arm
and a few ribs. The glass cut me up pretty bad, but
it was all fixable. It took me a while to get back in
shape, though. I used to compete in triathlons, but
now I'm just in training."

"You seem like an exercise nut."

"I just like staying healthy."

They jogged a block or two, then Jocelyn said,
"Let's talk about the contract now, and what level
of protection you want from me."

Donovan settled into a comfortable pace, his
breathing controlled. "Since you're going to be in
my house anyway, we might as well go for the highest level."

"It'll cost you."

"Not a problem."

They jogged down to the lights and crossed the
street.

"First," she said, "let's start with your penthouse.
Do you want me to arrange every improvement possible? Or stick with just the alarm system? Either
way, I'll need to see your deed to ascertain if there
are any conditions of occupancy that might limit
what we do."

"I'll get you the deed right away, and if we can, let's go the whole nine yards. The only thing I ask is that you keep the improvements from standing out too much. I don't want my home to look like Fort Knox."

"That can be arranged. I already put together some ideas last night with that in mind, since I figured cosmetics would be important to you."

Donovan swerved around a spilled ice-cream cone on the sidewalk. "There you go again."

"What do you mean, 'there I go again'?" Her voice got a little haughty, and Donovan couldn't deny that he liked it. She was inching off that rock of indifference.

"The way you figured cosmetics would be important to me. Now you're implying that I'm shallow."

She laughed out loud, and it was everything he had hoped it would be—throaty, from the heart and unbelievably sexy. "I implied no such thing!"

They crossed the street and headed toward Lincoln Park, their running shoes tapping the ground in perfect unison. Donovan had to admit he enjoyed needling her to open up a little, and he wasn't sure why. He never felt the urge to prod the women he usually dated and get to know more about what they were like deep down. It was usually the other way around.

She was quiet for a moment. "Can we get back to the contract now?"

They jogged onto the running track in the park, and passed other runners along the way. "Sure. You were talking about the penthouse."

"Yes. I'll act as your contractor, hiring the appropriate experts to install a new alarm system, as well as to come in and make your doors and windows more secure. As far as personal protection, I'll accompany you everywhere for a daily fee, which will be payable every thirty days."

"Even to work?"

"You said you wanted the highest level of protection."

"I do, but I'm a heart surgeon. You'll have to sit in the waiting room all day. You won't find that tiresome?"

"It's my job, Dr. Knight."

"What about days off? Surely you'll need holidays."

"I take holidays between jobs."

"What if you get sick?"

"I have colleagues I trust with my life, and we spell each other off in emergencies like that."

Donovan felt sweat cooling his back between his shoulder blades. Jocelyn had a healthy glow on her face, too, but she wasn't working too hard, not by a long shot. She was clearly in great shape. "I thought you worked alone."

"I do, but I didn't always."

"These colleagues…buddies from the Secret Service?"

"You got it. There are a number of us who work privately now. We contract each other out whenever we require team details."

They jogged in silence along the water, in perfect sync with each other, enjoying the fresh, early morning air. For a long time neither of them said anything, until they came to the end of the park.

"Ready to turn back?" Jocelyn asked.

"Yeah, I usually go that way." He pointed.

She stopped and bent forward, her hands on her

knees as she tried to talk through deep breaths. "Really? We should go a different way then, and run somewhere else tomorrow."

He understood what she was getting at—it was a security thing—and nodded in the other direction. "That way through the park'll take a little longer, but we'll end up back where we started."

"Great." They began to run again, both of them covered in a shiny film of perspiration, but still keeping perfect pace. When they arrived back on Donovan's street, they walked for a bit to cool down before going inside. They passed by the security guard, who politely waved.

Jocelyn got on the elevator first, and like before, checked the ceiling before letting him get on.

"What are you checking for?" he asked, as he stepped inside.

"If the hatch is ajar, there could be someone up there."

On the way up to his penthouse, Donovan was intensely aware of the silence between them, and had to stop himself from gazing down at her just for the sheer pleasure of it.

God, she smelled good. Like the outdoors and fresh, clean sweat. What he wouldn't give to touch her now. To rub his fingers along her slick, bare shoulder.

His blood began to pulse in his veins, and for the first time in years, he felt nervous around a woman.

"Maybe on the way to your office this morning," she said, "we could talk about suspects."

He tried to imagine that. "We could, if you don't mind people listening in."

"What do you mean? What people?"

"The people on the El."

The doors opened, and he stepped off, but Jocelyn stayed on the elevator. Donovan had to put his arm in front of the door to keep it from closing while she was still inside.

"You take the train to your office?" she asked, sounding more than a little shocked.

Donovan couldn't help smiling, and this time, she smiled back.

"I'm doing it again, aren't I?" she asked.

"Yes, you are. I suppose you expected me to drive a Jag? Or maybe have a limo and driver?"

At last she stepped off the elevator and held her hands up in mock surrender. "Okay, I'm guilty this time."

Donovan paused in the vestibule. "Why do you have those impressions of me, anyway? Is it because I was wearing a tux last night? Do you think my life is one big cocktail party?"

She shrugged. "Something like that. You have to admit, though, appearances haven't exactly made you out to be Blue Collar Joe."

Laughing quietly, Donovan bent down to get his key out of his shoe wallet, then straightened. "I'm a pretty normal guy, you know."

"Sure. A normal guy who has the best of everything in one of the most expensive penthouses in downtown Chicago."

"You're very observant, I'll give you that, but what you see is not always all that's there. You can't possibly know what's going on *inside* a person, by seeing what kind of beer they drink or what kind of house they live in."

She rubbed her perspiring forehead. "Appearances

speak volumes about a person. Already I know that you like things to be perfect in your physical life, and you lack depth in the relationships in your personal life.''

Donovan felt his hackles rise. ''Lack depth? God, it's one insult after another! Why would you think that about me?''

''Because I see how perfect everything is in your penthouse, and clearly with all the exercise and working out you do, the perfection of your *physical* appearance is very important to you. You don't have any close friends or family who visit you, and you have seven women on your answering machine, all waiting to be called back.''

He brow furrowed. ''You listened to my messages?''

''You said I could go through your underwear drawer if I wanted. I didn't think your messages were too far a stretch, and I was looking for clues about possible stalkers.''

''And you think you found them.''

She shrugged again. ''Disgruntled ex-lovers are classic suspects.''

Donovan inserted the key into the lock but didn't open the door. There was a lot he could tell her about his personal life to correct her on her impressions, but the last thing he wanted to do right now, while he was boiling mad, was become defensive and pour his soul out on the floor at her feet. Instead, he turned the tables on her.

''You think you've got me figured out, but what I want to know is, who are *you* to judge *me,* when you are clearly hiding inside a tough, cold exterior that shouts to the world to keep out? Answer that, Ms.

Mackenzie, and I promise I won't ask you any more personal questions for the duration of our professional relationship.''

He took some pleasure when he saw that he'd knocked her composure off-kilter. Her full lips were parted in astonishment, as if she had no idea what to say.

Then he added with a bite, ''That is, *if* this relationship lasts beyond a day. Cuz I sure as hell didn't intend to hire a bodyguard who thinks she's a therapist.''

Four

Hiding behind a tough, cold exterior that shouts to the world to keep out? Was that how he saw her?

For a few uncomfortable seconds, Jocelyn reflected upon his assessment of her. God, when had she turned into such a cold fish? Had she been alone too long and forgotten how to connect with people? Or was she dispassionate because she'd been dragged through the dirt by the people she'd allowed herself to trust in her life?

Her heart stung suddenly with a memory of being about five, climbing onto her father's lap for a hug, and being shoved off and yelled at because her fingers had been sticky.

Was that why she'd stopped trying to be close to people? Because of all the times like those in her childhood?

Jocelyn gazed up at Donovan, then consciously

swept away any concerns about her personality or demeanor, for it was not in her nature to feel sorry for herself, nor was this the time to be reflecting on her less than perfect childhood.

And hey, it was her job to be tough and cold!

She would have liked to tell him that, but she decided it would be completely unprofessional to enter into a debate with a client about the workings of her inner self. Best to just back down.

"I'm guilty again," Jocelyn said, holding her hands up in surrender as they stood outside his door. "I judged you, all right? I admit it. You're right, I don't know you very well and I'm sorry. Obviously there's more to you than I thought."

A great deal more, or you wouldn't be so interested in what's going on with me, her inner voice added.

"Now you're just trying to please your client."

"I'm sorry, all right?"

He looked taken aback. "You give in awfully easy for a tough bodyguard."

Jocelyn huffed. "It's my job to *prevent* showdowns, not engage the enemy unless absolutely necessary."

"And now you're calling me the enemy."

She shook her head. "No, I'm not."

"Well, I'm glad we got that clear."

They stood in the vestibule for a long time, staring at one another.

Jocelyn looked up at his finely chiseled cheekbones and smoldering green eyes, and felt her insides quiver with pleasantly erotic responses—responses she had no right feeling, especially when he had just tried to interrogate her about her personal life.

She wasn't used to questions like those. Clients never wanted to know about her situation. They always wanted to remain apart.

She was still shaken. Her belly was fluttering with nervous butterflies.

God, what was it about him that made her react like an adolescent schoolgirl when that's not how she wanted to react? What was it that made her forget who she was—an untouchable, invisible Executive Protection Professional—and want to melt like hot cream into his capable hands?

Obviously, he was well-practiced in the art of seduction. That's probably what those questions were about. He looked for a woman's weakness and leaped on it.

He blinked slowly at her. "You should give in more often, you know."

A sudden image of giving in to him *on his bed* burned in her brain. "I beg your pardon?"

Get a grip, Jocelyn. You're reacting to his masculine appeal and reading too much into everything he's saying. He isn't making a sexual reference.

"Your face…" He reached one hand up to touch the center of her forehead with his thumb. "All the tension right here. It's gone. You look…softer."

His thumb feathered along her eyebrow while his warm palm cupped her cheek, and her knees, damn them, turned to pudding. Who would have thought a man touching her eyebrow would have such a debilitating effect on her?

She didn't know what to say. The line had been crossed, and she wasn't used to being on this side of it—weak-kneed and foggy-brained with a client, after an inappropriate conversation about her character, a conversation that had left her contemplating the ramifications of her childhood.

She wet her lips and struggled to keep her breathing steady, struggled to keep herself from wondering what it would feel like to kiss those beautiful full lips of his.

''You can relax,'' he said, ''I'm not going to fire you.''

''I'm perfectly relaxed.''

''Yeah? I don't think so.'' He gave her an amused grin that told her he was arrogantly aware of his ability to reduce women to happy blobs of jelly whenever he felt the urge.

Jocelyn tried to steel herself against his liquefying effect. ''I'm not one of your girlfriends, you know.''

''I never thought you were.''

Why wasn't he lowering his hand? He was tickling her ear now, and goose bumps were shimmying their way down her entire left side.

''I mean,'' she said in her best tough-girl voice, reaching up to gently remove his hand from under her hair—and it was one of the hardest things she ever did—''you're my client and this isn't exactly appropriate conduct.''

That look of amusement never left his eyes. His mouth lifted in a wicked, sexy grin. ''I knew that was coming. Maybe I should fire you after all.''

''And risk opening that door to your stalker?'' she said in a deep throaty voice.

Something had taken over—the same flirtatious spark that had bucked when she'd made that remark in the elevator the night before, about going to get her jammies and toothbrush. Her voice had taken on that teasing tone again. Now *she* was sounding seductive!

Where was this coming from? This was nothing like her. She wasn't acting professionally; she was playing hard to get.

He glanced at the door with the key still in the lock, then back at her face. His gaze dropped to her lips.

She could see he was impressed by her "apparent" immunity to his charms. And tempted. He wanted to kiss her. For a heart-stopping moment, she thought he might, and she was glad in a triumphant sort of way that she was turning him to jelly, too.

She quickly reminded herself, however, not to get cocky, when she wasn't entirely sure she would be able to resist him if he did try to kiss her.

Thank God he backed off. He tilted his head as if he were disappointed she'd stood her ground. "I guess not."

He pushed the door open, but she wrapped her hand around his firmly muscled upper arm to stop him from going in first. It was damp with perspiration and the intimacy of touching his warm, wet skin at that moment—after what had just occurred between them—was painfully erotic. She felt the heat of the connection straight down to her toes.

Pushing those feelings down into the deepest reaches of her being, and summoning her acute, well-honed bodyguard senses, she went through the door first. "Mrs. Meinhard? Are you here?"

"In the kitchen!" she heard the woman call out.

"Is everything all right?"

"It's fine!"

Nevertheless, Jocelyn had Donovan wait inside by

the door while she checked out the penthouse. "It's all clear," she said when she returned.

But it wasn't all clear. Not by a long shot, because her heart was still pounding out a cacophony in her chest. All because of her client's blatant sexual appeal, his discerning ability to see through her tough-girl image and her own inability to keep her head on straight about it.

That night, after a long day in the hospital, Donovan changed into a pair of faded old blue jeans and a T-shirt, then sank into his plush, white sofa. He crossed one leg over the other on the glass and wrought iron coffee table. He had just ordered Chinese food, and Jocelyn had gone into her room for a few minutes to make sure the alarm system would be installed tomorrow as scheduled.

He stared at the dark windows, enjoying the silence for a moment, thinking about their conversation in the vestibule that morning.

When he'd gone up against all her judgmental observations with one of his own, he had completely disarmed her. She'd backed down quicker than a spooked rabbit.

What was her story? She didn't want him getting into her personal life, yet she was perfectly comfortable and eager to get into his.

She would probably argue that it was the nature of her job—to learn everything she could about the people she was sworn to protect—but he didn't buy that. When he'd asked her about *her* personal life, the shock and fear on her face had come from deep down inside. He'd seen panic in her eyes, as if no one had ever tried to reach in and pull out her soul before. It had been disturbing to her.

Why also, he wondered, did she have such strong negative opinions about his lifestyle? He wasn't a criminal, yet she looked upon him—and everything he owned—with disapproval and disdain.

He stood up, went to the CD player and inserted *Eric Clapton, Unplugged,* to try and clear his head. Sounds of a jazzy guitar filled the large room, and within seconds, Jocelyn came down the hall, still wearing her brown trousers and white blouse, though she'd unfastened the top few buttons. The blazer was gone, the part in her hair was crooked; her blouse was slightly untucked. To be honest, she looked a little bedraggled from the day.

She was completely adorable.

There was a different expression on her face to-night, one he hadn't seen before. It was…mellow.

She raised her eyebrows. "You listen to Eric Clapton?"

"All the time."

Jocelyn stood in the arched entry to the living room with her hand on one of the white columns, listening for a moment, then she began to move slowly, languidly into the room. Her voice was nostalgic and lighthearted when she spoke. "I haven't heard this in ages. I used to listen to it in my car. I drove to Florida once for a vacation, and played it over and over. It was great."

He smiled at her personal reminiscence and sat down. "When was that?"

"Oh, four years ago. I haven't had a vacation since."

"Sounds like you could use one."

"Not really. I like to work."

He sat down on the sofa again. She sat at the other end.

"Everybody needs time off."

"I get time off between assignments, although I'm usually doing the advance work for the next one. But you know what they say—a change is as good as a rest."

"Maybe." Just then, the doorbell chimed. "It's the food." Donovan stood to answer it, but Jocelyn stopped him.

"Let me." She went to the door and used the peephole, then opened it using the chain. "How much, please?"

The delivery man told her. "Just a minute." She closed the door again and locked it.

Donovan was right behind her with a couple of bills. "He can keep the change."

She opened the door and paid the man, then closed it and turned all the locks again.

"You are certainly thorough," he said, carrying the large paper bag toward the kitchen.

"It's what you pay me for."

She followed him into the kitchen. They pulled the white boxes out of the bag and set them on the large, marble-topped center island.

Jocelyn pulled out the wooden chopsticks.

"I have better ones here somewhere," Donovan said, pulling open drawers until he found his good set. He fetched plates, then sat next to Jocelyn on one of the stools.

They popped open a couple of cans of ginger ale, then served themselves and began to eat.

"You have a beautiful formal dining room, and I suppose you eat here most of the time."

"Yeah, I do. Everything's handy here, and it's just usually me anyway."

"But I thought you liked to cook." She poured her fizzing ginger ale into a glass. "I'd imagined you inviting dinner companions over, to impress them with your gourmet meals and fancy cutlery."

He drew his eyebrows together to give her a look that told her she was doing it again.

She covered her mouth with a hand. "God, I'm sorry."

He swallowed. "Apology accepted, on one condition."

"Uh-oh. I don't like the sound of that." Her playful tone sparked an awareness of her as a woman again. Damn his libido.

"Don't worry," he replied. "It's nothing indecent. Not that I wouldn't enjoy a little indecency with my very attractive bodyguard, but somehow I doubt it's in your job description."

She grew serious. "Even talking about it is inappropriate, Donovan."

Hearing her use his given name for the first time— after urging her unsuccessfully more than once in the past twenty-four hours—sent his pulse on a bumpy road trip.

"I understand that," he said soberly. "I don't mean to make your job difficult. I just can't help it every once in a while. You're a very attractive woman."

He saw her swallow hard. "And you're an attractive man, but we're both adults and more than capable of controlling our baser instincts, especially when there's danger involved. Someone might be trying to kill you, and I can't afford to lose my focus.''

He nodded, feeling somewhat disappointed in her unwavering proclamation of ''self-control.'' Feeling that way was completely ridiculous, he knew. He'd hired her to do a job and do it well, not act negligently and become his lover. He *wanted* her to be reliable. Didn't he?

Jocelyn sipped her ginger ale. ''You still haven't told me the condition involved in your accepting my apology.''

''Ah, yes. The condition.'' He wiped his mouth with a napkin. ''Well, you've expressed these somewhat biased perceptions of me more than once, and I would like to know why you have them, or more importantly, why you seem to disapprove of me.''

She inhaled deeply and moved her spring roll around on her plate with a chopstick. ''I don't disapprove of you. I barely know you.''

''You *do* disapprove of me, and you're also great at avoiding questions.''

''And you're great at being bold.''

''Still avoiding.''

She gazed directly at him, incredulous. ''You don't give up, do you?''

''Nope.''

Eric Clapton's ''Layla'' started to play in the other room, its sexy rhythm lightening the tension-filled silence. Donovan watched Jocelyn lean against the wrought iron back of the bar stool. Her lips were glossy from the cherry sauce.

What he wouldn't give to taste the flavor of those sweet, sticky lips....

His body began to react tumultuously to the image of his mouth on hers, so he swerved his thoughts back around to what he and Jocelyn had been talking about a few seconds ago. He'd asked her a question and she hadn't answered it.

He waited.

And waited.

She poked a chicken ball and swirled it around in the red sauce. "All right, if you must know, I used to be involved with a doctor, years ago. Only he wasn't a doctor at the time. He was in medical school."

"What, the guy was a jerk, so all doctors are jerks? Or you're not over him, and I remind you of it?"

"No, it's neither of those things."

"What is it then?"

Lord, talking to her was like getting blood from a stone.

She took a drink. "We lived together when he was going through school, and I supported both of us while I put off going to the police academy. Then, as soon as he graduated, he dumped me and went off to marry a rich debutante, and basically changed his whole identity. He bought a Mercedes Benz, started going to the opera and ballet, when he was never into that sort of thing with me. We used to go to hockey games and sports pubs where the draft was cheap. I guess the worst part was that he'd been seeing this woman while he was still with me. He lied to me and left me with all the debt I'd incurred to support us while he was in school, and never looked back. I met him once a couple of years ago in a bookstore, and he was with his wife. He never even acknowledged me. They treated me like I was dirt under their shoes—in another class far below them.''

"So that's why you disapprove of me? You think that just because I own a penthouse and go to the opera occasionally, I'm a stuffed shirt?''

He hoped she realized how mistaken she was. He didn't grow up with this wealth. He had come into it later when he would have given anything to trade it for what he had lost. God, he'd trade all of it today and live like a pauper, if it would mean he could erase the tragedy from his childhood, and see and touch the parents he never really knew. Even just for an instant.

He swallowed over the aching sense of loss that still lived deep inside him—the fleeting, vague memories, like little fragments of a dream: his mother's loving smile, his father's boisterous laughter as he swung Donovan around in circles. If only he could remember more...

He brushed the grief aside, like he'd learned to do years and years ago, and brought himself back to the present.

"It's not just that." Jocelyn gestured around the room with a hand. "Tom became a doctor to have this very thing. For the prestige. It had nothing to do with wanting to help people. This kind of lifestyle was more important to him than any person ever could be.''

"I see, and because I'm a successful doctor and live alone and have women leaving messages on my answering machine, I don't care about people, either?''

She shrugged.

"You really don't know much about me, Jocelyn. You realize that, don't you?"

Nodding, she seemed to agree. He was glad. Maybe he'd give her the whole story sometime.

"I said I was sorry before," she replied. "Old habits and values die hard, that's all."

Donovan gazed at her face while she fiddled with her food. She'd barely eaten half of what was on her plate.

"Look," he said, "I didn't mean to put you on the spot or make you feel bad or anything."

"I don't feel bad."

He lightened his tone, smiling. "Yes, you do."

Thank goodness she smiled, too. She picked up her fortune cookie, wrapped in plastic, and hurled it across the corner of the island to hit him in the chest. "I don't."

Donovan laughed. "Okay, okay." He looked at the cookie in his hand. "Is this yours or mine? I don't want to mess with fate and get the wrong fortune."

She picked up the other one. "It's yours. I want this one."

They both opened their packets. "What does yours say?" he asked.

"It says, 'You are a deep, complex individual.' What about yours?"

"Hmm. Let me see." He broke the cookie and unfurled the little piece of paper. "Wow. It says, 'You're going to get lucky tonight.' What do you think it means by that?"

Her face lit up like a baseball park at night. "Let me see that!" She grabbed it out of his hands. "It does not say that you big jerk! It says 'You like to fix things.'"

She handed it back to him, then rose to clean away the dishes and put the leftovers in the fridge. "Nice try though."

Donovan watched her from behind. Unfortunately, not nice enough.

Five

He was a brilliant heart surgeon, Jocelyn learned from just about everyone she talked to about Donovan at the hospital. The best around. Nice man, too, they all said, including the nurses, who didn't seem to imply that he ever tried to make moves on them, which was somewhat surprising to Jocelyn, considering how many moves he'd tried to make on her the past couple of days.

The thought sent a shiver dancing down her spine, as she sat in Donovan's waiting room reading a magazine and remembering all the times he'd given her ''that look.''

It was like he thought she was hot stuff....

Another shiver went down her spine, close on the trail of the first one.

She couldn't deny that she enjoyed those looks from him. It was flattering, especially because she'd never imagined herself as "hot." She wore plain suits and flat shoes to work, sensible cotton underwear. She had a conservative shoulder-length hair cut, and she was definitely *not* a flirt. In fact, she made a conscious effort *not* to give off signals—at least the kind that alerted hungry male hormones to a potential meal. She didn't spread her scent around. Consequently, she was dull. Downright dull.

In her defense, being dull came with the job. She didn't go places with her principals to be a part of their social lives. She wanted to blend in, to be polite and generally not speak unless spoken to, and where possible be invisible. In addition to that, she had to be paranoid all the time and keep an attitude that no one was to be trusted, which didn't exactly make her Miss Charisma at social functions.

Hence—she was dull.

Jocelyn lowered her magazine, feeling suddenly dissatisfied. Throughout her life, it seemed like she'd always made a conscious effort to be dull, whether it was in the way she dressed or the way she talked.

Why? Was it because she'd grown up being pushed to act cute in front of the neighbors and wear fancy dresses with lace, her hair in shiny curls? Was it because that was the only time anyone seemed to approve of her—when her appearance was perfect or noteworthy—and this was some sort of rebellion against that kind of shallow thinking?

She continued to flip through the fashion magazine, looking at all the skinny, glamorous models with big hair and small boobs. *Blah.* She didn't want to compare herself to them. She'd spent her whole life reminding herself that it was what was on the inside that mattered....

She shut the magazine and tossed it onto the table in front of her chair, thinking more about Donovan and the way he flirted with her.

How long had it been since she'd had a date with a man? she wondered. Ages. Sure, she went out with her professional colleagues for a beer occasionally, and they were mostly men, but those weren't dates. They all treated her like one of the guys.

It was the female signal thing.

She wouldn't know how to send one out if her life depended on it.

Not that it did.

Yet, Donovan was responding to something....

The door to his office opened, and a middle-aged woman walked out. Donovan, wearing a cotton shirt and jeans and sneakers beneath his lab coat, followed her out. She stopped at the reception desk to speak to the nurse, and was laughing at something Donovan was saying to her.

Carrying his clipboard, he turned away from her and said, "Enjoy yourself at the golf tournament, Marion."

He was certainly charming, and very caring with his patients. He seemed less and less like Tom every day. No wonder everyone liked him.

He passed through the waiting room and glanced down at Jocelyn—who sat in a chair like the other patients—and winked at her.

Heat licked all the way down to her toes and back up again. She forced herself to smile politely and open up another magazine, but God! He was so gorgeous! She couldn't breathe. She didn't have a clue what she was even looking at. Ads? Articles? Little green men?

Jocelyn cleared her throat and tried to calm her clanging heart, but she couldn't. She discreetly glanced around the quiet room, wondering if anyone else could hear it. Apparently not.

She watched Donovan invite the next patient in— an elderly gentleman with a walker.

"George, how are we doing today?" Donovan said to the man, just before he closed the door behind him.

Jocelyn continued to flip idly through her magazine, repeating to herself over and over in her head: He's your client, you idiot. Your client, your client, your client.

Contrary to Donovan's usual routine of taking the El to work and back, they started taking his car, as Jocelyn didn't feel it was safe to walk to the train at the same time each day, nor to stand in the crowded compartment, where anyone could pull a knife without warning and be gone just as fast.

In the parking lot after work, she conducted her usual vehicle search before allowing Donovan to get in. She began by checking the small pieces of tape she routinely affixed at inconspicuous spots along the door, hood and trunk openings, to detect if the vehicle had been tampered with during the day. Then she proceeded with a detailed search of the interior and exterior of the car, looking for trip wires, stripped screws, leaking fluids and such. Donovan waited nearby, watching.

She gave the vehicle a clean bill of health and got in. Donovan got behind the wheel and they headed home.

"How about dinner and the theater tonight?" he

asked her, shifting gears and gaining speed out on the road.

The question caught her off guard. Principals didn't usually ask her to dinner with them—not phrased like that anyway.

He gave her a perceptive, sidelong glance, taking his eyes off the road only for a brief second. "Sorry. What I should have said is, 'I'm going to eat out tonight and take in a play. I'll need you to work late.'"

Jocelyn smiled, appreciating his courteous rephrasing of the invitation. "Yes, sir."

"I'd like to go to an upscale place for dinner, so if you're going to fit in, you won't be able to wear that."

She glanced down at her suit. "Uh, I don't really have anything with me that's—"

"We'll get something for you on the way home." He turned down a street in the opposite direction from where he lived.

"Really, you don't have to buy me clothes," Jocelyn said. "We can stop by my apartment and I can pick something up."

"You live on the other side of town. This'll be much quicker. I know a great spot."

She reluctantly agreed, and they drove down a narrow, tree-lined street. Donovan pulled up in front of an exclusive ladies' boutique on the bottom floor of a late-Victorian mansion, and turned off the car. "What are you...a size five?"

"Seven, actually," she replied awkwardly.

"Great. Let's go."

He led the way in, and bells chimed over the door as they entered. An older lady with her hair in a bun, wearing a pale yellow silk suit and pearls, approached. "Dr. Knight, what a pleasure. What can I help you with today?"

They know him here?

"Actually, Doris, you can help my friend. We're going to La Perla tonight."

"Lovely." She turned her warm gaze on Jocelyn, who felt more than a little out of place in this high-end clothing shop. It was not a place she would ever set foot in on her own.

"I have some stunning gowns over here that would look wonderful on you," Doris said. She gestured for Jocelyn to follow. Donovan followed, too. Doris picked a gold, sequined dress off a brass rack. "What about this?"

Jocelyn glanced down at the tag. The dress cost nine hundred and fifty dollars. Good God. "Uh, that might be a little too…"

"Too flashy?" Doris said. "I understand. What about this?" The smiling woman moved to another rack and presented a deep crimson off-the-shoulder dress. It was twelve hundred dollars.

Jocelyn touched her index finger to her lips. "That, I think, is…um…"

"Not the right color?"

Not the right price! "Yes, exactly."

"Okay, I think I know exactly what you're looking for." Doris moved to the corner of the boutique and found a black, sleeveless, curve-hugging dress with a train. "Perfect for La Perla."

"Perfect for Jocelyn," Donovan said, moving past her and touching the delicate fabric.

Jocelyn didn't dare look at the price tag on that

one. The odd thing was, Donovan didn't look at it, either.

She shook her head in utter disbelief. *The rich.*

Feeling more than a little uncomfortable with all this, Jocelyn looped her arm through Donovan's and gently pulled him away from Doris. "Could I have a word with you?" she whispered politely.

"Sure." They moved behind a mannequin dressed in a sailing outfit.

"This is too much," Jocelyn whispered. "I can't let you buy me a dress here."

"Why not?" he asked innocently.

"Because it's too expensive. I couldn't possibly accept a gift like this."

"It's not *that* expensive. Not relatively."

"Relative to what?"

"To...to other shops. Really, twelve hundred's not that much for a dress like that."

"What, twelve *thousand* would be more in line with what you'd call expensive?"

"Well, yeah."

She felt the difference between them like a deep chasm at that moment. Twelve hundred dollars was pocket change to him.

"And how do you know about prices of dresses anyway?" she asked, still whispering. "And how does Doris know your name? Do you often come here to buy clothes for your lady friends? The ones who leave messages on your answering machine? The ones you never call back?"

He raised his eyebrows, looking amused. "You sound jealous."

"I am *not* jealous. I just find it odd that the clerk here knows you by name and—"

"What about this one?" Doris said, appearing unexpectedly behind Jocelyn, who felt her face color.

"I liked the other one better," Donovan said.

Doris went away, and he took a step closer to Jocelyn to whisper in her ear. "Why don't you just try it on? I really want to see you in it."

His hot, moist breath sent goose bumps tingling down her body. Oh, where was her iron hormonal resistance mechanism when she needed it?

"Why?" she asked. "This isn't a date we're going on. I'm just there for your security. You don't need to dress me up in something I guarantee I'll never wear again."

"You said yourself that you need to blend in. This is appropriate for where we're going."

Jocelyn gazed at his imploring expression for a long time, then remembered one of the strict rules of her profession: *It's not my job* should never be thought or spoken.

It was her duty to always ensure that her principal felt secure and comfortable, whether that meant raising an umbrella over his head if it started to rain, or making sure that his luggage didn't get lost on a flight across the country. In this case, if seeing her dressed to "fit in" with the clientele at the restaurant would make her principal feel more at ease, then she had to do as she was asked.

With a deep sigh of defeat, she raised her hands in the air. "All right, I'll try it on."

"Thank you," he whispered close to her ear, causing another torrent of goose bumps to tickle all over her skin.

Doris led her into an enormous wallpapered change room with a small mahogany table and lamp inside, as well as a brocade settee. There were three pairs of patent leather shoes on a low shelf, for the customers to use.

Lord, this was not her life.

She tried on the floor-length gown, slipped the heels on her feet, then turned to look at herself in the mirror.

Good God. Her heart almost skipped a beat. It had to be someone else's reflection she was looking at. The dress hugged all her curves—curves she wasn't even aware she possessed—and made her look sophisticated and radiant, like a movie star on the red carpet. *Like a woman.*

A knock sounded at the dressing room door. "How are you doing?" Doris asked. "Can I get you anything?"

Feeling uncertain and turning around carefully— for she wasn't used to walking in high-heeled shoes—Jocelyn slowly grasped the crystal knob and stepped out. She tried to ignore how uncomfortable and ridiculous she felt.

Doris smiled and nodded. "That's the one."

Jocelyn, who had kept her head down since she'd opened the door, finally looked up. Donovan's lazy gaze was moving slowly up and down the length of her body.

Her heart held still, waiting for what he would say, while she chided herself for letting it matter. She shouldn't care what she looked like in his eyes. In fact, she should hate the fact that he wanted to dress her up like her father used to do. She wasn't a doll or an ornament.

Yet, another part of her felt oddly liberated seeing herself this way. All through her life she had resisted her natural urges to wear something pretty, to feel soft and feminine, because she didn't want to be valued for that. She wanted to be valued for something deeper.

Contemplatively, Donovan tilted his head to the side and stared into her eyes. "Yes, this is definitely the one."

The restaurant was small, intimate and very romantic.

Located in the low-ceilinged basement of an old stone mansion in a quiet part of town, it was dimly lit with flickering candles and staffed with soft-spoken waiters in tuxedos. White-clothed tables—set with sparkling crystal wineglasses and shiny silver utensils—were spaced apart in little alcoves or surrounded by creeping ivy plants to provide privacy. It was the perfect place for a discreet affair.

Jocelyn had called ahead to arrange for cooperation regarding Donovan's security, and had ascertained that this would be a low-risk detail, judging by the floor plan the manager had faxed over to her. Still, she kept her gun strapped to her ankle and looked around the restaurant with discerning eyes as they were led to their table in the back corner.

"So this is where the theater crowd comes?" Jocelyn commented, sitting down while Donovan stood behind her and slid her chair forward.

He took the seat across from her. Behind him, a trellis of greenery closed him in; the gray stone wall provided enclosure. The waiter poured water for them and Donovan ordered wine.

"So you never told me how you know Doris,"

Jocelyn said, making conversation after the waiter disappeared.

Donovan's lips curved up in a slow-burning smile. "Have you been carrying that question around all afternoon and evening?"

"Really, I haven't given it a thought until now."

He gave her an exaggerated, knowing nod that told her he was completely aware that she had been curious since they'd left the shop, and was amused by it.

How was it possible a man could be so arrogantly sure of himself regarding her thoughts and feelings?

"If you must know, Doris was a patient of mine," he said.

Oh.

Jocelyn continued to gaze at him, realizing she'd jumped to conclusions again, and deciding that tonight, she was going to at long last figure this man out, and prove or disprove every first and last mistaken impression she had of him.

"I can't tell you more than that," he continued, "because of doctor-patient confidentiality, only that I trust her good taste."

"I see. I thought…"

He was amused again; the playful tone in his voice revealed it. "I know what you thought—that I take all my lovers there to dress them up to my liking, or impress them and buy favors."

Jocelyn shook her head at herself and grinned apologetically. This was ridiculous. She had to get her act together.

"Donovan," she said point-blank. "If we're going to have any kind of normal working relationship, it's time I did some intelligence gathering."

"Intelligence gathering? Jocelyn, you're a riot. How about we just have a conversation, like two normal people out to dinner together, getting to know each other?"

She nervously cleared her throat. Where were her social skills when she needed them? She supposed—on top of her glamorous attire this evening—she wasn't used to clients taking her out to quiet, romantic restaurants for dinner. Usually, she, in her flat brown shoes and starchy white shirt, sat at a nearby table alone while her clients had dinner with *other* people.

But apparently, Donovan wanted this to be like a date, and she had no idea how to behave with a rich, handsome doctor who knew which fork to use and how to order the wine.

Add to that the complexity of her trying to behave professionally and *not* be charming—as if she would know how—for she didn't want this to be too enjoyable for either one of them. That could lead to dangerous places.

"All right," she said nonetheless. "Let's get to know each other. How about we start with the messages on your answering machine? How is it possible that you could be seeing seven women at the same time? Do they know about each other?"

She made sure she kept her tone light and friendly, so she wouldn't come off sounding like a jealous, judgmental shrew.

He leaned back in his chair. "I'm not really *seeing* any of them. We're all mostly just friends."

"Mostly."

He wet his lips. "I'm thirty-four years old, Jocelyn. I'm not a monk."

If this wasn't such a high-class joint and she wasn't wearing these strappy heels, she would have crawled under the table and cringed, and stayed there until after dessert was served. "Of course, I didn't mean to imply…"

"It's okay. That's what we're doing tonight, isn't it? Cutting to the chase? While we're on the topic of those women, I might as well tell you that I'm not involved with any of them now. I've been busy lately and keeping to myself. I haven't had much of a social life, and contrary to what you think, those messages you heard didn't all come the day you arrived. They've been accumulating over the past couple of months, and I've been saving them only because I never seem to get around to returning the calls."

"But what if they've all been sitting by the phone all this time, waiting for you to call?"

"I doubt any of them have been sitting by their phones, at least not over me. They'd move on to the next guy pretty quickly."

"How can you be so sure? Maybe one or two of them truly are waiting for you to call. Maybe you're treating them carelessly and you don't realize it."

"No, Jocelyn, I wouldn't do that." His voice was so direct, his tone so indisputable, she couldn't even contemplate not believing him. "Besides, none of them ever had their hearts invested in me. It was only their ambitions."

"Their ambitions?"

"Yes. You know, the Won't-Mother-be-proud-if-I-snag-myself-a-rich-doctor kind of ambitions."

"How do you know?"

"I *just know*. And I never wanted that kind of a

superficial relationship, no matter how attractive or successful a woman was.''

She gazed into his smoldering, green eyes, stunned by everything he was saying. She knew she had been misjudging him all this time, but she'd had no idea to what extreme. She'd imagined he was the kind of man who would use other people for his own enjoyment, but in fact, it seemed to be the other way around. He was the one being used, and he—as far as she could see—didn't like it.

Shallow, he was not.

''Is that why you've never married?''

''Yes and no. I haven't met the right woman, certainly, but I haven't really been looking, either. Marriage just isn't at the top of my to-do list these days.''

''So what's been keeping you so busy lately?'' she asked, changing the subject. ''Besides watching out for stalkers?''

''I've been raising funds for a grief counseling center for children.''

''No kidding.'' The waiter brought the wine and Donovan tasted it and gave it the proverbial thumbs-up. The waiter began to pour some in Jocelyn's glass, but she stopped him after the first splash. ''That's enough, thank you.'' She never drank on the job.

''Are you ever going to let your hair down around me?''

''My hair is down.''

''You know what I mean. Are you ever going to forget that you're my bodyguard, and just be a woman?''

Jocelyn cleared her throat. The implications of that question were disturbing to say the least, especially the way she'd been feeling lately.

"That might be dangerous. If I let down my guard, even for a minute, that would be the time something disastrous would happen. Rule of the trade."

That wasn't the only reason why it would be disastrous, but she didn't want to go there.

Donovan sat across from Jocelyn, admiring the way she looked in the flickering candlelight, wearing that elegant off-the-shoulder black dress with the earrings Doris had helped her pick out to match.

He could tell by the way Jocelyn carried herself that she had absolutely no idea—not a clue—how incredibly beautiful she was.

Or how she was driving him insane keeping him on this side of the table, with the bodyguard-principal lines so firmly drawn. He'd chosen this restaurant for a reason, so she could relax for a few hours between walking in and walking out, and he could have a chance to try and bring out the woman in her.

Because he knew there was a real woman in there—a fascinating and passionate one—buried somewhere deep down inside and anxious to come out. He could see it in her dark, mysterious, dazzling eyes.

He wasn't imagining that there was something between them, either—something she was fighting with all her might.

The waiter returned and took their orders, then made a slight bow and departed.

"So why have *you* never married?" Donovan asked before taking a long sip of wine. He noticed she didn't touch hers.

She leaned forward, put her elbow on the table and rested her chin on her hand. "I don't really believe in happily ever after, and I prefer being on my own."

"Do you really?"

"Yes, I really do."

"What about your parents? Where are they?"

"My mother died six years ago, and my father is somewhere in the Midwest."

"You don't know where he lives?"

"No, my parents divorced when I was fourteen, and he never kept in touch. It was best that way. It would have been too hard on my mother to see him. He broke her heart when he left her for a younger woman."

Donovan reached across the table and touched her warm, slender hand. "I'm sorry to hear that. She never remarried?"

"No, and I can't blame her. After what Dad did, it would've been pretty hard to trust anyone again."

This tough, untouchable bodyguard was becoming more clear to Donovan by the minute. The only two men she'd ever been close to had both left her and never looked back. She was bound to be wary of relationships.

A few minutes later, their appetizers arrived, and they talked about other things. Jocelyn told him about her experiences in the Secret Service, as well as what it was like going through the police academy. Some of her stories were downright hilarious, and she had him in stitches with a few of her tales. There were some hair-raising incidents, too, when she'd come face-to-face with attackers and had to use her combat skills. Mostly, though, she described her job as being pretty quiet. Prevention was everything.

After dinner, they drove to the theater where they sat in Donovan's regular box seats, and Jocelyn seemed to enjoy the play immensely. When they finally arrived home it was almost midnight, and they rode up in the elevator, smiling and talking about the actors.

When they reached the top floor, Jocelyn removed her heels in the vestibule, disarmed the new, state-of-the-art alarm system inside, then searched the penthouse thoroughly. Once she'd ensured everything was normal, she returned to where Donovan waited near the door.

"Everything's fine. We can relax now."

"We can?" He tried not to think of all the ways he would like to relax with this incredible woman he had invited into his home. This beautiful, appealing, sexy woman who set his loins on fire.

"Since you put it like that, how about joining me for a nightcap?"

"You know I don't drink on the—"

"On the job, yeah I know, but we're home now and you've already searched the place. The new alarm system is up and running for later in the night. Surely you can consider yourself off duty for the next hour. Just one glass of wine. Or pop. Your choice."

Jocelyn sighed heavily. "I haven't had a glass of wine in eons."

He spread his hands wide. "I have just about every kind you can imagine—Shiraz, merlot, sauvignon blanc, Chardonnay—you name it."

"Well, I did want to talk to you some more about who could be stalking you."

"We can talk about whatever you want."

She hesitated for a few seconds. "I guess one glass of merlot wouldn't hurt."

"Excellent." He backed away from her toward the

kitchen. "Don't go away. I'll bring it to you. Just make yourself comfortable."

Donovan left Jocelyn in the living room and went to pour two glasses of the best red wine he had in his collection.

Six

Donovan brought the wine into the living room where Jocelyn sat, curled up on his huge white sofa.

He stopped in the entranceway. God, he couldn't get over how incredible she looked in that slinky, black dress. It set off the ebony color of her hair and complemented the creamy whiteness of her complexion; it brought out her full, rose-petal lips. She looked like a goddess.

"This really is a beautiful home you have, Donovan," she said, looking up at him. "I haven't said it before, but it's very inviting. And this sofa—I could get lost in it."

She stroked the soft upholstery with a graceful hand.

Donovan stood motionless, watching her long slender arm move back and forth across the cushions.

His blood quickened in his veins. What he wouldn't give to be one of those cushions now....

Groping for his equilibrium, he fully entered the room and handed a glass to her, then sat down on the sofa.

"I had a great time tonight," he said. "We should do it again."

She looked at him with those big brown eyes over the rim of her glass as she took the first sip, then set her glass on the coffee table. "I had a nice time, too, but I'm not so sure we should do it again."

"And why is that?" But he knew why.

"Because I wouldn't want us to end up having *too* good a time together."

"I see. Better that we have completely lousy conversations and get on each others nerves every minute of the day?"

She peered down at her glass. "You know what I mean."

He gazed at her feminine profile, feeling the pulse of his heart, the hum of his blood through his body. "No, I don't. Tell me."

He wanted this woman. There was no point denying it. She was the most intriguing creature he'd ever encountered in his life. Brave. Intelligent. Witty. Independent. Unimpressed with the fact that he was a millionaire.

He set down his wine. Reaching one arm across the back of the sofa, he stroked her bare shoulder with a thumb.

She didn't push his hand away; all she did was wet her deliciously full lips, which were already moist from the wine.

"I mean the same thing I've said before," she said. "That you're my client and there's—"

"Something happening between us."

He could see the gentle pulse at her neck begin to beat with fervent intensity. He half expected her to get up off the sofa and walk out on him. But she didn't. For a long, tense few seconds, she just sat there while he stroked her shoulder.

"Yes, there is," she finally said in a breathy voice that sent him hurling over the edge.

He couldn't fight it anymore. Desire was burning through him like an all-encompassing fire. He couldn't remember the last time he'd wanted a woman this badly.

How did she do this to him, and why?

He didn't care why. All he knew was that he had to have her. He had to satisfy this searing need to touch.

Slowly, cautiously, he leaned toward her. Close enough that he could smell the perfumed fragrance of her hair, feel her wine-scented breath against his face.

He hovered there, inches from her lips, waiting to see if she was in agreement, and when she made no move to pull back, he pressed his lips to hers.

Tentatively at first. Exploring. Seeking. Then she let out a soft little erotic whimper that fired his blood to the breaking point.

Her willing response sent a surge of voracious lust whipping through him like a cyclone. He cupped her head in his hands and felt her lips part for him, then he swept his tongue into her hot, wet mouth and deepened the kiss.

She whimpered with pleasure again....

He inched across the sofa, close enough so that he could take all of her into his arms. She melted into him like warm butter, reaching around his shoulders and raking her fingers through his hair. She was bewitching.

He slid his hand down the side of her gown and around her curvaceous bottom, feeling his tuxedo trousers tighten over his growing arousal.

"You taste great," he whispered at her cheek, trailing tiny kisses down to her neck while he shifted her in his arms. She tilted her head back to give him full access, and he devoured as much of her as he could, kissing her bare shoulders and tasting her jawline.

Within seconds, he was easing her onto the soft cushions beneath him, glorying in the potent sensation of her hands tangled in his hair.

She wrapped her legs around his hips, and he settled himself upon her, pressing his erection against her through all their clothing, pulsing his hips and reveling in the unmitigated pleasure of her thrusting her own hips forward in return.

"Mmm," she whispered, kissing him deeply, eating at his mouth as if she'd been starving for him for days, in the same way he'd been starving for her.

A hot, searing flame ignited and flared inside him, followed by something resembling panic. He wasn't sure he'd be able to stop things if they went much further—and he was surprised he'd gotten *this* far. He was dangerously close to the edge of reason. The feel of this woman beneath him was like a tidal wave of undiluted, intoxicating ecstasy storming his senses.

He slid his hand down her thigh and gathered the

fabric of her skirt in his hand, carefully lifting it inch by glorious inch. Her legs were bare beneath the skirt—no stockings—and the warm softness of her smooth leg wrapped around him gave him the most exhilarating palpitations in his chest. Finally, his hand was up under the skirt and at her soft hip, his fingers reaching the narrow band of her bikini panties.

He slid his fingers inside and around to her bottom and she began to kiss him faster, lifting her head off the couch pillows to deepen the kiss.

This was getting out of control. He wanted to make love to her here and now, half-dressed on the sofa, and again afterward in his bed. He brought his hand around to her flat belly, then slid it down to reach inside her panties....

Like a predictable clock chiming midnight, signaling the end of the ball, she squirmed and turned her face away. She pressed a palm to his chest. "Wait. Donovan, we shouldn't be doing this."

He froze, immobilized while his heart continued to pump heated blood through his veins. Closing his eyes for a moment to try to gain control of his breathing, he fought the crippling urge to kiss her again and continue this achingly pleasurable indulgence. He removed his hand from the intimate place it had *almost* been, and sighed.

She shifted slightly beneath him. He recognized her uneasiness—and knowing a woman was uneasy beneath him was about as effective as a bucket of cold water splashing over his head.

He backed off immediately and retreated to his side of the sofa, pushing his hair back off his perspiring forehead. "Sorry." He paused, catching his breath. "I didn't mean to take it that far."

God!

All he'd meant to do was kiss her....

Jocelyn pulled and tugged at the neckline of her gown to try and put herself back together. "It was my fault, too."

An awkward silence ensued.

"Look…"

She didn't let him finish. She stood. "Maybe this was a mistake."

"No, Jocelyn—" She started to leave. "Don't go. Let's talk about this." Damn, he'd really done it now. He followed her down the wide hall.

"There's no point talking," she said. "I knew this was going to happen. I could see it coming, yet I couldn't stop it, and that's dangerous, Donovan. I can't do my job this way. I should resign."

He caught her arm. "Resign! All we did was kiss, really.…"

He knew how ridiculous that sounded. It was a hell of a lot more than just a kiss.

"But it might not be just a kiss next time, and where does it go after that? I'll be honest, I'm very attracted to you. So much so, that I'm finding it hard to keep my mind on my work. I'm supposed to be watching you constantly, but I'm not watching you the way I should be. I'm not thinking about potential dangers, I'm thinking about *you*. About how badly I want to…"

Her chest was heaving.

"To what, Jocelyn?"

"To do what we just did."

He released her arm. "I won't lie. I've been thinking about it, too, and it's been getting a little crazy, but please, don't leave. I need you here. At least until the stalker is caught. Then…then maybe we could think about us.''

For a long moment she stood there, staring into his eyes, considering what he'd said.

Please don't leave, he tried to say without words.

But when she spoke, her voice was cool and back under control. His heart sank.

''If it's protection you need, Donovan, I'm no longer the best person for the job. I'm sorry. I'll make the necessary arrangements for another E.P.P., and stay with you until the new operative can take over, but after that, I'm gone. It's for your own safety.''

She went into her room and closed the door behind her.

Donovan backed up against the wall and pinched the bridge of his nose. His chest ached, his safety the last thing on his mind as he thought about what she'd just said, and the fact that she hadn't said a word about the *us* part.

''I'm in trouble, Tess,'' Jocelyn said to her assistant over the phone the next morning, after she escorted Donovan safely to the O.R. She now stood in the waiting room outside. ''I need your help.''

''Why? What's wrong?''

Jocelyn felt some of the tension in her shoulders drain away momentarily. Tess was not only her capable and competent assistant, but her truest confidante and dear friend. She was blond, beautiful, an aerobics fanatic and she'd been with Jocelyn since she'd opened her private agency four years ago. She was a great listener who always told it like it was.

"I gave notice to resign last night," Jocelyn said, "and Dr. Knight needs a new agent immediately."

There was a brief silence on the other end of the line. "What in the world happened? He didn't make a pass at you, did he? Like that slimy old retired senator in New Jersey?"

Jocelyn cupped her forehead with a hand. "No, it wasn't anything like that. Well, it was…I mean, he did make a pass at me, Tess, but the problem was, I was all for it. I think I might have even encouraged him. I'm not sure. I can barely remember what happened. It was all such a blur."

Silence again. "How old is this guy?"

"He's young. Thirty-four, and gorgeous."

"You didn't tell me that!"

"I know. I guess I didn't want to admit that I'd noticed."

She heard Tess take a deep breath and whistle. "As long as I've known you, you've never let this happen. Do you think you're falling for him?"

Jocelyn closed her eyes. "I don't *want* to say yes. I don't want to admit to it or give in to it, but…Lord help me, yes, I think I am. In fact, I think I already have."

"Why don't you want to give in to it? Because he's your client? If that's the problem, we can fix it today. I can find someone else to take over, then you'll be free to go for it."

"No, no, no, I don't *want* to go for it. I want to get as far away from him as possible. I don't want to see him again."

"Why the hell not?"

"Because…" Oh, how could she answer that? It was personal and complicated and would take too long to explain, and it would sound ridiculous. "I just don't want to get involved with anyone right now."

"I'll say it again. *Why the hell not?*"

Why did Tess always insist on acting as her conscience? "Because I'm busy. I don't have time for a relationship."

"That's crap and you know it. You're afraid to get involved with anyone because you're worried he'll be like Tom or your father."

So much for "complicated and too lengthy to explain." Tess hit the mark in one sentence.

That was Tess. Direct and to the point, even when Jocelyn wasn't quite ready to feel the point jabbing her in the behind.

Jocelyn gathered her resolve. "It's not just that. Donovan isn't my type. He's not looking for commitment—he said it himself over dinner last night—and from what I've learned about him, he's never had a serious, long-term relationship with anyone, at least not in his adult life. Why would I want to get involved with someone like that, when the possibility of getting my heart broken is practically a sure thing?"

"Did you ask him why?"

"Why what?"

"Why he's never had a serious relationship with anyone. Maybe he got burned once, too."

"No, I didn't ask."

"Aren't you curious?"

Yes, she was. She was curious about a lot of things.

"I really don't want to ask, because that will only add fuel to the fire. I don't want to get any closer to him. I want to get out of this assignment before I end up in his bed."

"And what would be wrong with that? You're a grown-up, Jocelyn. You deserve a few guilty pleasures every now and then, and you can handle them if you want."

Jocelyn sat down on a chair. "Are you implying what I think you're implying?"

"I'm not implying anything. I'm saying it loud and clear. Do I need a megaphone? If you're attracted to him and he's attracted to you, why not steal a little enjoyment while you can? It wouldn't hurt you to ditch your professional, tough-girl attitude for a night. Especially if we find him another bodyguard. There wouldn't be any ethical problems then."

"You're saying I should have casual sex with him? I'm not good at casual sex. Call me needy, but I have a problem with the 'casual' part."

"Maybe it wouldn't end up casual."

Jocelyn ran a hand through her hair. "I couldn't, Tess. I'm a chicken."

"No, you're not. You're the bravest person I know. Think about what you do for a living. You can tussle with the best of 'em."

"That's different. It's my job."

"So let me get this straight. You're fearless professionally, but scared stiff personally."

Lord, Tess was blunt. It wouldn't be so bad if she wasn't completely bang on.

"Okay, okay, you get the insightful award for today," Jocelyn said, twirling a loose thread from one of her buttonholes around her finger.

"So what do you want me to do?" Tess asked.

Jocelyn considered it a moment, then let out a deep sigh. "Try to find Dr. Knight a new E.P.P., and look into the waiting list to find me a new assignment. Preferably an out-of-town detail."

"So you're not going to take my advice." Tess didn't even try to hide the disappointment in her voice.

Jocelyn stood up to peer through one of the windows on the swinging doors to the O.R. All she saw was her own reflection, which she didn't really want to look at right now.

"Sorry, Tess. I'm not interested in taking risks with my heart. I'll be back in the office as soon as you can get me out of this. The sooner the better."

Jocelyn and Donovan were halfway home when he turned up a side street and pulled over. He turned off the car and draped an arm over the steering wheel, looking at her. "We have to talk."

Heart suddenly racing in her chest, she looked out the windows, checking for cars that might be following them. "There's nothing to talk about, Donovan. My assistant has been working all day to find you another E.P.P."

"No luck?"

"Not yet," she said, still looking out the windows. "So far, the only person available is a guy I don't trust. He's a hothead who would prefer to beat up on an attacker just to prove he's tough, when he should be shielding and evacuating his principal."

"Why won't you look at me?" Donovan asked.

She swallowed nervously. "I'm just trying to do my job."

And I can't bear to look at the tender, pleading expression on your handsome face.

"There's no danger. No one knows we're here," he said.

"Let me be the judge of that."

He sat for a few seconds, waiting for her to assure herself that there were no potential dangers in the neighborhood, then tried again. "You don't have to quit."

"Like I said last night, it's for your own safety."

His gaze was direct and penetrating. "I trust you to take care of that, even after what happened last night."

Jocelyn tried not to notice the way his jeans were pulling tight over his muscular thighs and the way her pulse was thrumming wildly in response. Tried not to think about what Tess had suggested that morning—that Jocelyn go ahead and seek pleasure with her soon-to-be ex-client, for the mere sake of self-indulgence....

"What happened last night *shouldn't* have happened," she said, trying to purge those imprudent, reckless thoughts from her muddled brain. "It's one of the first laws of my profession—*never* get involved with a principal."

He tapped his thumb on the steering wheel and faced forward. "All right, I'll accept that, Jocelyn, because I respect your judgment and your professionalism. If you want to resign and find another E.P.P. for me, that's fine. I'll take another E.P.P. Maybe it *would* be best."

That seemed a little too easy, but she suspected it was merely the calm before the storm....

Donovan shifted on the leather seat to face her. "Last night was incredible, Jocelyn."

Oh, God.

"It took every ounce of self-control I possessed," he continued, "not to follow you into your room after what happened, and pick up where we left off, when I knew I should be promising never to do it again. If I thought I could make that promise, I would try harder to convince you to stay, because I am completely willing to place my life in your hands. But I'm not that strong, Jocelyn. I can't make that promise. I wanted you last night like I've never wanted any woman in my life, and that feeling's not going away. I was in agony today. Agony. I can't fight it, nor can I resist touching you if you're anywhere within reach."

I'm within reach now, she thought, struggling with feelings of desire and longing that were bombarding her senses and becoming impossible to ignore.

Why did he have to smell so good? Look so good? Sound so good? The moist texture of his mouth, his lips parting seductively, and the heated glimmer in his eye—it was all so erotically, achingly sweet. Here in the car, she didn't feel like a bodyguard...she felt like a woman. A woman tingling all over. A woman struggling to resist the power of this man's appeal.

Her breaths came in short little gasps. They stared at each other for a long, pulse-pounding moment.

This was insane.

"If I could resist you," he said, "I would. The unfortunate thing is, I can't."

He swayed toward her, just a little, and it was enough to break down every wall of defense she had tried to build around herself today while he was operating on people. Her cover came crumbling down in a great, chaotic descent.

Donovan cupped her cheek in his hand and gazed at her for a shuddering instant before he pressed his mouth to hers.

The world spun stormily around Jocelyn as she reached her arms around this man who drove her wild in the most ground-shifting way. He somehow managed to make her forget who she was and what she was doing here. All that mattered was the erotic delight of his hands touching her.

The drenching heat of arousal between her thighs hit like a tidal surge.

He whispered in her ear. "Come home with me, Jocelyn." Gooseflesh tickled down her body and caused another wave of creamy heat between her legs. "I want you in my bed...."

Tess's words resounded in her mind again: *Why not steal a little enjoyment while you can?*

Lord, how she wanted to...

He kissed her neck and stroked her shoulders and back, then devoured her mouth again with another skillfully wet kiss that dissolved most of what was left of her resistance. She wanted this man inside her, and she didn't care what the consequences were. Surely she could deal with her fears another day.

Then she heard laughter from somewhere outside her hazy consciousness, somewhere outside the car. She pulled back and turned. Two teenagers were standing outside her window, watching them! How long had they been there?

Realizing they'd been discovered, the youths immediately turned and took off down the street, but the damage was already done. Jocelyn had fallen down in her duties, to an unimaginable degree.

"They're gone," Donovan whispered, leaning forward to continue kissing her, but she held him back with a hand.

"No, that was a sign."

"Don't tell me you're superstitious now."

"No, I'm *awake* now, thank God. What if that had been your stalker? This is crazy, Donovan, and you know it."

He grabbed hold of the steering wheel with both hands and tapped his forehead against it. "This *is* crazy. It's a good thing you resigned, because if you didn't I'd have to fire you. Because I don't want you as my bodyguard anymore. I want you as a woman. In my bed."

"That can't happen." She tried to fight her impossible desires. "Not yet. Not now."

"But someday? Can I at least entertain some hopes?"

She couldn't seem to answer right away. What just happened had spooked her, doused her with a healthy splash of reality. Her heart was racing inside her chest. Besides that, she wasn't sure she could handle this with Donovan, not if it was going to blow up in her face in a month's time.

At her hesitation, his eyes narrowed, then he blew out a breath of air. "I need a second or two to get a hold of myself." He flicked the latch on the door and got out.

"No, wait! Donovan!" She got out, too, meeting him around the front of the vehicle and taking him by the arm. "Get back in the car. I can't be sure we're safe here."

Just then, a navy blue sedan came speeding out from behind the car that was parked to the rear of them. Jocelyn's senses thrummed to life, and she pulled Donovan across the sidewalk to the shelter of a huge oak tree. She shielded his body with hers, just as the driver opened fire out of the passenger side window.

Seven

Tree bark exploded beside Jocelyn's head, then tires squealed and the car sped off. She tried to see the license plate, but it was too late.

Donovan stepped back onto the sidewalk, staring after the attacker.

"Get in the car," Jocelyn ordered. "I'll drive."

She flipped open her cell phone to call the police as she ran around the front of the vehicle. She had the emergency number on speed dial. She gave the particulars about the assailant while she got in and started the engine. "You better buckle up," she said.

Donovan watched her squeal out onto the road. "What the hell just happened?"

"We were being watched, and not just by those teenagers. Look out the rear window. Did he come back around? Are we being followed?"

"No, there's no one behind us."

She pulled a U-turn and started back in the other direction, got onto the main road and shifted quickly in and out of lanes.

Donovan kept one hand on the dash to brace himself. "You're quite a driver."

"Comes with the territory. Anybody else shifting around behind us?"

He turned to look. "No. It's clear."

She turned left at a busy intersection and went up and down some side streets to avoid the direct route home. They finally reached his building, and Jocelyn parked out back instead of in his usual spot inside the garage. She escorted him out of the car quickly and skirted through a back entrance for which she had a key.

"I didn't even know this door was here," Donovan said. "You did your homework, didn't you?"

"Preparation is everything." She checked around corners in basement halls, moving quickly to the elevator and keeping an eye out until he was safely inside. They rode up the twenty-two floors in complete silence.

Jocelyn took all possible precautions entering Donovan's penthouse and locking the door behind them. She searched the place, then closed all the blinds and curtains and told Donovan to stay away from the windows.

Once they were sure they were out of immediate danger, Jocelyn led the way into the kitchen where Donovan sat on one of the stools at the center island.

"Are you all right?" she asked. "Can I get you anything? A glass of water?"

"That would be great, thanks. Things were pretty nutty back there."

She went to fill a glass from the water cooler in the corner. "This is obviously a very determined stalker, and what happened today will happen again and again until he's caught, so I want to do everything I can to assist the police in their investigation." She set the glass of water down in front of him. "They're going to be here soon, so let's try again to figure out who would want to hurt you. We need to give the police something more to work with. You mentioned the grief counseling center you're working on. You don't have any plans to pave over a park or anything like that, do you?

"No, the location hasn't even been decided yet. We're still in the fund-raising stage."

"What else can you think of? Have you lost any patients lately? Could there be a grieving loved one who blames you?"

"I guess it's possible. I'm a good surgeon, but I'm not God. I've lost my share."

"Can you get me their names? Maybe the police could look into it."

He nodded.

Jocelyn flipped open her phone to call the police and see if they'd apprehended anyone. Unfortunately they hadn't, which was not surprising, since the assailant had sped off too quickly and she hadn't identified the plate number.

She was told an officer would be there soon to ask questions, and that they would be heightening the investigation.

Two hours later, after Jocelyn had dealt with the police and called Tess to report what had happened, she found Donovan in the kitchen, cooking.

She took a seat on one of the stools. "How are you doing?"

He stood over the stovetop on the island, whisking something in a saucepan. He wore his faded jeans and a white T-shirt, tucked in.

"Better," he replied. "Cooking relaxes me. Want some bacon-wrapped scallops?" He set down the whisk, opened one of the stainless steel ovens behind him, and pulled out a pan of sizzling hors d'oeuvres. He set them on a china platter, and after sticking toothpicks in them, set the platter in front of Jocelyn.

"Don't mind if I do. Oh, sweet heaven, these are delicious." Then she realized how hot they were and opened her mouth to wave a hand in front of her face. "Ow."

Donovan smiled as he returned to his whisking. "Burn yourself? If only you would exercise such a lack of caution and restraint with me."

She couldn't help smiling. "I'm sorry, Donovan, but you have to admit I'm right. Especially after today."

He whisked faster. "Yes, and I must say, you were pretty impressive driving my car." He lifted his sexy gaze. "You, my dear, are no debutante."

She laughed. "And you, kind sir, are an excellent cook." She popped another tender, juicy scallop into her mouth. "What are you making?"

"Grilled chicken with lemon cream sauce over angel hair pasta, and sautéed snow peas. Are you hungry?"

"I'm starved and that sounds amazing. We forgot to eat dinner, didn't we? For obvious reasons, I guess."

He tilted his head, not bothering to speak about why.

"Listen…Donovan," she said cautiously, "before we sit down to eat, I'd like to clear the air about what happened today."

His gaze lifted again. "I got shot at by a stalker."

"Before that."

"You mean what attracted the voyeuristic teenagers? Yeah, that was interesting, too, wasn't it?"

"It was more than interesting," she replied, feeling like she was treading into dangerous territory, but needing to get this out in the open so it wouldn't happen again. "It was excruciating."

He set the saucepan aside and flicked off the burner. Slowly, sensuously, he moved toward her like a confident panther on the prowl. Her blood began to race faster through her veins.

"In what way was it excruciating?" He took her hand and pulled her gently to her feet. She stared at him for a shaky moment while he raised her hand to his lips and kissed her knuckles. Tremors of delight danced across her skin.

"In *that* way."

His wicked gaze met hers.

"You're cruel, Donovan," she said in a low, breathy voice while she tried to fight the powerful emotions that were tugging at her from all directions.

"No more cruel than you are, not allowing me to have hope."

She swallowed over the huge lump of anxiety in her throat. "We shouldn't be thinking about this kind of thing right now."

"You're the one who brought it up."

This was agonizing. "Yes, I did, because I thought

we should—'' He laid a few more soft kisses upon her knuckles, and the cool, lingering moisture from his lips seemed to tingle all the way up her arm. She forgot what she was going to say. Damn him....

"You thought we should clear the air," he said for her.

"Yes." *Thank you.*

"Let's clear it, then. I promise I'll be good." He gave her hand back to her and let his own hands fall to his sides. "I'm listening."

Her heart did a few wild little somersaults in her chest. How was it possible that he could reduce her to a stammering idiot, when she'd promised herself she would be a brick wall?

"I know I said I was going to resign," she told him, "but in light of what happened today, and the fact that Tess can't seem to find anyone to replace me on such short notice, I think it's important for me to stay on for a little while."

He wet his too-inviting lips. "Ah. I suppose the next thing you're going to tell me is that the kissing has to stop."

"Precisely." She waited with apprehension for his argument, prepared her rebuttals in her mind....

"Done," he said flatly.

She shook her head in disbelief; her voice revealed her utter amusement. "Done? I don't believe you."

He laid his hand on his chest, looking dismayed by her lack of confidence in his ability to keep his hands to himself. "You don't trust me."

"I do trust you, it's just that...well, you haven't exactly been agreeable to my requests before now."

He considered her point. "Maybe not, but I've had

some time to think about things, and I feel differently about everything tonight."

"Differently? How so?"

"I realize that in addition to the fact that I'm your client, and the fact that I was shot at today and you feel responsible, you're nervous about getting involved with me because you don't know me very well and you're afraid I might turn out to be the playboy you thought I was when you first met me. A little more time together will give me the chance to prove to you that you're wrong. And maybe prove it to myself, too."

The last thing he said went straight through her. He was revealing something of himself. A deeper vulnerability. A desire to improve some of his shortcomings.

She hadn't imagined he was aware that he even had any.

"So you're going to be good?" she replied, trying to recapture the mood from a few minutes ago—when it was a little more simple. A little more casual. "You're not going to try to tempt me?"

He touched her chin briefly. "I'm going to do my very best, hoping of course, that there will be a reward at the end."

"Like a dog treat?" she replied, finding this all very hard to believe.

"No." He backed away and opened the oven to serve up dinner. "Like your heart."

A ripple of unwelcome anticipation coursed through Jocelyn. *My heart?*

Damn him for being so impossibly, wonderfully charming.

* * *

They ate dinner by candlelight in the formal dining room, on the shiny, polished mahogany table, and sipped sparkling, alcohol-free cranberry cocktail from crystal goblets. After the dishes were cleared, it was past ten o'clock.

"One last chance," Jocelyn said, "to cancel your surgery tomorrow morning. We could stay here and watch TV and avoid risks."

"I would if I could, but it's an important procedure. It's not something that should be postponed."

She nodded, helping him load the dishwasher. A few minutes later, they were yawning.

"Will you be able to sleep?" she asked.

He walked her to her bedroom door. "I doubt it."

"Would you like to stay up a little longer? We could watch a movie if it would help."

"No, I have to be in the O.R. at 6:00 a.m. I should at least try to get some shut-eye."

"All right. Well, don't worry. I'm here, and remember I sleep with one eye open, the monitor's on and your new alarm system is second to none. You'll be fine tonight."

He settled one broad shoulder against her door-jamb, and relaxed there, just looking at her. "Will I?"

Jocelyn's insides began to quiver at the awesome effect of his words in the wake of his sexy green eyes, half-shuttered in the dim light.

"Of course," she replied, even though she knew he was referring to another kind of danger. The kind that went hand in hand with temptations and consequences.

His voice was calm and soothing after the madness of the day. "I'm sure you're right."

Still, he remained at her door, gazing into her eyes, then down at her lips, back up to her eyes again.

"You're hovering," she said in a playful tone. "Remember what you promised."

"I promised I wouldn't kiss you. I didn't promise I wouldn't look at you. It's not easy to pry my eyes away, you know."

"Well, you'd better if you're going to be able to keep them open during surgery in the morning."

He visibly snapped himself out of it, and stepped away from the doorjamb. "You're right, you're right. I should go." He started to back away. "Thanks, Jocelyn."

"For what?"

He paused in the hall. "For being here."

"It's my job."

"No, it's more than that. You make me feel…" He shrugged, starting to back away again. "Happy. I've never been so happy to have a woman stay overnight, when there wasn't any chance of you know what."

"Parcheesi?"

He laughed. "Is that what they call it these days?"

"God only knows."

He laughed again, still backing away. "You're adorable, you know."

Jocelyn began to close her door. "Good night, Doctor."

"And you're breaking my heart."

"While you're breaking a promise. Good night," she repeated, closing her door until it clicked, but remaining there with her ear against it, just to hear the sound of his footfalls until they disappeared into his room.

* * * *

At 3:00 a.m., Jocelyn awoke to a knock at her door. "Yes?"

Donovan answered from the hall. "You awake?"

Her shoulders heaved with a sigh, and she climbed out of bed and opened the door to find him standing there looking sleepy, disheveled and delicious, shirtless with nothing on but a pair of black pajama bottoms.

"I woke you, didn't I?"

"It's okay. I had to get up to answer your knock on my door anyway."

He smiled, and she wasn't quite sure how she'd managed to speak, with that smooth, golden chest at eye level, scrambling her senses into a jumbled mess.

She noticed his eyes were bloodshot. "Can't sleep?"

"I haven't gotten a wink so far. I think it was everything that happened today. I'm still wired."

"I know the feeling. What can I do? Want some hot milk or something?"

"Hot milk? What, am I twelve?"

"You don't drink hot milk?"

He raised his eyebrows and shook his head. "I didn't think *anybody* drank hot milk. At least not since the fifties."

"I do, and it works. Truly." She started toward the kitchen. "Come on, I'll prove it to you."

They both walked barefoot to the kitchen and turned on the lights. Jocelyn poured some milk into a mug and stuck it in the microwave. While the appliance hummed, she explained the hot milk technique.

"If you want it to work, you have to make sure you close your eyes as soon as the sleepy feeling hits, because if you don't, you'll miss it. It's like a wave you have to catch. So you shouldn't drink it in the living room, because then you'll have to get up and go to bed, and that alone might make you miss the wave. Drink it in bed."

"I see. Sounds like you've got it down to a science."

"I do." The microwave beeped, and she removed the steaming cup and stirred it with a spoon. "There you go."

He took the cup and smelled it. "Hot milk. Hmm."

She put her hand on his back to usher him to bed, and the warm feel of his well-toned muscles beneath her fingertips sent shivers up and down her spine. She tried to ignore them, but it was no use. She gave up trying, and resolved to go back to her own bed ASAP.

They reached his bedroom, and she hesitated for a fraction of a second before going with him inside. She'd never escorted a principal to bed before—and certainly not a principal who looked like Donovan, bare-chested and devastatingly masculine in nothing but his drawstring pajama bottoms. It would never have seemed appropriate with any of her previous clients, nor had any of them ever attempted to push the boundaries like Donovan did.

Still, his comfort and safety were her concern, so she entered the room. "You'll be all right now?" she asked, pausing at the bottom of the king-size bed while he set the mug on his side table and climbed in.

"I don't know. It depends on the hot milk."

She was about to say good-night when he gestured

toward the chair in the corner. "Have a seat. Stay and talk to me for a few minutes. Tell me something personal."

She swallowed nervously. "Like what?"

"I don't know. Like what kind of person you were in high school. Were you popular—you know, the student council type, the prom queen—or did you hang out with the druggies?"

Jocelyn moved to the chair and sat down. "I wasn't anything. I just went to class, got average grades, had a few friends I hung out with most of the time."

"Your basic invisible kid, ignored for being normal," he said, a little too perceptively. "Did you have any boyfriends? Or was the social climbing med student your one and only love?"

"No, I didn't have any boyfriends in high school. I had a couple of guys who were friends, and we hung out some times, but I didn't even go to the prom. None of us did. Looking back on it, maybe we were geeks. I was a bit of a loner. Still am."

"But why? You're gorgeous and funny. You should have been snapped up by now."

She sat forward. "It's simpler this way. I've gotten used to living alone and I like to focus all my energy on my work. I don't have to worry about disappointing anyone when I don't come home for weeks on end. But hey, who are you to point the finger, Mr. Single-Man."

He took the first sip of his milk. "Point taken, but I've had some really good excuses. First it was medical school, which kept me busy constantly, then there were years of residencies, where I was sleep-deprived and stressed out most of the time. I haven't had time for a relationship.''

''What about now? You've been here in Chicago for a couple of years, and you appear to have a social life. You go to the theater and you have women calling you.''

He took another sip. ''Yeah, but I never really got to know any of them.''

''Who's fault is that?''

He gave her a playful look. ''It couldn't be mine. I'm perfect, don't ya know.''

Jocelyn smiled.

''Seriously though,'' he continued, taking another sip from his mug, ''I know I haven't seemed like much of a family guy, and maybe I'm not. I've been on my own for a long time.''

''You must have some family. Brothers? Sisters?''

He shook his head. ''I'm an only child. Not that my parents ever intended it to be that way. They died when I was two.''

A flash of grief flared through her. ''I'm so sorry, Donovan. I didn't know. I mean, I knew they weren't alive, but I didn't know when you lost them. What happened?''

He gazed at his mug as he spoke. ''Car accident. I was in the back seat, and we hit a patch of ice and went over a low cliff. Somehow I survived, and someone heard me crying the next morning. A woman found me outside the car, sitting in the dirt, suffering symptoms of exposure. My parents had been dead all night. It's a miracle I survived.''

''My God, do you remember any of it?''

''No. I barely remember my parents, though my grandmother raised me and always talked about them. She was good to me. She died when I was seventeen and I received my inheritance then, which—aside from a small monthly allowance for my upbringing—had been held in trust. This penthouse was part of it. My parents had bought it together when they married, and wanted to spend their lives here. I lived in it with them when I was very small, before they died. Then, like the rest of the estate, it was held in trust. So you see, I didn't always have money, and I didn't ask for it, nor do I consider it a part of who I am. I'd give it all away this minute to have my parents back.''

Jocelyn's whole body ached with empathy for Donovan's loss and his lifelong yearning. She had already realized that he wasn't shallow. This only reconfirmed it. ''I had no idea. What about becoming a doctor? When did you decide to do that?''

''I always knew that's what I wanted to do. Unlike your ex, it wasn't because I wanted a fancy penthouse or expensive car. I think it was because I wanted to feel like I had some control over saving people's lives, because I sure as hell felt powerless after I lost my parents. I didn't know why I had been so lucky to be spared, and wanted to give something back and make my survival worthwhile. So I used part of the inheritance to put myself through medical school. When I was finished my residencies, that's when I came back here to live. It was kind of strange—like coming home, even though I barely remember living here when I was little.'' He was quiet for a moment. ''Too bad air bags weren't standard back then. They might have lived.''

Jocelyn got up and went to sit beside him on the bed. She reached forward and stroked the hair off his forehead, then cupped his cheek with her hand. "I'm so sorry that happened to you."

"Me, too. From what I heard, my parents were great people."

She rubbed his forehead again. "Is that why you're trying to raise money for the grief counseling center for children?"

"Yeah. I know what it can do to a child. The fears and the grief, the abandonment issues and survivor guilt." He finished the last of his hot milk and sat forward to set the mug on his side table. When he reached across, she saw there was not only a scar on his shoulder—which she had noticed when they'd gone running that first day—but more scars under his arm, along his ribs.

She reached to touch them while he was still leaning. "That's two car accidents you've been in. These look like they were serious."

He raised his arm to inspect them himself. "They've healed nicely though, don't you think?"

"I guess so." She continued to touch them, feeling the warmth of his skin, wanting very badly to rub away the pain he must have suffered, both as a child and a year ago when he'd been hit by that other car. "You said a woman went through a red light and rammed you?"

"Yeah."

"Did she live?"

"No. She wasn't wearing a seat belt."

Jocelyn considered that. "Was she drunk?"

"No. Apparently she and her husband had just had a fight, and she was pretty messed up."

Jocelyn continued to touch the scars, tilting her

head to the side as she stared down at them. "What was the date of the accident?"

He told her.

"That's exactly a year to the day before the intruder broke into your house and left you the letter. You don't suppose…"

Donovan sat forward. "That the husband has it out for me?"

"It's a possibility." Jocelyn went to get her phone. "I'll leave a voice mail message with the cop who was here today and have him check it out."

She made the phone call from the kitchen, then returned to Donovan's bedroom. She was about to tell him not to think about it anymore, to try to get some sleep, but she didn't have to.

She approached the bed. His eyes were closed, his breathing deep and heavy.

"See? Hot milk works." She bent forward and placed a gentle kiss on his forehead.

She pulled the covers up over his legs and watched him for a moment, gazing at the perfection of his face—the strong line of his jaw, the straightness of his nose, the beauty of his eyes, even when they were closed.

He was handsome, yes, but there was so much more to him than that, she thought, her heart still aching from what he'd told her about his parents.

She imagined him making the decision to start a grief counseling clinic for children. He must have spent his whole life pondering and mulling over his childhood and upbringing, longing for what had been taken from him, and wishing someone had been able to ease the pain. Now, he wanted to help other children, to help ease *their* pain.

Jocelyn swallowed over the huge lump in her throat. There was a very big heart in there, she realized, gazing down at Donovan's chest, fighting the urge to lay her hand upon his skin and feel his heart beating. It was a fragile, wounded heart that had never found the courage to love anyone. It was no wonder. *I know what it can do to a child. The fears and the grief, the abandonment issues.*

She suddenly understood what he'd meant earlier that night, when he'd said he wanted to prove to himself that he wasn't a playboy. He obviously had some understanding of the damage done to his heart, and blamed that for his single lifestyle.

Feeling suddenly sleepy, Jocelyn pulled the covers up to Donovan's shoulders and turned from the room. Something tugged inside her—an intense, aching desire that shot through her soul like a rocket. A desire to protect this man, no matter what it took, no matter how long.

Never in her career had she experienced anything like it.

Eight

The next night, they returned home to Donovan's penthouse after a long, stressful day at the hospital. Stressful for Donovan, because of the two back-to-back surgeries, and stressful for Jocelyn, who didn't relax or let down her guard, even for a minute, grilling everyone and anyone who wanted to get within ten paces of Donovan, and constantly watching over her shoulder. Realizing her limitations, she had called Tess to look into retaining a few more operatives to make this a team detail and increase security temporarily, at least until they gained some leads on the stalker.

Shortly after they entered the penthouse, the phone rang. "I'll get it." Jocelyn answered the telephone in the front hall. "Hello? Sergeant O'Reilly, have you learned anything?"

Donovan approached, watching her and waiting,

curious about what the police had managed to discover during the day.

"I see." She looked at Donovan. "Yes. We were lucky. I'm not sure yet. Yes, I'll do that. Thank you for letting me know." She hung up the phone.

"What happened?"

Jocelyn moved toward him and placed her hand on his arm. "You won't believe what I'm going to tell you. Maybe we should go and sit down."

She led the way into the living room, where they both sat on the sofa. Jocelyn took Donovan's hand in hers, and held it. "The man whose wife died in that car accident is the man who's stalking you. His name is Ben Cohen."

For a long time, Donovan gazed at her. "How do the police know?"

"Because after I gave them the information, they went to his apartment to question him. He wasn't there, but the landlady told them some things that gave them enough reason to get a search warrant, and when they got inside, they found pictures of you on his wall, newspaper articles about the accident, pictures of your smashed SUV, among other things."

"Did they arrest him?

"That's the problem. He wasn't there, and he hadn't been there for a while. The landlady said a week or two. The police don't know where he is. He hasn't been to work in a week, either. Hasn't even called in sick."

"It sounds like he *wants* people to know he's the one."

"Yes, which makes him all the more dangerous, because he has no fear. This is a personal vendetta for him, and he doesn't care about the consequences.

He doesn't seem to care that he's going to lose his job or his apartment, and most likely go to prison."

Donovan cupped his forehead in his hand and squeezed his pounding temples. "The accident wasn't even my fault. *She* was the one who ran the red light."

"I know, but he's obviously not rational. He wants someone to blame, and from what the police found in his apartment, he's angry about the issue of SUVs being like tanks on the roads. He thinks it's a conspiracy to wipe out the lower classes, and the fact that you're a rich doctor only added fuel to that fire."

"This is crazy!" He stood up and paced around the living room. "I didn't get an SUV to kill people! I got it because it was good in the snow and in my line of work—trying to *save* people—I can't afford to get stuck on the way to the hospital."

"I know, I know," Jocelyn said, rising to her feet and going to his side. "None of this is your fault. He's a nut, but at least we know who he is and the police are keeping an eye out for him. They'll catch him. It won't take long."

"But in the meantime? Am I supposed to go about my life, waiting to get shot at again?"

She took his hand in hers. "No. You're not supposed to go about your life, not if I have any say in the matter."

He met her gaze directly. "What are you suggesting?"

"It's my job to protect you, Donovan, and the risk-level—now that we know what's going on—has skyrocketed in the past twenty-four hours. You can't continue to do the things you normally do, because he's been watching, waiting for the chance to strike—like yesterday on the sidewalk. I don't want you to be a sitting duck. I want you to come away with me.''

"I can't tell you where I'm going," Donovan said to his friend, Dr. Mark Reeves, over the phone, "because I don't know. She won't tell me."

"I had no idea it would get this serious," Mark said. "I half thought the intruder was a burglar, like the police wanted to believe, and thought maybe the letter was unconnected. Or maybe I was just hoping."

"Look, don't worry. Jocelyn is a professional. She knows what she's doing and I have complete faith in her."

"So you're on a first-name basis," his friend said with a curious tone.

Mark was single, but didn't have many women in his life. Not that he didn't have his share of females trying to bang down his door. He was just too busy with his work to stop and smell the roses. Which was why he enjoyed hearing about all of Donovan's dates. Donovan supposed it was Mark's way of having a vicarious love life.

"You're not just making this up, are you?" Mark said. "So you can take off with her on a wild Jamaican weekend while I cover your patients?"

Donovan rolled his eyes toward the ceiling. "No, Mark."

"Don't fault me. A guy can't help wondering. She's a looker, and I've seen the way you looked at each other at the hospital. There's heat between you—the sizzling kind. Is she still sleeping in the guest bedroom?"

The direction of the conversation unnerved Donovan suddenly. He tried to laugh it off. "Mark, you need to get a life. I've got to go."

"But wait, why won't you tell me anything?"

Donovan considered that with more than a little profundity. Why wouldn't he say anything? Because this was deeper and more personal than any affair he'd had in his past? Because he didn't want to jinx it? Or because he himself was still completely in the dark about what was going on?

"This is different, that's all," he replied with the intention of being vague. "She's my bodyguard, and just for the record, she *is* still in the guest room."

Mark whistled. "No kidding. She must be pretty tough. I haven't known a woman yet who's been able to resist you."

"Well, she is an original, that's for sure. I've never met a woman like her."

Mark's voice lowered. "I was right. There *is* something going on between you. Just tell me this, are you going to lure her out of the guest room any time soon?"

Donovan stared down at the dial pad on the phone, shaking his head at his friend's typical tenacity. *I'm doing my best,* he thought.

"Enough nosy questions, Mark. My kiss-and-tell days are over. Thanks for covering my patients, and I'll see you when I get back."

Donovan hung up the phone, anxious to get on the road with Jocelyn, to wherever they were going. He was looking forward to being alone with her. Somewhere safe, where she would be able to relax a little and, for once, let down her guard.

He didn't mean professionally.

* * *

After a long, careful trip out of Chicago in a rented car under Tess's name, Jocelyn turned up the winding, woodsy road that led to the cabin. No one would ever be able to trace them here, and it had the added benefit of being familiar to Jocelyn, who had come here twice before. It was the perfect hideout.

They drove through the shady woods for a few miles, churning up dust on the dry road while rays of sunshine gleamed like dappled light through the trees.

Donovan looked out the window. "This is really isolated. "You're sure we'll be safe here?"

Safe from the stalker, yes. Safe from her growing attraction to Donovan? Not likely, considering this was probably the most romantic place on earth.

"Positive." She tried to sound confident and ignore her personal feelings. "No one knows where we are, and I took the necessary precautions when we left the city."

They finally pulled up in front of a cedar, prow-fronted cabin overlooking a lake, with huge floor-to-ceiling windows and a multilevel deck with patio furniture, a round table with a sun umbrella and a barbecue. Rich green grass went all the way down to the water, where a small cruiser was tied up at a private wharf.

"This is beautiful," Donovan said. "You sure know how to pick a spot."

"Well, I figured if we're going to be forced to leave town and be inconvenienced by Cohen, we might as well at least be comfortable, and maybe even enjoy ourselves."

Enjoy ourselves. She shouldn't have said that. It

inspired all kinds of inappropriate images in her mind.

Jocelyn turned off the car. The silence was astonishing. All they could hear was a single bird chirping, and the sound of a light breeze whispering through the pines and leafy elms.

Donovan stared up at the cabin. "You've been here before?"

"Twice, yes. Wait till you see the inside."

They opened their doors and breathed in the clean scent of the woods, then stepped onto a carpet of soft, brown pine needles in the driveway. Fetching their bags out of the trunk, they made their way up to the door, where the key and a welcome note from the owners were waiting for them in the wooden mailbox. Jocelyn opened the door and let Donovan enter first before following him inside.

Nothing had changed since the last time she'd been here. Everything was rustic pine—the kitchen table and chairs, the hutch full of china, the plank floor and the pine walls, as well as the honey-pine ceiling, supported by solid cedar timbers.

"Wow," Donovan said, looking up at the cathedral ceiling in the great room and the huge, gray stone fireplace. "Looks like we're going to get that vacation we've both been needing. How long do we get to stay?"

She set down her bag. "That depends on how long it takes the police to find Cohen. Could be twenty-four hours, could be a month."

"Let's hope it's a month. Though I doubt the hospital would be happy about that."

Jocelyn locked the door behind them. "Come on, I'll show you the bedrooms."

"A woman after my own heart," he said.

Fighting the thrill that charged through her like an electric current, Jocelyn poked him in the chest. She couldn't afford to be knocked off-kilter by something as minor as a suggestive joke. "Behave yourself, Doctor. Our rooms are on opposite sides of the cabin."

Gathering her composure, she picked up her bag and led the way across the open concept kitchen and living area, to the bedroom on the ground floor. A four-poster pine bed stood against the wall; white wicker furniture was arranged in a corner beside the glass sliding doors that led out onto a deck.

"I'll take this room," she said, then led him across to the other side of the cabin, where they climbed stairs to a loft.

The master suite had its own balcony and private bath, as well as a skylight over the bed.

Donovan set down his bag. "That'll be great for stargazing."

"For sure. You'll be comfortable enough here?"

He walked to the bed and pressed his hands onto the mattress. "Well, let me see…nice and firm. It's perfect. Want to come try it out?"

She laughed. "I'll trust your diagnosis, Doctor, and stay on this side of the room, thank you very much. Besides, I've already tried it out, the last time I was here."

His eyes narrowed playfully. "Alone, I hope."

Jocelyn folded her arms over her chest. "That is none of your business."

He raised his hands in mock surrender. "You're right, I'm sorry. I'd just like to know you better, that's all, and I'm curious about certain things."

She gazed at him intently. "About what, exactly?"

"About your life before I met you. Did you bring other clients here? Or were you here just for pleasure?"

Jocelyn sighed, wishing she didn't feel so inclined to answer his questions, wishing that this desire to be closer to him on an emotional level would go away. But ever since the night in his bedroom, when he'd told her about his past and she'd told him things about her personal life, she'd felt more connected to him. She had felt like she was talking to a friend she'd known for years.

"I wouldn't exactly call it pleasure," she replied, "but it wasn't for work reasons, either."

He sauntered toward her. "Now you've got me *really* curious. You can't leave me hanging."

Her pulse began to race as he approached, stopping in front of her, close enough that she could smell his musky male scent. Oh, this was going to be a very difficult assignment over the next few days....

"All right, I'll tell you. I came here the first time with my mother when I was fourteen, just after my father left us. She wanted to get away, so she wouldn't have to answer the phone and explain to everyone what had happened. We stayed for two weeks. Then I came back alone, years later, after Tom and I broke up."

Donovan stared at her for a long moment. "So this place doesn't exactly have pleasant memories for you."

She shook her head.

"Why did you choose it?"

"Because it was the safest place I knew, and I'd basically already done the advance. I know the layout of the property and the inside of the cabin like the back of my hand."

"Always a professional," he said.

"I try."

He gazed at her pensively for a few more seconds, then thankfully dropped the subject. She had the feeling, however, that it would come up again at some point....

"Want to get the groceries out of the car?" he asked.

"Sure." Jocelyn led the way down the stairs.

They brought in the food—a week's supply that Tess had picked up for them and delivered just before they left Chicago in the middle of the night. They stowed it away in the fridge and cupboards.

"What would you like for dinner tonight?" Donovan asked, checking out the cooking utensils in the drawers. "I don't want to influence you, but I make a perfect barbecued steak."

"Sounds great."

If his steak was half as good as his chicken and lemon sauce, and he continued to be such an enjoyable dinner companion, Jocelyn was going to find it very difficult to remember that she was not here on a quest for pleasure. Epicurean or otherwise. She was here to do a job.

That evening after dinner, they walked down to the beach. The water was calm, except for tiny, circular ripples from fish bobbing to the surface. The sun was setting just beyond the treeline on the other side of the lake.

It was a hot night, so Jocelyn had changed into a black T-shirt and khaki walking shorts with Nike sandals, but Donovan still wore his jeans. Jocelyn spread a blanket on the sand.

"Listen to the crickets," he said. "What a gorgeous night."

He began to unbutton his shirt.

"What do you think you're doing?"

He unbuttoned it all the way down and shrugged out of it, then hopped on one foot while he pulled off a shoe. "I'm checking out the lake."

"Are you wearing a swimsuit under those?" she asked, pointing to his jeans, trying not to stare at the sheer magnificence of his bare chest in the glimmering, red twilight.

"Nope." He pulled off the other shoe.

"Hold on a second!" Jocelyn blurted out, realizing what he was doing. "You can't do that here!"

"Why not? It's a scorcher tonight, and there's no one here but us."

"*Us* being the operative word! I'm here, and I don't particularly want to see your—"

Good God.

He pulled down his jeans, and she caught a flash of his bare hip just before she shut her eyes and whirled around to face the other direction. The next thing she heard was the sound of bare feet running onto the wharf and a huge, resounding splash.

Jocelyn opened her eyes, turned and looked down at Donovan's clothes on the blanket at her feet.

All of them.

Right down to the baby blue boxers.

She walked to the edge of the wharf just as Donovan resurfaced. "The water's great!" He flipped his wet hair back off his face. He was one beautiful man. "You gotta come in!"

"I will most certainly *not* come in!"

He laughed. "Why not? It's a gorgeous night, Miss Executive Protection Professional. There's no one here. Relax for once, just for a little while."

"I've said it before and I'll say it again, Donovan—that's precisely when something would happen—as soon as I relaxed in my duties. You've hired me to do a job, and I intend to do it. I'll watch."

She chose not to tell him that watching felt equally as dangerous. For her, anyway.

"Have it your way."

He dove under the water, and she saw more than she wanted to see—a tight, muscular bare butt to die for. Her insides quivered with excitement. Was he trying to drive her mad on purpose? She cupped her forehead in her hand and shut her eyes again.

Feeling slightly desperate, she glanced all around, looking for anybody who might suddenly appear for some unknown reason. The owners, perhaps? A lost hiker? Of course there was no one—it was only wishful thinking on her part—so she looked back down at Donovan, frolicking in the water and damn well driving her insane with both exasperation and yearning.

He treaded water and looked up at her with a tempting smile. "Sure you won't change your mind?"

"I'm sure." But she wasn't sure. What she really wanted to do was dive into that lake and cool off. Because she sure as hell needed to.

"I can see you're changing your mind," he said teasingly, still treading water.

How in God's name did he know that? she wondered miserably. Was it written on her forehead in great big letters—I'm Hot For You, Doctor Knight?

He continued to try to coax her in. "Just for five minutes. You said yourself no one could possibly know we're here. Why can't you just enjoy yourself?"

Now he was making her feel like a prude. A boring old stick-in-the-mud.

Which she was! When was the last time she'd enjoyed herself? Or gone out on a date that didn't involve work? When had she laughed, outside of these last few days with Donovan?

"I'd like to, but…"

"No more buts. Just dive in. I'll even turn around while you get undressed."

She stood for a few more seconds, considering it while Donovan continued to tread water with his back to her. Oh, what would it hurt? Five minutes. He was right. She'd done her job and done it well. No one could possibly find them here.

"All right," she said reluctantly, pulling her T-shirt off over her head. "But I'm not getting naked. I'm wearing undergarments that are perfectly respectable for swimming."

She was glad she'd worn the new black bra and matching panties that Doris had picked out for her, to go with the black dress. It almost looked like a real bikini.

He laughed. "Whatever floats your boat."

Shaking her head, Jocelyn stepped out of her shorts and folded everything neatly in a pile. She walked to the edge of the wharf.

"Okay, you can look now." She reached her arms

out in front of her, paused, then did a double forward flip through the air into the water.

As soon as she surfaced, she heard Donovan clapping and whooping. ''That was amazing! What, you were an Olympic diver in your past life?''

She rubbed the water from her eyes. ''No, but I was on a recreational swim team when I was a kid.''

''You do everything well, don't you?'' He swam closer.

She shrugged, trying not to think about the fact that he was completely naked in the water, not two feet away from her now, and she was in her underwear. If she moved any closer, she'd be able to touch him.

Lord, how she wanted to. Her body was practically humming with the desire to wrap her arms around his neck. To feel his cheek next to hers.

She wanted to let go of all her inhibitions—just this once—and do what Tess had suggested. Take advantage of this romantic summer night with the most handsome man on earth here beside her....

She took a deep breath and dunked her head, still trying to cool off, but realizing it was hopeless and she might as well resign herself to a painful, heated lust for the next half hour or so.

They dipped and dove and swam around each other as the sun disappeared behind the trees. The sensual feel of the water on Jocelyn's skin was sinfully erotic.

After a few minutes, Donovan came closer, treading water. ''I have a goal,'' he said. ''Concerning you.''

She managed to keep her breathing steady as she

spoke. "What is it? You're not going to teach me to cook, are you?"

"No."

"To perform heart surgery on a raccoon?"

He laughed. "No."

"What then?"

Donovan's eyes smoldered with determination. "I want to make our time here pleasant for you."

As she gazed into his glimmering eyes, she couldn't think of a single thing to say. She wasn't quite sure what he was suggesting, though something about it made her feel warm inside.

Thankfully he elaborated. "The last two times you were here were some of the worst times in your life. This is a beautiful place, Jocelyn, and you should have happy memories of it. Feel as if those sadder times are over."

Beginning to understand his meaning, she slicked her wet hair back. "You mean you want to *cleanse* the cabin of its past for me?"

"In a matter of speaking, yes."

She was now treading water, very close to Donovan. "Why?"

He slowly blinked. "Because I want to see you smile."

"You've seen me smile."

"Not very often." The way he was looking at her now—with tenderness and caring—it was softening all her female powers of resistance. She didn't think she could keep herself from touching this incredibly charming man.

Yet it wasn't a sexual seduction that was going on here. He was just being inconceivably nice to her.

"What's this about?" she asked.

"It's about me wanting to make you happy."

She grinned at him. "That fortune cookie was right. You do like to fix things. It's why you want to open that grief counseling center to help children. It's why you became a heart surgeon. It's why you want to work on me now."

"I don't want to *work* on you."

"Yes, you do, but I'm not complaining. It's nice. No one's ever wanted to make me happy before. They always wanted to use me for their own happiness. But what about you, Donovan? You deserve joy in your life, too. Maybe I should have a goal as well."

They swam in circles around each other. "What are you suggesting?" His voice was a low murmur.

It was almost completely dark now. The moon was high in the sky, stars were sparkling. "I'm suggesting that if you feel the need to do something nice for me, I should do something nice for you in return."

"You already are. You're here, protecting me from a stalker."

"And you're paying me to do that, so we're even in that department."

"But if I try to make you happy while we're here…"

"Then I should do something similar for you."

Her heart was pounding against her ribs now. How far was she going to take this?

"And how do you intend to do that?"

She swam closer until she was nose-to-nose with him in the water. The magic of the night enveloped her; a brief shiver rippled through her body, followed by a juicy, delectable arousal between her legs.

She was tired of being the consummate professional, day in and day out, every minute of her life.

For once, she just wanted to be a woman.

"Like this." Then she slowly pressed her lips to
his.

Nine

The kiss was hot and wet and way overdue, Jocelyn thought, as she stroked her hands over Donovan's dripping hair and settled them on his shoulders. He folded her into his strong embrace, and in response, she let go of her reserve and wrapped her legs around him. His erection was already rock-hard, pressing against her, sending waves of wicked pleasure straight to her womanly center.

Before she knew what was happening, she was spinning slowly and deliciously through the water, then he was carrying her toward shore.

They emerged out of the water onto the beach, her legs still wrapped around his torso, his hands supporting her behind. Kissing deeply and passionately, they reached the blanket and Donovan sank with ease to his knees. He laid her on her back and came down smoothly on top of her.

Jocelyn opened her legs for him and tipped her head back and whimpered, while he kissed her neck and shoulders and heated her blood, and made her feel free and out of control. She could hardly believe this was happening—a beautiful, wet, naked man wanted her and was kissing her, outdoors beneath a star-speckled sky.

"Donovan, this is crazy," she whispered. "What if someone comes by?"

His discerning gaze scanned the yard around them. "I'll be listening."

All at once, she was on the other side of the fence, laying her safety and comfort in the hands of another person. It was peculiar to her, and infinitely wonderful.

Satisfied that he had eased her worries, Donovan pressed his lips to hers again and she swung eagerly into the pleasure he offered. He slid his hands down the side of her body, over the curve of her hips and back up to her breast, where he unhooked the front clasp of her bra, then began to stroke her. Tingling waves of delight moved through Jocelyn, followed by a sharp, intense ecstasy when he took her nipple into his mouth and brought her to the brink.

"Are you cold?" he whispered in her ear a few minutes later, his hot breath sending glorious little shivers down her spine.

"No, I'm burning up."

His gaze found hers and he smiled—warm, open and adoring. "Then I'll try to cool you down, though it won't be easy, love, considering I'm on fire, too."

He was still smiling when he kissed her again, and she cupped the strong muscles of his buttocks and pulled him tight against her. He continued to kiss and stroke her until she felt a surge of wild, impetuous lust. Her patience dissolved like sugar in liquid. She took his hand and guided it down, and like a skillful, insightful artist, he began to pleasure her with his finger.

She took him in her hand as well, and tried to give him the kind of pleasure he was giving her, but soon it was not enough and she wanted more. She wanted to feel him inside her. She was tired of holding back.

"Please tell me you have protection in your wallet," she said breathlessly.

"As a matter of fact, I do. I was hopeful about this."

She smiled while he reached into the pocket of his balled up jeans, pulled out a condom and put it on.

Jocelyn wiggled out of her panties and slid them off. She sat up, gently pushed him onto his back on the blanket, and straddled him. "I just want to make sure you know that this is me making you happy tonight, and not the other way around."

He smiled wickedly, taking her hips in his big hands and shifting beneath her. "Ah. You're trying to set this up so that I *owe* you."

"Absolutely. And I'll expect payback as soon as you're able." She reached down to place him where she wanted him, then let her body glide down.

He filled her with a tantalizing completeness that sent her passions soaring.

His voice became breathless. "Don't worry, it won't take me long to be able."

He pushed her hair back from her face and pulled her down for another deep, soul-drenching kiss.

Their bodies moved in the moonlight, thrusting and withdrawing. Jocelyn's thoughts seemed to come to her on a floating cloud. How long had it been since she'd made love? Years. Not since Tom, and quite frankly, that had never been like this. Tonight she was overcome with rapture. She felt beautiful and erotic. Like a real woman. She felt cared for and protected, all of which was unfamiliar to Jocelyn, who was always on the other end of that spectrum.

This was pure bliss.

She plunged herself down and rubbed against him, again and again until a rushing flood of sensation overwhelmed them both. Jocelyn threw her head back and cried out; Donovan ground his hips forward, pushing into her with all his might. They climaxed simultaneously. It was the most incredible orgasm Jocelyn had ever experienced.

Weak and out of breath, she collapsed upon him. He held her for a few minutes, then rolled her over onto her back. She gazed up at him adoringly for a long, long time.

He leaned on one elbow looking down at her, caressing her face, playing with her hair. "What changed your mind about this?"

She took a moment to think about that. "It wasn't really a rational decision. If I was being rational, I wouldn't be here like this, naked and completely vulnerable on a beach with you. It was more of a surrender. I just couldn't fight it anymore."

"*It* being…?"

She ran her fingers through his hair. "The way I feel about you. The way you make me forget what I've somehow become, and make me remember that I'm a woman."

"You're *all* woman, Jocelyn. Even when you're pointing a gun at a stalker or speeding through the streets of Chicago. You turn a guy on. Don't ever forget it.''

She smiled up at him, wishing this moment could last forever, but knowing it couldn't. She had to go back to being on guard. She could not relax like this again. Or at least not without some preparatory safety precautions.

''Tell me,'' he said in a low, sexy voice, ''when would you like your services returned? I'm willing, and surprisingly enough, considering the brevity of our conversation just now, I'm quite able.''

Jocelyn laughed. ''*You* may be, but *I* need a break. My legs are like jelly!''

''Not to worry. You don't even have to move, just relax and stay on your back.''

She slapped his chest. ''You sound like you'd have me sleep through it.''

''Your comfort is my first priority. If you want to sleep, that would be fine.''

''While you're doing *that?*''

He laughed again. ''I'm joking Jocelyn. Why don't we go for another swim before we go inside?''

She gazed up at his warm, friendly eyes and felt relaxed. Safe. It was an unfamiliar sensation indeed. ''All right.''

He stood and helped her up. Jocelyn pointed down at her bra and undies on the grass. ''I guess I don't need those now.''

''Definitely not. Let's go.'' She took his hand, and laughing, they dashed naked across the dark beach and splashed with abandon into the lake.

Later that evening, after Donovan had a shower, he went downstairs to make popcorn. He could hear the shower still running in Jocelyn's bathroom, so he took his time getting things ready—lighting some candles, pouring their drinks, fluffing up the pillows on the blue chintz sofa.

She was taking a long time in the shower, he thought, as he opened the popcorn jar and went searching for cooking oil. He hoped she didn't regret what they'd done. He certainly didn't. In fact, he'd never been so ecstatic about making love to a woman before. Then again, he'd never known a woman like Jocelyn.

He found the oil and poured some into the heavy pot he'd set on the stove, then stood and stared down at it while he waited for it to heat up.

What was it about her that drove him so unbelievably wild? He wanted her, but more than just sexually. He wanted to be close to her—to get to know her and to reveal himself to her as well. He wanted to know everything about her childhood and her adulthood and her job and her personal life. He wanted to tell her about all his shortcomings and all his successes. Everything. He wanted her to know everything.

His insides stirred with an odd mixture of elation and fear. Was this love, or the beginnings of it?

Maybe it was, but how could he be sure? He'd never loved a woman before. He'd felt lust for them, yes, and been infatuated with girlfriends during high school and med school, but never had he loved any of them. He'd never felt a desire to enter into a commitment, or spend every waking minute of every day with them. He'd never felt connected to any of them, not like he did with Jocelyn. Perhaps it was her down-to-earth nature. She didn't put on any false airs. She was real, and he felt like he knew her as deeply as he knew his own soul.

An unfamiliar warmth moved through him, and he exhaled a deep sigh of tranquillity. It was one of the most pleasant sensations he'd ever experienced. He smiled.

A half a second later, something deep inside him warned him to be careful. He'd never given his heart to anyone before, and it wasn't so easy to let go of years of independence. There was also the fear that a relationship with Jocelyn might not work out. How the hell would he handle it if she disappeared from his life?

He'd been there before, to that devastating place.

In fact, he'd *always* been there. The sense of being alone was a part of his identity, even when he was with other people.

Except for Jocelyn.

A ripple of apprehension flowed through him. This was dangerous. In addition to his skepticism, she was still his bodyguard and he knew she wouldn't be ready or willing to shirk her responsibilities in order to become his full-time lover. She'd made it clear that she didn't like to get involved with clients, nor was she looking for a committed relationship. How many times had she told him that she didn't need anything in her life outside of her work?

Feeling suddenly nervous and uncertain about what was going on between them, he poured the popcorn kernels into the pot and covered it.

Jocelyn came out of her room a moment later, wearing a white terry cloth bathrobe and huge white socks that pooled around her ankles. She was rubbing a towel over her wet hair.

Donovan was mesmerized. "How is it possible you can look so good, just coming out of the shower?"

She gave him the bright, sparkling smile he'd been waiting to see. It almost knocked him backward into the pot.

Relief poured through him. He'd been worrying that she would feel awkward and uncomfortable when she came out, or be full of remorse. He'd been preparing himself for her to avoid meeting his gaze entirely.

"You're a charmer." She moved toward him and kissed him on the cheek. He wanted to laugh out loud with joy.

"What's cooking?" she asked.

"Popcorn."

She glanced at the pot. "You're making it on the stove? What a treat."

"*You're* the treat," he replied, enjoying the way she winked flirtatiously at him, then turned around and walked, hips swaying, into the living room.

He returned his attention to the stove and shook the pot continuously until a mouthwatering, movie-theater aroma filled the kitchen and the popcorn raised the lid right off the pot. He poured the popcorn into a bowl, then he melted butter to drizzle over the top.

Jocelyn was sitting on the sofa, twirling her hair around a finger, waiting for him. As soon as he set the bowl down on the coffee table, she pulled her legs up under her. "Donovan, we really have to talk about what happened between us tonight."

He was about to sit down, but found himself frozen on the spot. He couldn't move. "You asking me to politely back off is becoming a regular routine."

She took his hand. "I know, I'm sorry. Please sit down."

He gave in and did as she asked, though he would have preferred to go back to the way he'd felt five minutes ago when she'd given him that dazzling smile.

"Sounds like you did some thinking while you were in the shower."

He tried to fight the dread that was seeping into his gut, but it was worse this time. There was more at stake. The other times, his feelings for her hadn't had the chance to burrow too deeply inside him. He hadn't made love to her. He hadn't felt her warmth in his hands and in his heart. But now…he was too far over the edge.

"Yes, I did, and I think we need to set out some parameters."

"Parameters?"

Damn, he wasn't ready for the disappearing act yet. Despite his fears, he wanted more of her. He wanted to get inside her soul. He'd certainly come a long way toward that end, but as of now, there was still so much he didn't know about her. "I don't like the sound of that."

"I know, but it's important, considering the situation. I can't risk your safety."

He leaned forward and rested his elbows on his knees. "Look, I know you feel like you lost control down there at the lake, and I'm sorry if I pressured you into coming in, but you have to admit, what happened because of it was pretty great."

She squeezed his hand. "I'm not denying that at all. It was incredible, Donovan."

At least she was giving him that.

"We can manage this," he said. "You told me that we're safe here, that it's low-risk. The chances of anyone finding us are—"

She touched a finger to his lips to hush him. "You don't have to talk me into anything. I had a great time, too, and I want to do it again. I have every intention of it, actually."

His whole body flooded with relief, followed by heat and desire, in response to her blatantly sexual confession. "I beg your pardon?"

"I told you I'd done some thinking in the shower. I decided that because this is a low-risk detail at the moment, and since we've already broken the ice, so to speak, that we should set out some parameters to make sure that we can work it out. To make sure that we can make love again, and still exercise caution." She waved a hand toward the lake. "That was definitely *not* cautious."

"So, you're saying…"

"I'm saying I think we should stick to your bedroom from now on. With the door locked and the monitor on."

Donovan felt all the tension drain out of his shoulders like liquid. It was replaced by another type of tension—the kind that required a very satisfying cure.

He leaned back on the sofa and raked his fingers through his hair. "Thank God!"

Jocelyn laughed. "What, did you think I was going to torture you for the next few days? Torture both of us?"

He shook his head. "I don't know what I thought. I was afraid of that, I guess."

She swayed toward him and took his face in her hands. "What happened down at the lake was amazing, Donovan. I have no regrets. We're here in this great spot, I'm attracted to you and you seem to be attracted to me. We're both adults, so I don't see why we shouldn't enjoy each other, as long as we act responsibly and take precautions."

She was making it sound like a casual, temporary fling.

A part of him wanted to talk her out of that—to convince her that they could be so much more than that, if they tried.

But in light of the uncertainty he still felt about how willing he was to risk his own heart, he decided it would be best to just nod and say yes. She was offering a few days of no-strings-attached lovemaking. Maybe it was all she could give. For all he knew, maybe it was all *he* could give. He couldn't possibly predict, because this was uncharted territory.

This was a good thing, he decided, smiling at her and leaning in for a kiss. It would give them both time to get to know each other, without ever really committing to anything more. Then, if it didn't work out, it wouldn't be too serious.

At least, he didn't think it would be. Considering the way he felt at the moment—all hot and bothered and emotionally exhilarated—there might not be any way to prevent it from becoming serious.

Jocelyn raked her fingers through his hair and kissed him deeply, distracting him from his thoughts. Heady temptations seared his brain.

He tried to ease her back onto the sofa, but she

rested her hands on his chest. "Remember what I said."

"Precautions?"

"Yes. So why don't we take that popcorn upstairs and eat it later?"

He smiled down at her and kissed her one more time. "I like the way you think."

She raised a flirty eyebrow and got up, taking him by the hand and leading him to the stairs.

He would just have to be patient, he decided, and see where the next few days would take them....

"You know, I was actually surprised that you hired me," Jocelyn said the next morning as she pulled the drapes open across the huge windows.

Donovan leaned up in bed on one elbow, the white sheet slung across his waist. "Why?"

"Because I'm a woman."

Jocelyn gazed down at the awesome sight of his handsome face and muscular, sun-bronzed chest, and felt her insides melt, but she fought the urge to get back in bed and make love with him, because they'd already made love twice that morning, and they needed breakfast.

"You had a great reputation," he said.

She went to get her bathrobe, on the floor by the door. "Yes, but I didn't think you considered me a real bodyguard. Part of me thought you just wanted me to come and stay in your penthouse because you thought I was cute and it would be fun."

He smiled, looking taken aback. "It *was* fun."

She picked up one of his socks on the floor and flung it at him.

"Seriously," he said, "I did need a new alarm

system, and for some reason I trusted you to provide the security I needed.''

''But would you have given in so easily to Mark and hired me if I had been a short, bald man?''

He gazed at her for a moment. ''What's with the questions?''

She pulled on her robe, tied it around her waist, and shrugged.

He pointed at her. ''You just want to know if I'm still the playboy that you thought I was when you first met me, and if you're my most recent diversion.''

Jocelyn combed her fingers through her hair, wishing he wasn't always so perceptive where her emotions were concerned. Even though she'd come to realize he wasn't at all shallow, she was still afraid of something. She wasn't quite sure what it was yet. ''You can't blame me. I suppose I want to understand what's going on between us.''

His chest heaved with a sigh. ''I thought last night you said this was just about enjoying each other while we're here.''

Was that really all he wanted? she wondered, surprised at how hurt she felt by his reminder. She should have asked him what his intentions were at that moment, but she couldn't. A question like that would be too needy and demanding, and he was right, she *had* said they would just enjoy each other. She'd offered him a few nights of pleasure, nothing more—it was what she'd wanted herself—and she had no right to change her mind now.

Was she changing her mind? The thought terrified her. Everything had been so wonderful last night down at the lake, and through the night in his bed.

Donovan had not only given her more pleasure than she'd ever dreamed possible, he'd been gentle and caring and loving.

It was all so new. So overwhelming. She didn't know what to make of it.

"Hey, I'm sorry," she said, trying to hide the depth of her unbidden fears. "I shouldn't have brought it up."

"Brought what up, exactly?"

A flurry of panic coursed through her. He was staring at her intently. Watching her. Wanting to know what she was getting at.

Oh God, was she scaring him off?

She was scaring herself.

"The fact that you hired me," she replied, skirting the *real* question, for him as well as for herself. She needed time to sort out her feelings. "Some people don't trust a woman to do the job. Come on, let's go get some breakfast."

He tossed the sheet off and got out of bed, then fished through his suitcase for a pair of shorts. He pulled them on and followed her down the stairs.

"I hired you because I trusted you," he said. "You have a competent air about you."

Jocelyn entered the kitchen. "Thank you. Why don't I cook breakfast this morning?"

"All right." He sat down on one of the stools at the counter, while she pulled eggs and bacon out of the fridge and set to work. She laid the bacon slices in a skillet to fry.

"So tell me," he said, "why did you leave the Secret Service?"

"To be honest, for the money." She cracked some

eggs into a bowl and began to beat them with a whisk.

"That's surprising. I thought you hated that kind of thing."

"I hate people attaching more value to their cars and boats than to their loved ones. I don't hate money. In fact, I appreciate it very much when I can put it to good use. I'm sending my younger sister to Juliard."

He perked up at that. "You never mentioned that before."

"It never came up."

"Do you have any other brothers or sisters?"

"No, just Marie. She's eighteen and a very talented cello player. She moved in with my aunt after my mom died and no one could afford to send her to a good music school, so I went out on my own to try to cover the expense. Besides that, I like the independence of running my own business."

"Are you musical, too?"

She smiled and poured the eggs into the frying pan she'd set on the stove. "I like to sing."

"You are full of surprises. Sing something."

"Not while I'm cooking! I need to concentrate."

"Oh, yeah, I forgot. Cooking is one of the things you *don't* do. But it looks to me like you're doing it pretty well."

She gave him a look over her shoulder. "I didn't say I *couldn't* do it. I just said I didn't like to."

He rose from the stool to come around the counter and approach her from behind. "Seems to me, you're good at everything. This especially..."

He slid his hands around her waist and nibbled her

neck, while she stirred the eggs on the stove. Goose bumps erupted and tickled all over her body.

"You're distracting me. I'm going to burn the eggs."

She felt his erection pressing against her bottom. Desire coursed through her. Incapable of resisting the heated power of it, she set down her spatula and turned around to kiss him. She wrapped her arms around his neck and reveled in the feel of his wet, open mouth and his tongue mingling with hers. How was it possible a man could press all her buttons with such unbelievable intensity?

After a moment or two, the bacon snapped and sizzled in the skillet, reminding her that she was in charge of breakfast. She smiled and pushed him away. "We can't do this constantly, Donovan. We're human. We need to eat."

He kissed her on the cheek and returned to the stool. "Being a doctor, you'd think I'd remember that."

While Jocelyn cooked breakfast, they talked more about her sister, Marie, then about Donovan's plans with the grief counseling center.

They sat down to eat, discussing what would happen after the police caught Cohen, and how involved Donovan would be in the legal proceedings.

After breakfast, Donovan rose from the table and picked up both their plates. Jocelyn made a move to rise.

"No, you stay here and enjoy your coffee," he said. "I'll get this."

He's a dream, she thought, thanking him with a kiss. Still in her bathrobe, she pushed the sliding door open, then stepped out onto the deck to enjoy the view of the lake. She sat down on a lounge chair and sipped her coffee, remembering how incredible Donovan had been in bed the night before, how he had brought her to tears when she'd climaxed. Tears of joy. Tears of hope.

God, she was losing control. He may be a dream, she told herself, but he's still your client. A client who has never had, with any woman, a relationship that lasted.

She shifted uneasily in her chair. What in the world was she doing? She was a professional, and she'd broken the cardinal rule: Never get emotionally involved.

Yet here she was, happier than she'd ever been in her entire life, wanting to touch Donovan and feel his arms around her, wanting to talk to him and fill whatever void still existed in his heart from losing his parents. She wanted to help him find true happiness and show him how wonderful a lasting love could be....

Her mind suddenly clouded with self-doubt. Lasting love? What did she know of that? She'd been single for years since Tom left her. She still carried around anger at her father for leaving her mother. What did she know of the kind of happiness that came with lifelong love? Nothing.

A fine pair they made.

Jocelyn heard the sound of pots clanging in the kitchen, and took another sip of her coffee.

Yes, she cared deeply for Donovan, maybe she was even falling in love with him, but was she brave enough to throw all caution to the wind, and jump in headfirst? She wasn't sure.

All she knew was that for now, she had to keep

her feet on the ground and remember that this was a week of pleasure, nothing more. She didn't think she had what it took to lead Donovan out of the lonely place he'd known all his life, and he most likely didn't have what it took to keep a relationship going—even though it was no fault of his own.

Together, they were probably ill-fated. She would do well to remember that.

Ten

Over the next three days, when they weren't making love in a locked bedroom, Jocelyn and Donovan went fishing, swimming and hiking in the woods. The owners of the cabin delivered live lobsters one night, which Donovan cooked for supper with melted butter and Italian bread. The other evenings, Donovan barbecued, and afterward, they went skinny-dipping in the moonlight.

It was the most romantic few days Jocelyn had ever known in her life—and the most confusing, because everything was perfect. Donovan was affectionate, attentive and a generous lover. He cooked for her, rubbed her shoulders and listened to whatever she wanted to talk about.

She couldn't imagine that life could be like this every day—that this wasn't some special dream world. There had to be a hitch. There always was.

"Tell me something," Donovan said in bed one night, after they'd made love. "When you were trying to convince me not to buy that black dress for you, you said you could guarantee it was something you'd never wear again. Why? And why do you always wear that plain brown suit and flat shoes, when you'd look terrific in something…else?"

Jocelyn sat up and smiled. "That's a tactful way of telling me I dress like crap."

He laughed. "You know that's not what I mean. You just seem to want to play *down* your looks."

Jocelyn lay back down, resting her cheek on Donovan's shoulder. "I guess I've never been able to stop fighting what I always had to fight as a child."

"What was that?"

"My father's wayward sense of what was important. He wasn't the warmest individual on the planet, and the only time I ever got a smile or a compliment from him was when I was dressed up like a little doll. He couldn't stand to see me in jeans, or dirty from playing outside, and he was completely unattracted to my mother when she was wearing her terry cloth bathrobe around the house. Then, when he left, he told her it was because she didn't care enough about her appearance. He took off with a younger woman who wore short skirts, glittery earrings and lots of hairspray. I'll never forget what she looked like, and my poor mother, who was the kindest, most loving person in the world, never got over that. She became insecure and self-conscious, even when I tried to tell her every day that she was the most beautiful woman in the world to me. I guess I just don't ever want people to like me because I *look* good. I can't stand the superficiality of that."

Jocelyn couldn't believe she had just told Donovan all of that. She'd never told anyone those things, except her assistant, Tess, and that had been after two years of working together.

He rubbed a thumb over her shoulder. "It doesn't matter what you wear, Jocelyn, you *always* look good."

She kissed his bare chest. "But you're not shallow, Donovan. Lots of people are, and I don't want or need to dress up to impress *them.*"

"But by trying to look like one thing—a tough, untouchable bodyguard—you're doing the same thing your father was doing, only the opposite way. You're still putting a lot of emphasis on your appearance, trying to give off a certain impression, when it doesn't matter. You can wear short skirts if you want to, and you'll still be the same person. You'll still be smart and funny and tough."

She sighed. "That's a unique way to look at it."

"Maybe. I just wonder if the real reason you've always played down your looks was to keep people away, because you said yourself that you don't believe in happily ever after." He kissed her forehead, brushing her hair back with his lips. "Jocelyn, I don't want to be one of those people you try to push away."

She leaned up on one elbow to look him in the eye. "You're trying to fix me, aren't you?"

His expression was open, friendly, adoring. "I just want you to know that you could wear *anything* in front of me—fancy or plain—and you'd still be extraordinary. And I'm sorry that your father couldn't love you for the person you were on the inside. He was very wrong to take his family for granted. He had no idea how lucky he was to have you both. Maybe someday he'll realize it.''

She rested her head on his chest again. "How did you get to be so optimistic?"

"I don't know, maybe it's because of the ideals I have about my parents and the things I remember about them. My grandmother told me they were like two peas in a pod. They had everything in common and cherished each other, and when they had me, they grew even closer. We were a tight unit, the three of us, and nothing was more important to them than our little family—not their jobs, not their money, not their belongings. Gram told me they were soul mates.''

"That's beautiful, Donovan. You were lucky to grow up with a promising outlook on relationships.''

He gazed down at her. "Why do I get the feeling you think I'm being unrealistic?"

She shook her head defensively. "I don't. All I know is what I've seen in my life. Maybe the kind of happiness your parents knew is possible for some people.''

"But not you?"

She looked at his face, contemplating what she believed. What she thought was possible. Until now, she'd been a skeptic, but Donovan was touching something inside of her. She was dreaming of happiness now, imagining a beautiful future with him even though she was scared to death that she was setting herself up for disappointment.

Still, she'd never been inclined to dream of a perfect future before, and that said something. Donovan had given her hope. "I...I guess I would like to believe that maybe it is possible.''

His face warmed at her words—words that signified a lowering of her shield. Words that gave him
hope, too.

"You're beautiful." He gathered her into his arms
and pressed his mouth hotly to hers. Jocelyn let all
her worries go, and gave herself over completely to
the pleasure of his lovemaking, which tonight was
like a wonderful, erotic dream.

She would worry about reality tomorrow.

"Want to go upstairs and play Monopoly?" Donovan asked, after supper when it looked like it was
going to rain.

Jocelyn smiled at him. "Monopoly…is that some
fancy term for the horizontal mambo?"

He laughed. "No, I think the fancy term for 'the
horizontal mambo' is 'the horizontal mambo.' I mean
play real Monopoly."

"Why upstairs?" she asked suspiciously.

"I thought we could play it on the bed, in the
nude."

Oh, he was delicious. She sauntered up close to
him and slid a hand down his pants. "It's only fair
to warn you, I used to be addicted to Monopoly when
I was a kid. You don't know what you're getting
into."

He took a deep breath but didn't let it out. "I think
you're the one who's getting into something dangerous at the moment. If you're not careful, we'll never
even get near the game."

Jocelyn slowly removed her hand from Donovan's
jeans, and backed away toward the stairs. "And
which game would that be?" Then she started to run.
Donovan chased her.

They bounded up the stairs, laughing and hooting. Donovan caught up just as she neared the bed. He leaped on top of her and flipped her over onto the soft mattress, coming down, kissing her mouth and pressing his pelvis into hers.

"Let's play Monopoly later," Jocelyn whispered, her body tingling with sweet, lusty sensations.

They both rose up on their knees on the bed to take off their T-shirts, still kissing whenever possible. Within seconds, they were out of their jeans and falling back onto the bed.

"Wait!" Jocelyn said. "We didn't lock the door."

"I'll get it." Donovan scrambled off the bed. He flicked the lock and turned on the monitor, then turned to where she lay, naked on top of the covers.

Completely overwhelmed by the loving expression on her face, he stopped at the foot of the bed to gaze down at her, then rested his open palm on his chest. He spoke softly. "You are so beautiful."

Donovan's heart was aching. Aching! He couldn't take his eyes off Jocelyn. She was a tiny piece of heaven, there on the bed, waiting for him, her eyes honest and adoring. How could he ever walk away from this?

He gently came down upon her slender body and held her in his arms.

He felt joyful, more complete somehow as his lips brushed hers and her body melted perfectly into his. They were made for each other, and he was completely in her power, overcome by the compulsion to hold her tighter and closer, to make love to her tonight and every night until the end of their days.

His blood quickened in his veins at the frightening decision—that he wanted her forever.

The absolute certainty was strange and foreign, and so potent that he felt it like a blazing inferno inside his chest. He didn't want to ever let her go.

She wrapped her long, beautiful legs around him and kissed his neck, ran her hands up and down his spine, and he squeezed her tight against him. Soon, she was inching down the bed and taking him in her mouth, bringing him to the brink of insanity. He couldn't take it. It was so good....

"Jocelyn," he whispered, running his hands through her hair. "I've never felt like this. Come here." He pulled her up beside him and reached into the drawer for a condom. He put it on, then he rolled on top of her, and with a swift, urgent need, he entered her in a single thrust.

She whimpered amorously. "I've never felt like this, either, Donovan."

He made love to her in the twilight, slowly. Very slowly, with deliberate attention to what she was feeling, intensifying the things she liked, rising up on his forearms and using his legs and hips to build the pleasure.

She moved with him in harmony on the bed. Sexually, he had come to know her very well these past few days. He knew what stirred her into that whirlwind of excitement, and what sent her soaring. He knew how to move inside her, how to work the friction—when to ease it, when to build it.

He took his time delivering the pleasure tonight. He spent each passing heartbeat watching her face and giving her all that he had. He wanted to give her everything, and he wanted this to last.

She opened her eyes and gazed up at him lazily, then cupped his face in her soft hands. They watched each other moving in the dim light. Time seemed to stand still. Donovan's heart swelled with love.

Yes, it was love.

"Jocelyn." He was approaching that place…the burning eruption. His mind began to spin. He lowered his body to hers and held her tightly in his arms, recognizing the signs. She was approaching that place, too. "I don't want this to end."

He didn't just mean their lovemaking. He meant all of it.

Then he quickened the rhythm, bringing her with him to the edge of desire, then over the edge to the beyond where all their needs were sated, and euphoria enveloped them completely.

It was different this time. The deepest places in his heart were involved and committed.

He held her tightly afterward, squeezing her close, wishing he could get even closer. "Jocelyn."

For a long time they lay in each other's arms until the twilight turned to darkness and rain began to tap on the skylight over their heads. Seconds later, it intensified to a torrential downpour, drumming noisily on the glass.

Jocelyn snuggled in closer. "Guess we won't be stargazing tonight."

Donovan kissed her forehead. "I like the sound of the rain. It reminds me of camping with my grandmother in her trailer when I was a kid. We always had the worst luck with weather, but it was nice all the same. Cozy."

"My parents took me tenting when I was really little, but only a few times. We weren't much into family vacations, then when Dad left, we didn't do

much other than the usual routine. I'd love to go to
a campground someday.''

"Let's do it," Donovan said.

"Yeah, sure."

He tipped her face up to see her eyes, but he
couldn't see the expression in the darkness. "No, I
really mean it. Let's go as soon as they catch Cohen.
As soon as he's behind bars. We'll bring a bottle of
champagne."

She nodded, but he sensed a sadness in her.

"What's wrong?" he asked,

"Nothing."

He sat up. "No, something's wrong. You seem
down."

"It's nothing, Donovan."

"It is something. Tell me what's the matter."

For a long moment, she lay in silence, then she sat
up, too. "Reality is settling in."

"What do you mean?"

"I mean, we're going to have to leave this place
eventually, and I've been having such a great time."

"So have I, but we can have a great time in Chicago, too."

She shrugged. "I just think that when we go back
to our real lives, this will seem like a dream."

He leaned away from her to flick on the light.
They both squinted as their eyes adjusted. "Didn't
you hear what I said before? That I didn't want this
to end?"

"I thought you were talking about—" she waved
her hand over the bed "—this."

He shook his head. "No, I was talking about *all*
of it with you. I want to keep seeing you, Jocelyn."

She swiveled to put her feet on the floor so that

he was looking at her bare back. "I'm not sure that would be a good idea."

His heart wrenched painfully in his chest. Was this the disappearing act? No, that couldn't be....

He was sure she cared for him. He couldn't have mistaken the way she touched him, the way she looked at him and spoke to him. They'd talked about so many personal things over the past few days. They'd opened up to each other. They'd made love.

"Why not?" he asked. "We're great together, and once you're no longer my bodyguard, there won't be any reason to resist this."

"There's a big reason."

He swallowed hard over the sickening lump of dread in his throat. "Is there something you haven't told me?"

She turned slightly on the bed to look at him. "No, it's nothing like that. It's what I've told you before— that I don't believe in happily ever after." She must have seen the expression of shock and hurt on his face, because she reached for his hand. "It's not that I don't trust you or care for you. It's that I don't trust myself not to fall so hard for you that I would never be able to recover from it when it ended."

"What makes you so sure it would end?"

"It always ends."

"That's not true. Lots of people spend their whole lives together."

"Not people like you and me."

Donovan couldn't speak for a moment. He raked a hand through his hair. "Jocelyn, I felt that way, too. Maybe I still do a little. I can't see into the future, and hell, I'm as scared as you are about how this might turn out, but I've never felt this way about anyone before. This is different. So if the circumstances are different, maybe we can be different, too.''

She shook her head. ''I don't know, Donovan. My parents were in love once, and look what happened to them. My dad left my mom for a younger, prettier woman and never looked back. My mom was devastated, because she really, really loved him. She never got over it. She was still crying years later when she looked at his picture. It was heartbreaking for me to see, and I don't want to go through that. I don't want to be like her someday.''

''So you're going to pass up on what we have together, because there's a *chance* it might not work out? Jocelyn, you might be missing out on a happiness that could last forever.''

''I'm not a risk taker. I do what it takes to prevent dangerous things from happening.''

''That's a fine philosophy for your work, but not for your life. If you don't risk the bad, you'll never experience the really great stuff. I've been alone my whole life, and you're the first person I've ever felt close to. I can't let you disappear. I need you.''

She turned her back on him again. ''You're just feeling this way because of the situation. You're feeling vulnerable, and I make you feel safe. What you feel isn't permanent, Donovan. When Cohen is caught, you won't need me.''

''I will need you, and it has nothing to do with Cohen. Don't you trust me? Don't you believe that I care for you deeply, and that I want you? Hell, Jocelyn, I'm in love with you.''

She turned to look at him, her face pale with astonishment. She sat motionless, staring at him.

"I love you," he repeated, sliding closer and pushing a lock of hair away from her face. "I've never said that to anyone before. Doesn't that count for anything?"

"Tom said those words to me, too, and my father said them to my mother."

"I'm not Tom or your father. I'm Donovan Knight, the man who loves you and wants to spend his life with you."

Jocelyn got off the bed like it had caught fire. "What are you saying?"

"I'm saying I want you to marry me. Marry me, Jocelyn."

Her eyes grew wide like saucers. She grabbed her head in her hands and paced to the door. "This is too sudden! You're not being sensible. We hardly know each other."

He tried to follow her. "That's not true. We know each other better than some people can know each other in a lifetime. We click."

Her face winced. She looked like she was going to cry. "Please don't do this, Donovan. You're pulling me in."

"That's my intention."

"But I don't want to be pulled in! I want to stay safe and be in control, at least until I can feel more sure of things."

"Love is not a security assignment, Jocelyn. There will never be guarantees."

"That's what scares me."

"But if it works out, think of how great it will be."

"*If* it works out? I can't hang my hopes or my future happiness on anything that begins with the word *if*." She reached for her clothes and pulled her T-shirt over her head. "I'm sorry, Donovan, I need to be alone for a while. I'll be in my room."

With that, she walked out.

What just happened? Jocelyn wondered frantically as she shut her bedroom door and leaned against it. How had a simple week of pleasure gotten so out of control? And who started the heavy ball rolling? Had she encouraged Donovan subconsciously somehow? Maybe she had been dreaming a little too much about happily ever after, and she'd communicated that to him.

Or was he right? Did they click like they'd never clicked with anyone else in their lives? Was this the once-in-a-lifetime fairy tale?

Jocelyn dropped her forehead into the heels of her hands and padded to the bed. If only she had more experience with this sort of thing. She'd shied away from dating ever since things went sour with Tom, and she was way out of her league here. For all she knew, maybe all infatuations felt like this at first—a burning fire that refused to be extinguished. Maybe it was just lust. Maybe it would pass for both of them as soon as they got home.

Or maybe it wouldn't.

She lay down on the bed she hadn't slept on since they'd arrived. What was she going to do?

Her cell phone rang in the kitchen, and she jumped. Jocelyn hurried out of her room to answer it. "Hello?"

"Jocelyn, it's Tess. How's everything going?"

Jocelyn contemplated how she should answer that question. "Oh, you know, everything's fine."

"Yeah? You've been having a good time?"

Jocelyn recognized Tess's playful, prying tone, but she wasn't about to give her the dirty details when she didn't even understand them herself. Tess probably wouldn't even believe it if she told her. *Yes, I've been having a wonderful time, and Prince Charming just proposed marriage....*

"What's up?" Jocelyn asked.

Thankfully, Tess stuck to business. "I have news. The police picked up Ben Cohen this afternoon. He's in custody and he confessed to everything."

"You're kidding me." Jocelyn sank into a chair at the table. "That didn't take long."

"Yeah, it's great, isn't it? You can come home anytime. Oh, and I tentatively booked you on a new assignment. An animal rights activist has been getting threatening letters."

Feeling numb all of the sudden, Jocelyn sat and watched the rain slide down the windows in fast-moving rivulets. It was over. They'd caught Cohen. It was time to go home.

"Jocelyn? Are you there?"

She snapped herself back to reality. "Yeah, Tess, I'm here. That's great. Uh…we'll pack up and leave tonight. I'm sure the police will want to speak to Donovan first thing in the morning."

"Yes, they did ask about that." There was a long silence on the other end of the line. "So what do you want me to do about the animal rights activist? Do you want to take that assignment? She's pretty anxious."

Jocelyn continued to stare at the rain-covered window. Lightning flashed somewhere in the distance.

Her heart throbbed a few times in her chest, then she took a deep breath and stood up.

"Yes. Take it, and tell her I'll start immediately. I'll do the advance work tomorrow."

She flipped her phone closed, and turned around. Donovan was standing at the bottom of the stairs, staring at her, his brows drawn together with anguish and disbelief.

Jocelyn's stomach flared with nervous knots. "I didn't realize you were listening."

His voice was low and controlled. "I can see that." He slowly strode toward her. "What's going on, Jocelyn? And why do I get the feeling that if you have it your way, after tonight I'm never going to see you again?"

Eleven

Jocelyn strode to her room to pack her things. "It won't be like that. We've gotten close, Donovan. We can keep in touch."

He followed and stood in her doorway. "The old 'we'll still be friends' routine? Come on, Jocelyn."

She opened dresser drawers and pulled out her clothes, balling them up and tossing them into her suitcase.

Donovan strode to her and took her arm. "Stop packing for a second and talk to me."

"We can talk in the car. I want to get going because it's a long drive and I want to get you back to your penthouse by midnight."

"You're just gonna drop me off and keep going?"

She paused for a moment to gaze into his eyes. "There's no more danger. Cohen is behind bars, and there's no point in you being charged my fees for another day.''

''Oh, so you're doing me a favor, is that it? Saving me a few dollars? I didn't realize I was paying for your services at *night*.''

Jocelyn's mouth fell open. She supposed she deserved that, for all the pain she was inflicting upon him. All because she was afraid to take a risk.

Feeling defeated, she sat down on the edge of the bed. ''Donovan, I'm sorry about this. I know I'm being a jerk.'' He stood a few feet away, listening. She gazed up at him imploringly. ''Maybe we could see each other but take it slow. Cool our jets and just try to bring it back a notch.''

He considered that a moment, then shook his head, his expression grim. ''I don't think I can do that. It would be hell for me. It would be like trying to swim upstream in whitewater rapids. I'm in love with you, Jocelyn. Passionately. I don't want to be away from you. I want to come home to you every night and wake up with you every morning. Life's too short to do it any other way.''

Jocelyn sighed heavily and stared down at the white T-shirt she was squeezing into a ball on her lap. ''I can't be that person, Donovan. I can't be your doting wife, who gives all of her heart to you. It would never be real. I would always be holding back and you'd know it. You deserve better. You *need* something better, because you've never had it, and I can see how much you want it. Believing that I'm the one for you...it's just wishful thinking. You're in love with the person I was here, but this isn't the real me, and frankly, it's not the real you, either. We were pretending. Pretending that life was perfect and nothing could touch us. It won't be like that when we go back."

For a long time, he stared at her in the lamplight, then he nodded and began to back away. "All right. I'll go pack my things."

He left the room. Jocelyn was shocked. Shocked by everything she had just said, and shocked that he was gone.

She continued to sit on the bed, staring after him in silence. Her eyes filled with hot, stinging tears. Her insides were churning.

She hated hurting him like this! But wasn't it better to do it now, when it was just an infatuation, before things got truly serious?

A tear trickled down her cheek and she wiped it away. God, when was the last time she'd cried? She couldn't remember. She'd spent her whole life trying to be tough, pushing pain away. She'd never cried when Tom left her, or when her father left. Anger and resentment had smothered any possibility of tears.

Looking back on it, she supposed she had never truly felt that Tom's heart was involved—or her father's, either. They'd been callous men, more concerned with appearances and what the neighbors thought than what she or anyone else was feeling.

Donovan was the opposite. He felt everything deeply, which was why he was working on a grief center for kids, because his heart was still enduring the hole left behind when his parents drove over that cliff and perished in front of his eyes. It was why he was still single. He was not cavalier about love.

Yet she had been savage toward his tender heart. What did that make her? How could she have done that? Was she really the cold, tough, unfeeling person she pretended to be? In not wanting to be like her mother, had she become like her father?

Her chest throbbed with a painful, squeezing agony. She didn't feel like her father on the inside. She felt more like a wounded bird, who couldn't manage to find her wings.

Yet she had found them briefly these past few days with Donovan, when she'd clutched at him and cried out his name in the darkness, or when she'd laughed with him or told him secrets about her childhood.

Was it too late for her to find her wings? Too late to believe in a love that could last forever?

She gazed up at the ceiling and heard Donovan slamming things around upstairs. She didn't know. She just didn't know.

After a long, silent drive back to Chicago in the pouring rain and darkness, Jocelyn escorted Donovan up to his penthouse. She did a thorough search to make sure everything was okay, then stood in his marble vestibule, preparing to say goodbye.

"So this is it," Donovan said flatly.

She flinched at his icy tone. "Donovan, I'm sorry. I've accepted another assignment and—"

"You don't have to explain. You already did that at the cabin."

They stared at each other for a few seconds, then Donovan stuck out his hand. "It was a pleasure working with you. If you need references, I'd be happy to give them. You did an excellent job with the security."

Feeling numb and confused, Jocelyn gazed up at

his beautiful face, listened to his detached tone, and shook his hand. "Donovan..."

She didn't know what to say! She wasn't any good at this. She'd never been in this situation before, and she'd spent half her life struggling to keep people at a distance. He was doing the same thing to her now, and it was killing her inside.

Rising up on her toes, she leaned toward him and kissed him on the cheek. "I had a great time with you. I'll never forget it."

"Neither will I." His voice told her he was shaken by the kiss. So was she.

"I should go. It's late and we both need to catch up on some sleep."

Donovan nodded.

She walked to the elevator and pressed the down button. With her back to him, she listened for his door closing, but it didn't. He was still standing there, watching her. Her stomach tightened into knots, her heart racing.

Something was tugging at her. Telling her to turn around and dash into his arms, kiss him and tell him how sorry she was. Tell him that she loved him and never wanted to let him go.

But her brain wouldn't let her. What about tomorrow, she heard herself asking, and the day after that? She couldn't make important decisions like this on a heart-splitting impulse. She had to think about the ramifications of her actions. She needed time....

The elevator dinged and the brass doors opened smoothly. She stepped inside.

She didn't want to turn around. She couldn't look at his face one more time, because she might change her mind. Yet she had to turn around to press the lobby button.

Jocelyn took a deep breath and faced the front. Whatever she was afraid of was a nonissue. Donovan's door was just clicking shut.

"I can't believe you got on that elevator," Tess said from her desk, tearing the paper off the bottom of her blueberry muffin. "Prince Charming wants to marry you, and you walk away."

Back in the familiar feel of her brown pantsuit, Jocelyn stood at the filing cabinet in the reception area of her office, looking for something in the top drawer. "Life isn't a fairy tale. It all happened too fast. People can't make important decisions like that based on a few romantic days with their bodyguard at a lakeside retreat, when their life's in danger."

"*He* did."

She threw Tess an impatient glare. "That doesn't make it sensible. He would have regretted it. I did him a favor last night. He'll realize that as soon as he gets back into his regular routine. I give each of us three days tops to forget about this. Where's the file on limo services?"

"How can you be so sure? And what about *you*? Did you do *yourself* a favor last night, turning down a marriage proposal to the most handsome man alive, who also happens to be a rich doctor and great in bed?"

Jocelyn held up a hand. "Don't go there. I don't want to think about that."

"Why not? If you don't think about it, you're not facing it and you'll be living in a bubble, out of touch with reality."

"Tess, I don't want to—"

The phone rang. Tess picked it up. "Mackenzie Security."

Her gaze lifted and she started pointing frantically at the phone, mouthing the words, *It's him!*

There could have been a power surge in Jocelyn's veins. She stood at the filing cabinet, panic filling every corner of her being, while she watched Tess and waited for her to say something.

Tess kept her gaze down, nodding and saying, "Certainly," in that professional tone she had down. A few seconds later, she hung up the phone and Jocelyn's heart broke into a thousand pieces.

"What did he want?"

Tess grimaced. "He wants me to fax him the bill instead of mailing it, so he can drop his check off today."

A lump the size of a grapefruit was forming in Jocelyn's throat. She couldn't talk.

"Maybe he wants to see you, and can't wait," Tess offered helpfully.

Jocelyn knew better. She shook her head and went back to what she was doing. Her fingers crawled over the tops of her files. "I don't think so. He wants to put a tidy finish on things."

"Maybe not. Maybe he'll show up with flowers."

Jaded as she was, Jocelyn sighed and shook her head again, fighting off the tiny fragment of hope that, despite her attempts to crush it, still lived inside her.

That tenacious little hope languished, however, later in the day, when a check arrived by courier.

* * *

Jocelyn had given herself three days to get over Donovan.

Three weeks had gone by.

After finishing her assignment with the animal rights activist, she sat in her apartment eating Cheerios and watching television at ten o'clock at night. She had no work lined up for tomorrow. She'd told Tess to give her a few days off. She'd never needed time off before, but she'd never felt tired before, either.

Tired. Lord, she just wanted to crawl into her bed and lie there for a week. Everything had gotten so…busy. There was nothing to smile about. The animal rights activist treated her like she was invisible—which was nothing new. She expected and even encouraged that from her principals. But since her week with Donovan, she'd come to realize that being invisible wasn't all it was cracked up to be. Sure it was okay on the job, but what about outside of her work? Who was she?

With Donovan, she had felt alive. She'd felt like a woman. Someone with an identity, even though she was away from everything that was a part of who she was—her apartment, her car, her office. Donovan had made her feel like she mattered in the world, even when she was naked, swimming in the lake.

What she'd had with him was the least materialistic thing she'd ever known. Yet it was the most real.

And she had walked away from it! Worse than walked away. She'd hurt him in the process, when he'd been hurt far too much in his life.

Would he ever forgive her? she wondered, longing for the bliss and tranquillity she'd felt in his arms day after day when she had been in his employ. She had thought it would fade away by now, but the hurt was only getting worse. She missed him. God, how she missed him. What a coward she had been.

She rose from the sofa to put her empty bowl in the dishwasher, then poured soap in and pressed the start button. She went to her bedroom and gazed at her empty bed, then at her treadmill and free weights, thought about what she did for a living, all the dangerous situations she'd been in. Wasn't she supposed to be tough and strong? What had happened to her? Where was her grit?

A vision of Donovan's beautiful face appeared in her mind, along with the memory of his kindness and tender generosity. Three weeks had gone by and she was nowhere near to being over him.

This was not just a fleeting infatuation.

A new sense of purpose filled her. She went to her closet and began rifling through her clothes, looking for something feminine to wear. She'd had three weeks to think about Donovan, and in her heart and soul she finally knew that this was not an impulse.

Tomorrow, she was going to see Donovan again, and come hell or high water, she was going to rise above her fears. For the first time in her life, she was going to take a risk with her personal life. How it would turn out, she had no idea. She would just have to have faith.

Jocelyn was getting out of the shower when her cell phone rang in her bedroom. Wearing a towel, she padded down the hall to answer it. "Hello?"

"Hi, it's Tess. Something's happened and I thought you should know about it."

Recognizing the sober tone in Tess's voice, Jocelyn sat down on the edge of her bed. "What is it?"

"Ben Cohen was released yesterday. Apparently, there was mix-up with the warrant they used to search his apartment. A couple of officers crossed wires and they each thought the other had the warrant, and they ended up using one that was meant for someone else."

"Oh, no."

"You might want to go and see Dr. Knight. You want me to call his penthouse?"

"Yes. Tell him not to go out, and that I'm on my way."

Jocelyn threw off the towel and got dressed.

Fifteen minutes later, she was in her car on her way to his place, when her phone rang again. "Yeah?"

"It's Tess. I've been trying his penthouse, and there's no answer. I called the hospital but he's not working today. I haven't been able to get in touch with him, Jo. I hope everything's all right."

A cold chill spurted through her. "Keep trying. Maybe he's out on the terrace or in the shower or something. I'm near his place now. I'll call you when I know something."

She parked, holstered her gun, and dashed into the lobby. "Briggs, is Dr. Knight at home?" she asked the security guard.

"No, Ms. Mackenzie. He's gone for a run. Left about a half hour ago."

"Thanks." She pushed through the revolving door and called Tess again. "He's gone for a run. I'm going to look for him, but you keep trying his penthouse in case we don't cross paths. Tell him to lock

his door and not to move until I get there, and call
me if you reach him.''

Jocelyn flipped her phone closed and slid it into
her pocket. She started running down the street toward the park which had been his regular route before he'd hired her. She was glad she'd worn her
sneakers.

The sun warmed her head and shoulders. She
worked up a sweat, running in her jeans and blazer,
but all she cared about was finding Donovan.

She reached the park and shaded her eyes. She
scanned the crowds of people on rollerblades and
walking their dogs. There were lots of runners on the
paths, but no sign of Donovan.

Then she spotted someone sitting on the ground a
distance away, leaning against a tree in the shade,
fiddling with a sprig of grass. It was him. A cry of
relief spilled from her lips. *Thank God.*

She perused the surroundings, looking for any sus-
picious-looking characters, and approached.

His gaze shot up. His face paled when she came
to a stop in front of him. ''Jocelyn, what are you
doing here?''

She had to work hard to catch her breath. She
wiped her forehead with the back of a hand. ''I'm
so glad I found you.''

He squinted up at her for a few seconds. ''Why?''

''Something's happened. Ben Cohen was released
yesterday. You're not safe.''

He said nothing for a few seconds. ''I see.''

''I need to escort you back to your place.''

Donovan stared up at Jocelyn's beautiful dark eyes
and full lips, her cheeks flushed from the heat, and
wondered how it was possible he could still be so

completely in love with her after the way they'd parted three weeks ago.

Between now and then, he'd flip-flopped between feeling furious with her one minute, to picking up the phone and dialing her number to ask her out the next, only to hang up before it rang. He hadn't been able to think of anything but her.

Damn, he'd thought she had come here for personal reasons. He'd thought he was finally going to be able to hold her in his arms again, but she was only here because of his stalker. He'd thought wrong, like he'd been wrong about everything else where she was concerned.

Rising to his feet, he tried not to look at her gorgeous face or the way her jeans clung to her long, sexy legs. If he was ever going to feel normal again, he was going to have to forget about her and convince himself that she'd been right. That what they'd had at the lake hadn't been real.

This was the real Jocelyn. All business. No heart.

"That's fine," he said coolly. "I'll go with you for now, but I think—because we were personally involved—it would be best if I hired someone else to be my bodyguard. You understand, I hope." If he was going to protect himself from falling under her spell again, he couldn't even consider hiring her and inviting her back into his home.

Her lips parted. With surprise? Or was it anguish? If it was anguish, it could be no worse than what he'd suffered when she'd insisted on ending things between them. He would not let himself feel guilty about it.

"All right, let's go this way." She recovered

quickly from whatever she'd been feeling. Always the professional, he thought bitterly.

Keeping her eyes on the path and the people approaching them from any side, Jocelyn walked beside Donovan. They didn't talk. He knew she was focused on what she was doing, and he, to be frank, couldn't have made his mouth work if he tried. He just wanted this to be over.

They approached his building and waited to cross the street. All of a sudden, from out of nowhere, a shot fired past Donovan's head and chiseled a piece of brick out of the building behind him. He instinctively ducked behind a telephone pole. Jocelyn put her arm around him and shielded him with her body, just like she'd done the last time. People on the street were screaming and running. His heart hammered inside his chest.

Another shot blasted by and missed.

"He's not giving up!" Jocelyn, holding her gun in her hand, looked around for better cover.

Donovan peeked out.

"Stay back!" she shouted.

"He's there!"

"Where?"

Donovan peaked out again. "Around the side of my building. He's pointing his gun at us."

Jocelyn leaned out, just as a bullet hit the telephone pole. Wood splintered next to her face. Seizing an opportunity, she fired at Cohen and miraculously knocked his gun out of his hand. Donovan heard Cohen groan with pain, then saw him bolt.

"He's running!" Donovan sprinted out into the street to go after him.

"Donovan, wait!" Jocelyn followed.

Sirens began to wail somewhere in the distance, but Donovan wasn't stopping. He had the chance to catch Cohen now, and he couldn't wait for the cops.

He chased Cohen down the alley and across a back street. Jocelyn's footfalls tapped the ground not far behind him. He knew she had her gun, and Cohen was unarmed. He wasn't giving up now. He leaped over a garbage can.

He was gaining on Cohen. The guy wasn't a runner.

A minute later, Donovan hurled himself through the air and tackled Cohen from behind, into a pile of wooden crates in another alley. He felt his arm scrape against something; his jaw cracked against the back of Cohen's head, and he tasted blood in his mouth.

Cohen scrambled beneath him to get away, but the sound of a gun cocking next to his head made him freeze.

"Hold it right there," Jocelyn said, both hands on her gun, her legs braced apart. "Move one muscle and you'll be leaving here in a body bag."

Donovan took one look at her—tough as nails—and backed off Cohen, who raised his hands in the air. Just then, a cop car skidded to a halt on the street at the end of the alley and a swarm of uniformed officers came bounding around the corner. Donovan wiped his bloody lip with a hand.

"Hey, Ms. Mackenzie," one of the cops said, just before he grabbed Cohen and cuffed him. "Good work."

She lowered her weapon. "It was Dr. Knight who did most of the work, Charlie." Her shoulders rose and fell with a deep intake of breath as she looked at Donovan. "Are you all right?"

He inspected the blood on his hand. "I'll live."

She stared at him, then something in her face changed. The tough-as-nails persona disappeared, and a softness took its place—along with a few tears spilling over her cheeks.

Donovan was breathing hard. So was she. God, he loved her, still.

Jocelyn took three long, fast strides toward him and threw her arms around his neck.

The whole world disappeared around them. Donovan didn't care what was happening to Cohen, he was barely aware of the cops reading the guy his rights. All that mattered was Jocelyn, here in his arms, shuddering with tears and weeping onto his shoulder.

"It's over," he said, stroking her hair. "He's in custody now."

She shook her head against him and sniffled. "That's not why I'm crying. I do this stuff all the time."

He couldn't help laughing. "Then why *are* you crying?"

She looked up at him. Her face was wet and her nose was running. "Because I was afraid I was going to lose you, and I'd never get the chance to tell you how sorry I was."

A warning voice whispered in his head. Maybe she was sorry for not preventing the shooting. Maybe she was sorry for hurting him at the cabin. He didn't want to let himself hope that she might regret saying goodbye....

"Sorry for what?" he asked, despite himself.

The officer named Charlie appeared beside them.

"I'm going to need statements from the both of you."

Donovan and Jocelyn stepped apart. Jocelyn wiped under her nose and quickly collected herself, then began to explain what had happened, as well as the fact that Cohen's gun had flown out of his hand back at Donovan's building and needed to be picked up. The officer had some questions for Donovan, too, then he closed his notebook and said he'd be in touch.

Donovan and Jocelyn stood in the alley, alone at last. Neither of them said anything for a moment or two.

"You okay?" Donovan asked, wishing they hadn't been interrupted before. Jocelyn had been in his arms. He wanted her back.

It wasn't going to happen, however. Not now. The moment had passed, and he wasn't sure what was going on anymore. She was staring at the ground, looking like a tough E.P.P. again.

"You want to go back to my place for a drink?" he asked, not sure where this was going to lead, but wanting to try anyway. "You're off duty now, and I sure as hell could use a beer. I've never apprehended a stalker before." He held up his hand and made it quiver.

He managed to get a smile out of her at least. "Sure. I'd love a beer."

She said yes.

Elation flowed through him.

The very next second, his gut twisted into knots as he smiled down at her and comprehended how much of his future happiness depended on the next half hour of his life.

Twelve

Donovan pulled his key from his shoe wallet and unlocked the door to his penthouse.

"Wait." Jocelyn touched his arm and held him back. "Let me go first and check things out. You never know."

Donovan exhaled deeply. She was dedicated to her work, and he respected her for it, even when it got in the way of his hopes to make this drink personal rather than professional.

He waited by the door while she disarmed the alarm and checked his penthouse for God knew what. A short time later, she came sauntering out of his bedroom.

What he wouldn't give to see her sauntering out of there every morning for the rest of his life....

Brushing those hopes aside, he smiled. "Everything okay?"

"Yeah, it looks fine. How about that beer?"

"Coming right up. Make yourself comfortable." It felt strange, treating her like a guest when she'd been his roommate not that long ago.

Donovan went to change into a pair of jeans and a clean shirt, then went to the kitchen and pulled two cold ones out of the fridge and twisted off the caps. He poured them into a couple of mugs and started heading down the hall.

He stopped in his tracks, however, when he heard his Eric Clapton CD playing. Memories of those early nights with Jocelyn came flooding back. He remembered discovering for the first time something of the real woman beneath the suit and the tough girl image. He remembered the way she'd smiled when she'd heard those songs.

He swallowed hard over his anxiety, his fear that today might end the same as that pivotal night at the cabin—when an argument and a breakup had wedged them apart.

"Here you go." He entered the living room and handed her mug to her. "Cheers. Here's to Cohen behind bars again."

"I'll drink to that." They clinked glasses and sipped their beer.

"Have a seat," Donovan said, feeling awkward and out of his element, trying to be casual when all he really wanted to do was take Jocelyn into his arms and kiss every inch of her.

That would probably scare her off, though—to put it mildly—and at this point, he was more than willing to go slow and cool his jets, like she'd asked him to do, that final night at the cabin.

Damn, he'd stand on his head for a week if it

would change her mind about ending their relationship.

She sat down and kicked off her shoes, then tucked her jean clad legs up under her. "Donovan, I'm glad you invited me here, because I really wanted to talk to you today."

He cleared his throat nervously. "About Cohen?"

For a moment she stared at him. "No. I…I know that's why I went looking for you at the park, but the truth is, I was planning to come and see you before I knew about his release."

Donovan remembered how he'd felt when he'd first looked up at her in the park, how he'd hoped she was there just for him. Then the disappointment…

He waited in silence for her to continue.

She lowered her gaze, drawing little circles on his upholstery with the tip of her index finger. "I…I've missed you."

All his nerve endings began to quake and buzz.

"The past few weeks have been hell," she said. "I haven't been able to stop thinking about you, and I hate the way things ended between us. That week at the cabin was the best week of my life, and I totally screwed it up."

"You didn't screw it up, Jocelyn," he said gently, covering her hand with his.

"Yes, I did." Her voice quavered, but she spoke with a candid resonance, looking him directly in the eye. "I'm sorry for being such a coward."

He sat there, dumbfounded, bewildered and shaken. "What are you saying?"

"I'm saying that I was an idiot. I was afraid to love you because of the things I remember about my father and Tom. I was afraid of getting hurt, but walking away from you hurt even more. I want to go back to what we had. I only hope that you can forgive me for causing you pain, and I hope you still…'' She lowered her face.

Donovan inched closer to her and cradled her chin in his hand. "You hope I still what?"

Her eyes were wet and bloodshot as she gazed up at him. "I hope you still want me."

His entire being heated from the inside out. Everything was pulsing with joy and excitement and profound relief. How could she even doubt if for a minute?

"I never stopped wanting you, Jocelyn. I wanted you the first second I saw you, standing at my door with that serious glare in your eyes, just like I want you now."

She blinked up at him, all woman—vulnerable, feminine. Her lips were moist and parted and a pulse of arousal began to throb in his loins. He took her face in his hands and covered her mouth with his own.

Jocelyn wrapped her arms around his neck and he pulled her into his embrace, deepening the kiss and letting his hands slide down the soft curves of her body. How many nights had he lain awake dreaming of this? How many nights had he wished she would come to him and tell him she wanted to go back to what they were when they were together?

Yet none of those dreams could compare to the exhilarating flesh and blood feel of her in his arms now, her mouth tasting deliciously of beer and her hair smelling of citrus. He couldn't get enough. He didn't think he would ever get enough….

"I love you," he whispered in her ear, nibbling at her lobe and feeling her writhe with rapture and delight. "You're the only woman who has ever filled the hole in my life, Jocelyn—the sense of emptiness, from never feeling ready to let anyone in."

"I don't know what I did to deserve you."

"You were just you."

He took her mouth again with a wild intensity, and drank in the luscious flavor of her whole being.

"I promise I won't get spooked this time," she said, tipping her head back as he dropped open kisses upon her neck. "These weeks away from you gave me time to understand that what we had wasn't just an infatuation. I needed time to think about everything, because as you know, I'm not impulsive. But I'm here now, Donovan, and I'm yours. Completely."

He drew back to look into her eyes. "You're sure about that?"

"I've never been more sure of anything."

He kissed her again, long and slow, then sat back. "Will you stay here for a second?"

"Sure." She watched him curiously as he kissed her on the forehead and left the room.

He went to the safe in his bedroom and turned the knob left, twenty-four, then right, sixty-eight, then left again to five and back to zero. He couldn't go fast enough. Damn, his hands were shaking!

Finally the safe clicked open and he reached inside for the little velvet box he'd been saving his entire life. His heart was racing.

He paused a moment and took a deep breath, feeling his world shift. Everything was changing. He slipped the box into his pocket.

Donovan walked down the hall and returned to the living room, where Jocelyn was waiting on the sofa, all smiles, looking flushed and beautiful, like an angel from heaven. He slowly made his way to her and knelt at her feet.

His heart was pounding against his ribs. He'd never been so nervous about anything in his life.

He took her hands in his and labored to keep his voice steady and controlled. "You're the one, Jocelyn. I know it as clearly as I know my own soul. You're the one I want to spend my life with, the one I want to grow old with, and I promise I will make you happy forever, and I will never, ever leave you, if only you'll say yes."

Her eyes were sparkling. She began to smile. "Yes to what?"

"Yes to marrying me. I didn't propose properly last time. This time, I'm doing it right." He reached into his pocket, withdrew the box and opened it before her. The diamond ring glittered magically. "This was my mother's. She left it to me in her will. She said it signified everlasting love, and that it would represent her love for me even after she was gone, and that she hoped I would pass it on to my own children. It means a lot to me. Will you wear it, and give it to our child some day?"

Jocelyn covered her mouth with trembling fingers and stared down at the one-and-a-half carat, pear-shaped diamond. "It's the most beautiful ring I've ever seen, Donovan." She took it out of the box and tried it on. "It fits perfectly."

Donovan got up off his knees to sit beside her again. He touched her cheek lovingly. "Meant to be, I guess."

She began to nod. "I think you're right. I feel good about this. I feel *really* good about it."

He exhaled a long sigh of contentment, then kissed her again, tenderly and passionately, stroking her hair and her shoulders and glorying in the feel of her body next to his. "I feel good, too. I'll always feel good with you in my life, Jocelyn. I hope you don't want a long engagement."

She smiled seductively. "I'll marry you tomorrow if you can get the time off."

A swell of arousal moved through him at the beguiling expression on her face and the sexy, silky sound of her voice. "Tomorrow might be a little difficult. How about the day after?"

"What's so important tomorrow?" she asked, laying teasing little kisses on his chin and neck. The feel of her wet lips on his skin sent a message to his nether regions, and he began to rise to this tantalizing occasion.

"Tomorrow I'm helping you move in here," he replied. "That is, if you *want* to live here."

"Of course I do." Her voice became serious. "It was your parents' place, Donovan, and look what they created while they lived here." She touched her warm palm to his cheek. "We have a lot to look forward to, don't we? But for now, I only want one thing."

"And what's that?"

Her eyes glimmered with desire. She pulled off her shirt to reveal a red, lace teddy. "I want you to carry me to your bedroom, so I can thank you for bringing out the woman in me."

His hunger for his new fiancée intensified. He

rubbed his nose up against hers. "We'll get there faster if we run."

She laughed and leaped off the sofa. "As long as you promise to go slow when we get there."

Desire burned through his body at the idea of making love to her slowly, for the rest of the day and long into the night, in the bedroom that would become theirs together, forever. "I wouldn't have it any other way."

* * * * *

Watch out for exciting new covers on your favourite books!

Every month we bring you romantic
fiction that you love!
Now it will be even easier to find your favourite
book with our **fabulous new covers!**

We've listened to you – our loyal readers, and as of
August publications you'll find that...

We've improved:

- ☑ *Variety between the books*
- ☑ *Ease of selection*
- ☑ *Flashes or symbols to highlight mini-series
  and themes*

We've kept:

- ☑ *The familiar cover colours*
- ☑ *The series names you know*
- ☑ *The style and quality of the stories you love*

*Be sure to look out for next months titles so
that you can preview our exciting new look.*

SILHOUETTE®
DESIRE™ 2-IN-1

0504/51a

AVAILABLE FROM 21ST MAY 2004

SCENES OF PASSION Suzanne Brockmann

Maggie Staunton's life was safe and dull until a stranger made her exchange predictability for passion. The stranger was a man she'd known since childhood—a man who stirred her imagination until she blushed—a man with a secret…

A BACHELOR AND A BABY Marie Ferrarella

The Mum Squad

Joanna Prescott had never stopped loving Rick Masters, and after he rescued the pregnant beauty from near death and helped deliver her baby they were soon setting each other on fire in the bedroom again. But could he forgive her past mistake?

HER CONVENIENT MILLIONAIRE Gail Dayton

Sherry Nyland had persuaded mystery millionaire Micah Scott to marry her. But what would it take to convince her seductive in-name-only husband to get up close and personal?

THE GENTRYS: CAL Linda Conrad

The Gentrys

When the tantalising Bella Fernandez came to look after Cal Gentry's children he wasn't prepared for the passion that her presence would spark. But danger had followed her to his home, to rival the peril of his sensual embraces.

WARRIOR IN HER BED Cathleen Galitz

John Lonebear was the most compelling man Annie Wainwright had ever met. And even though he didn't want her in his home, he couldn't deny the heat that blazed between them…

COWBOY BOSS Kathie DeNosky

Faith Broderick hadn't planned on getting involved in a matchmaking scheme to help Cooper Adams shake off his bachelor status. Once Cooper met her, though, he knew that promoting her from employee to wife would be all too easy!

AVAILABLE FROM 21ST MAY 2004

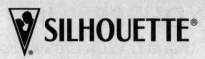

Sensation™

Passionate and thrilling romantic adventures

SHOOTING STARR Kathleen Creighton
LAST MAN STANDING Wendy Rosnau
ON DEAN'S WATCH Linda Winstead Jones
SAVING DR RYAN Karen Templeton
THE LAST HONOURABLE MAN Vickie Taylor
NORTHERN EXPOSURE Debra Lee Brown

Special Edition™

Life, love and family

SHOWDOWN! Laurie Paige
THE SUMMER HOUSE Susan Mallery & Teresa Southwick
HER BABY SECRET Victoria Pade
BALANCING ACT Lilian Darcy
EXPECTING THE CEO'S BABY Karen Rose Smith
MAN BEHIND THE BADGE Pamela Toth

Superromance™

*Enjoy the drama, explore the emotions,
experience the relationship*

A BABY OF HER OWN Brenda Novak
THE FARMER'S WIFE Lori Handeland
THE PERFECT MUM Janice Kay Johnson
MAGGIE'S GUARDIAN Anna Adams

Intrigue™

Breathtaking romantic suspense

ROCKY MOUNTAIN MAVERICK Gayle Wilson
HER SECRET ALIBI Debra Webb
CLAIMING HIS FAMILY Ann Voss Peterson
ATTEMPTED MATRIMONY Joanna Wayne

Spence Harrison
has to solve the
mystery of his
past so that he
can be free to
love the woman
who has
infiltrated his
heart.

The
Country
Club

Book 6 available from 21st May 2004

FREE!

2 Book

and a surprise gift!

We would like to take this opportunity to thank you for reading this Silhouette® book by offering you the chance to take TWO specially selected titles from the Desire™ series absolutely FREE! We're also making this offer to introduce you to the benefits of the Reader Service™—

- ★ FREE home delivery
- ★ FREE gifts and competitions
- ★ FREE monthly Newsletter
- ★ Books available before they're in the shops
- ★ Exclusive Reader Service discount offer

Accepting this FREE book and gift places you under no obligation to buy; you may cancel at any time, even after receiving your free shipment. Simply complete your details below and return the entire page to the address below. *You don't even need a stamp!*

YES! Please send me 2 free Desire books and a surprise gift. I understand that unless you hear from me, I will receive 3 superb new titles every month for just £4.99 each, postage and packing free. I am under no obligation to purchase any books and may cancel my subscription at any time. The free books and gift will be mine to keep in any case.

D4ZEE

Ms/Mrs/Miss/Mr ....Initials ....

BLOCK CAPITALS PLEASE

Surname...

Address..

....

....Postcode ....

Send this whole page to:
UK: The Reader Service, FREEPOST CN81, Croydon, CR9 3WZ
EIRE: The Reader Service, PO Box 4546, Kilcock, County Kildare (stamp required)